Hooked on a Demon

ISLA WINTER

WORDY
WHIMS

Also by Isla Winter

To anyone who has ever felt they aren't good enough. You are more than enough.

And remember, if they wanted to, they would.

A Play List of Sorts...

I am not an author who often listens to music while writing. However, I regularly have movies or TV shows playing in the background while I write. So, in no particular order, here are some of the stories that kept me company while I visited Leeside with Declan and Eliana.

Movies
- *Scream* franchise
- *Speed*
- *Spider-Man: No Way Home*
- *Jingle All the Way*
- *Jurassic Park*
- *Jurassic World*
- *Elf*
- *The Hunger Games* trilogy
- *Meg 2: The Trench*
- *While You Were Sleeping*
- *Book Club: The Next Chapter*
- *Dirty Dancing*
- *The Princess Diaries*

- *To All the Boys* trilogy
- *The Kissing Booth* trilogy
- *Cinderella*
- *Ocean's 11, 12, & 13*
- *Gone in 60 Seconds*
- *Death Becomes Her*

TV Shows
- *The Resident*
- *Gilmore Girls*
- *Survivor*
- *Virgin River*
- *The Sex Lives of College Girls*
- Hockey games (not really a show, but also not a movie, so it goes here…)
- *Bridgerton*
- *Buffy the Vampire Slayer*
- *Sweet Magnolias*
- *The Pitt*
- *You*
- *The Secret Lives of Mormon Wives*

About this book

Welcome back to Leeside! As with the other books in this series, this is a work of fiction that has magical characters dealing with life. They are messy and imperfect, just like us.

You can expect the following to be within these pages:

•Explicit sex scenes

•Swearing

•Emotionally abusive and manipulative relationship (occurred in the past, but discussed on page).

As always, protect yourself first.

Isla

CHAPTER 1
Declan

This—right here—is how he hopes to die, his face buried between the thighs of a gorgeous woman as she rides his face into oblivion. While she moans her release, screaming his name along the way, Declan releases a satisfactory groan into her delicious pussy.

Sitting on the edge of the bed, wiping his face, his partner for the night moves to the floor and spreads his knees. Taking his cock in her hands, she begins to stroke. Declan Grace is many things: expert mechanic, funnyman, upstanding citizen, and, of course, younger brother to the demon lord and supernatural council member Lachlan. But, according to the woman kneeling before him and now hungrily sucking his dick, he's also a god and the best she's ever had.

As tension builds at the base of his spine and his left leg starts to twitch, Declan drops his head forward. "Fuck you look good with my cock in your mouth."

As she swirls her tongue around the tip, he wraps her ponytail around his fist and thrusts into her mouth. She greedily takes every thick inch of him, moaning around him while gazing at him through her lashes. It sets him off, and he grunts his release, pouring his hot cum down her throat. Releasing her hair, she drags her tongue up his dick slowly, making sure to suck an extra time before fully releasing him. Her hand lands on his chest as she pushes him backward. Declan lies back on the bed, and she crawls up his body, meeting his mouth and kissing him deeply. He can still taste himself on her as it mixes with her lingering deliciousness on his tongue and fucking Hades, if it doesn't get him hard all over again. She palms his quickly hardening cock, opens a condom package, and rolls it down his length. She hovers over him, lining up with her slick cunt, and slides down to the base. Fucking hell, she's so tight. Her head tilts back. His hands find her tits, and she rides him into the sunset.

Waking a couple of hours later with her leg draped sleepily across his and her body curled into him, Declan feels the panic inside begin to rise. The contact feels nice, but he knows he can't stay here. He never does. Looking over at her, her face hidden behind her curly blond hair, he feels a pang of regret, but if he's going to sneak out, it needs to be now.

He groans internally, not wanting to make a sound, as he slides a hand under her leg and lifts it ever so slightly to give himself room to slide out of the bed. Once freed, he locates all his clothing and dresses hastily, checking occasionally to ensure he hasn't woken her. He glances one last time at her perfect ass and swears to himself before silently leaving her room, moving through her apartment, and out the door.

Standing in the hall, he releases a breath and shakes his head. This isn't the kind of guy he wants to be.

Is leaving before she wakes the cowardly way out? Absolutely.

But does it help prevent her from getting hurt? One hundred percent. He would rather risk an angry partner discovering he took off after one hot night than either of them getting attached and it inevitably ending because he's not boyfriend material. He never has been.

Making his way home, he stops and picks up a coffee and breakfast sandwich, knowing he won't have enough time to eat before heading back out again to get to the shop in time to open. He pulls into his driveway, throws his truck in park, and enters his home, where he is greeted by the most excited giant ball of black fur.

Two big black paws land firmly on his chest, nearly knocking him over. "Good morning to you, too, Buckley. Were you a good boy while daddy was out?" He ruffles his hands through the mop of fur on Buckley's head before leaning in to squish his face and kiss his forehead aggressively. "Do you want some breakfast?" Buckley drops to the floor and begins dancing around him. "Yeah? Let's go get you some grub, Bucks."

Dropping his keys on the counter, he sips his flat white, tilting his head back and relishing the taste of the creamy brew as it floats over his tongue. Buckley, eager for his food, headbutts the back of his leg, almost taking Declan out at the knee. "Alright, alright. It's coming." Declan gets the container from the cupboard and collects his dish from the sink. While Buckley is a Newfoundland, a giant-looking beast, he is friendly as all hell and would rather bowl people over and lick their faces. Declan adopted him about a year ago as a puppy, which was the best decision he ever made. When he was younger, he never really understood the draw of having a pet. But being able to come home and have someone eagerly awaiting his arrival, excited to see him no matter how long he's been away, is the best feeling ever.

Buckley almost knocks his food out of Declan's hand before it reaches the floor, causing Declan to laugh and pat the happy fool's head. "Here ya go, ya monster."

Leaving Buckley to his feast, Declan checks the kitchen clock and notes he doesn't have much time before he needs to be at the shop. He takes another sip of coffee, and his mind begins to wander back to the taste of last night's partner on his lips. His dick twitches in response. He single-handedly pulls his shirt over his head as he moves upstairs, heading to his shower. One last round would have been great, and despite his brain's reminder that they needed to get out of there as quickly as possible, his dick is insisting on another release.

His pants fall to his knees, and his dick springs out of his boxers as they slide down his hips. The fucker is standing at full mast as a bead of precum glistens on its head. He palms his hard cock, lazily stroking it as he reaches over with his other hand to turn the shower on.

With the water hot enough, he steps in, letting it run down his body. His eyes close as he leans forward, placing a forearm on the cool wall; he hangs his head, letting the water flow down his back while his other hand grips his cock more firmly and begins gliding up and down his dick with intention. His mind focuses on last night and the feel of her hot pussy wrapped tightly around his cock. The feeling of sliding into home, again and again, and the little noises she'd made as he slammed into her from behind. How she forced herself up and leaned back into him as he pounded into her delicious cunt. How his hand fit around her bouncing tit while she played with her clit as he filled her over and over.

His hand pumps furiously as he chases his release. Images of her mouth wrapped around his dick and how she looked up at him while on her knees flicker in his mind and the thought of how she so greedily swallowed his release leaves him grunting under the streaming water, spurting hot cum down the drain. Panting, he slowly glides his hand along his softening cock, getting out every last drop wishing he was covering her ass again instead of the drain.

Fucking hell. His dick is pleased for now, but he's going to have to make sure he keeps his thoughts on work during the day, or he'll have to write himself up for indecent behavior.

Once he composes himself again, he finishes showering, dries himself off, and dresses for the day before returning downstairs. He lets Buckley out the back door to do his business, and the jovial mop of fur bounds outside, chasing after birds and barking at them to get off his lawn. Thankfully, Buckley is quick about doing his business, and by the time Declan picks up his keys again, the giant beast is curled up on the couch, already snoring. With his mostly full coffee and breakfast in hand, Declan pats Buckley on the head and walks out the door.

On mornings like this, he's happy he moved to Leeside. One, he's now closer to his brother Lachlan and his sister-in-law Petra. Two, he doesn't need to drive the hour from Beckton to his garage in Leeside anymore. He loved living in Beckton but he realized that most of his life was taking place here in Leeside. Family, friends, work. All of it was here. So the move was an easy decision.

He makes it to the shop with minutes to spare before opening. He unlocks the door, turns off the alarm, and turns on the lights. He places his breakfast on the front counter, then flips the sign to open.

CHAPTER 2
Declan

While being the brother of a demon lord and a beloved supernatural council member has benefits, living in the same town as his powerful brother hasn't come without its troubles. Everyone knows who he is. Which means everyone seems to know his business, whether Declan wants them to or not. There are eyes everywhere, though Declan has to give his brother credit, as he does his best to stay out of Declan's business. Lachlan helped to raise him after everything with their dad went down, but no longer a trouble-making teen and a hefty thirty-two, Lachlan trusts Declan to make his own choices. For better or worse.

When he opened his auto shop, publicly backed by Lachlan's support, the Leeside community latched on quickly. Business took off, and because the community generally trusted Lachlan, they trusted Declan by association. For a new business, Declan knew it wasn't a bad place to be.

A few years later, the regulars have stuck and new customers are consistently coming in. Hellbent Motors has been busy enough and he's thought about expanding, but it's a lot of time and money he doesn't have at the moment. As such, they remain where they are, and he hires staff as needed to help meet the demand. And he's grateful for every single one of his staff who has found their way to him. They are clever, motivated, and make his days easier.

"Hey, Sebastian, can you watch the front desk for me. I gotta step out for a bit," Declan says to one of his service techs. "And can you let Chloe know she needs to check the rotors in bay three?"

"Sure thing, boss," Sebastian says before running into the shop to find Chloe. He returns a moment later, rag in hand, as he dries them off before sitting at the computer.

"Thanks, bud." Declan claps him on the shoulder before walking around the desk and heading out the front to his motorcycle.

A little bit later, Declan's flipping through a five-year-old magazine he found on the table, sitting in an uncomfortable chair at the doctor's office. Looking around, he's not sure how they manage to stay in practice. They are always running at least half an hour behind, the staff is miserable, and he's definitely gone into an exam room before with another patient's file still on the screen. If he ran his shop like this doctor's office, they would have closed after the first month.

Eventually, his name is called, and he follows the nurse back. What feels like ten minutes later, the doctor finally comes in.

"Good afternoon, Mr. Grace. How are you doing today?" she asks.

"Good, good. Thanks. And you?"

"The same," she replies, taking a seat on the little rolling stool by the desk. "What can I help you with?"

7

"The usual," he replies, rolling his sleeve up. He doesn't miss the stare she gives him as he does so, and while she's certainly attractive, he does his best not to mix business with pleasure. It took him a while to find a doctor who was comfortable dealing with demons and had knowledge of the differences in their bodies, so he definitely wasn't going to sleep with her and leave him with having to find a new doctor. Instead, he ignores the ogles and keeps his interactions as neutral as possible to avoid any confusion.

"Standard panel?"

"Yep."

She nods and gathers the supplies before coming over to stand in front of him. She wraps the tourniquet around his arm and waits for the vein to appear. As she takes his blood sample, he senses her need to say something and her growing hesitation.

"Say what you want to say, doc," he prompts.

"I mean no disrespect, Mr. Grace. But, as a doctor, I feel it is my role to note you come in here pretty regularly, getting tests done for sexually transmitted infections."

"Yes."

"While I appreciate your attention to your health, I do have to wonder if you would be better served, uh, reducing your activity."

He breathes in slowly, trying to find an appropriate way to tell her to mind her own fucking business. Fighting the angered demon within, he says, "Thank you for your concern. I will take it under advisement." His voice comes out harder than he intended, but frankly, he's tired of being judged for how he chooses to spend his time. Every partner consents and, as fully-formed adults, he and whatever companion he's with have the right to make their own choices.

She nods again, not pushing him any further. She finishes up a moment later and sends him on his way, letting him know the results will be forwarded in a couple of days.

After changing out of his grubby shop clothes, he grabs a cold beer from the fridge and flops down on the couch next to Buckley. Wisps of smoke unravel from him, spreading around the room as they relax, releasing the tension he's gathered throughout the day. He loves being a demon and all the power that comes with it. But he'd be lying if he said that it also wasn't exhausting. Holding his demon at bay all day, staying in his human form, keeping his smoke inside. It's a lot to manage. So when he gets home, he likes to let his power out, allowing it to stretch and relax as he does, which is why one of the wisps hovers over Buckley, petting him absent-mindedly. Buckley, like the ridiculous dog he is, rolls over, exposing his stomach to the smoke to provide premium access for optimal belly rubs.

He drops his head back on the back of the couch, closing his eyes. A loud *thunk* has him cracking an eye open, looking to the side of the room where a tendril of smoke has knocked over a plant stand, spreading dirt all over the floor. "Hey. Dipshit. Knock it off," he tells the tendril. The point rises and turns toward him. If it had a face, he's sure it would be giving him a mischievous grin. Rather than argue with it, he draws it back in. Calling the magic to return to its base. It tries to resist the command, stretching and wriggling forward, but eventually relents at Declan's insistence.

Placing his beer on a coaster on the coffee table, Declan gets a broom from the closet and cleans up the mess. After his precious marble pothos has been righted and its dirt replaced, he settles back on the couch, picking up the remote to watch last night's episode of *Liars & Thieves*, his favorite competition, following a group of selected liars attempting to deceive their way into winning a pot of money. Declan's phone vibrates next to him as the truth-seekers finally manage to eliminate a liar. Pulling it out, he sees a message from his best friend, Everest Oaks.

EVEREST

Hey loser

Are you done moping?

DECLAN

I'm not moping

But you are a loser

Fuck off.

Never!!

You'd be lost without me.

That's debatable

Anyway, what's up?

Wanna go for a drive?

I've already had a beer. Starting my second.

I'll come get ya

Declan pauses to think about it. He doesn't really want to go out. But he also knows that if he doesn't, he'll sit here for the rest of the night drinking and watching reality shows, which doesn't exactly scream healthy and well-adjusted.

Though, there is probably a lot about him that doesn't scream well-adjusted.

Sure.

Cool

Be there in 10

K.

He turns off the TV, puts the cap back on his beer, knowing full well it will be flat by the time he gets home, and puts it back in the fridge. He charges upstairs, turns on the shower, and hops in to quickly wash off the day's grime. Everest is comfortable enough to let himself in if Declan isn't ready right when he arrives, so he doesn't worry about rushing through it too much. When done, he rubs his hair with the towel, squeezes some gel on his hands, and runs it through the long strands that run down the center of his head before quickly braiding it. Unsure where, if anywhere, Everest wants to go, Declan feels it can't hurt to make sure his hair isn't a complete poof ball when it finally dries. He grabs a pair of dark wash jeans from the dresser drawer and a dark green Henley. By the time he makes it downstairs, Everest is already sitting on a stool in the kitchen, scrolling through Declan's phone with Buckley's head resting in his lap. *Traitor.*

"Dude. Who is Charlie? And why is she blowing up your phone?"

"None of your business," Declan says, trying to grab his phone from Everest's hands, but he twists to keep it out of reach.

"Pah! She says, and I quote, 'You were the best I've ever had, and I can't wait to ride your'—" Declan tackles him, wrenching the device from Everest's stupid hands as Buckley bounces behind them, grumbling playfully.

"You're such a dick. Why do I stay friends with you?" Declan grumbles.

"Apparently, you're the king of dicks, according to Charlie." Everest laughs. "Besides, you know your life would be boring without me."

After Declan's father passed and Lachlan became the new demon lord, Declan found himself accompanying his brother on some of his travels. Partly so Lachlan could keep an eye on him, and partly because Declan was curious what else there was out there. Soon enough, Lachlan found himself settling in Leeside, and Declan decided to stay on this side of the world as well. Hanging around Leeside so much led to joining clubs to keep busy.

As much as it pains him to admit it, Declan knows Everest is fucking right. They've been friends for years, meeting when they both signed up for a recreational football team. They were paired up for some warm-up drills and have stuck together ever since. Growing up in the underworld, Declan never thought he would befriend a human, let alone become best friends with one.

Declan has never been one to have a large group of friends. Instead, he prefers a small, tight-knit group of quality friends over quantity. Granted, the idea of keeping a small group of trusted individuals around him may have been a by-product of his father and how he felt the need to keep a close group of confidants during his reign as ruler of the underworld. But Declan has yet to unpack all the ways his father fucked him up, and he's certainly not about to do it right now.

"You ready to go?" Everest asks, pushing away from the counter.

"Oh. Yeah." Declan slides a pair of running shoes on, not bothering to untie them. He pats Buckley on the head, giving him a good scratch behind the ears and a kiss on the forehead before they exit the house. "Where are we going?"

Everest unlocks his truck and, as he climbs in, says, "That's for me to know and you to find out."

Declan buckles his seatbelt and rolls his eyes at his friend. "Nothing illegal, alright. Bucks needs his daddy to come home."

"Daddy, huh?"

"Fuck off." Declan laughs.

CHAPTER 3
Eliana

"So, tell me, how have things been going for you lately? It's been a couple of weeks since our last session."

"Really? That's the best you've got?" Eliana replies.

"Well, from your reaction, I assume everything has been going swimmingly."

Eliana rolls her eyes. Dr. Colson Reid has been her therapist since she moved back to Leeside two months ago. He came highly recommended, at least according to the random internet reviews she looked through before selecting him. He's generally pretty good at what he does, and he has helped her begin to work through her anxiety and other feelings as she navigates life in her hometown.

Huffing out a sigh, she crosses her arms across her chest and admits, "No, things are not going *swimmingly*."

Colson lifts his left leg and rests his ankle on his right knee as he lays his notepad on his thigh. His pen scratches across the paper, the sound of which is like nails on a chalkboard to her as he makes notes. Looking up from his pad, his gaze catches hers, and he suggests, "Why don't we start with what's frustrating you."

She resists the urge to grumble at him like a petulant teenager. Instead, she casts her eyes down to her hands, where she picks at the skin along her nail, trying to find the words. After what feels like ages with Colson waiting, for he never rushes her, she says, "I feel like I'm not me." Colson shifts, and she knows he's going to ask why, so she raises her hand to stop him before he can. "I know. We've talked about this before, and I've accepted my career path has changed, but it doesn't mean I don't still miss it. Long for it even. I miss the stage and the joy of dancing every night for a new group of people."

"How do you feel when you're with your pupils?"

Eliana smiles, thinking of her little group of toddlers who are pure joy in her class. "I love them. They are fun and adorable and embody the joy of dance."

"So, is it possible you could find joy with them, and your other students? They may not be a new group of people every night, but is it possible your joy still exists, but has taken on a new shape?"

She runs his question through her mind. Does joy for her still exist, but it wears a different mask? Instead of a new crowd, she gets to watch her littles grow and prosper in this art form. "Yeah, that's possible."

"If you have joy and dance, what leaves you feeling stuck?"

Eliana pauses before answering, almost afraid to admit what she's about to say out loud. "I left Leeside with the intent to never come home. I had big dreams. Aspirations. I was going to be the next principal dancer for the Harmony Dance Company—one of the largest and most prestigious organizations. As you know, my dream was cut short thanks to a ruptured Achilles, and after a lengthy time healing post-surgery and being on my own, unable to do what I loved, I moved back here. The problem is that I find myself still wanting *more*. I love teaching little ones now, but it doesn't quite fulfill me in the same way dancing professionally did. I live on my own. I basically go to work and go home. I have the odd brunch date with my best friend from childhood… but it's not enough."

"It sounds like you feel more lost than stuck, which is normal. You lost a big part of your life. Something you had been working toward for presumably the majority of your life. And now you're back in a place that you left behind. Does that sound right?"

"Yeah."

"You are allowed to grieve what once was."

She wipes away a single tear from the corner of her eye. She's been feeling this way since she returned home but had been worried that others would think it was her being dramatic. That her feelings weren't right. It's not uncommon for dancers who face career-ending injuries like hers to never set foot in a studio again. The pain—both physical and mental—is too much. She knows she's lucky that she's still able to have dance in her life, but that doesn't mean she feels any less out of sorts with her current situation.

"I know," she says softly, more to herself as an attempt to validate her own feelings.

Colson leans forward, resting his forearms on his thighs, pen and pad clasped in his left hand as it hangs between his knees. "Then the question remains: what do you think you need to help you find your footing again? To feel more grounded rather than like a bag in the wind searching for a place to land."

"I don't know."

He looks at the clock. "Well, I think for your homework, you need to think about that. Consider what you need. What do you think will help you feel less lost? We can talk about that next time."

"Okay," Eliana replies, gathering her coat from the arm of the couch as she stands. "Thanks, Colson."

Eliana pulls open the door to Strike a Pose dance studio and steps into the naturally lit lobby. "Good morning, Bellamy."

Eliana grew up coming to Strike a Pose for lessons. She loved her jazz classes but always felt more drawn to ballet. When she was old enough, Eliana started working here and helping out with some of the younger classes before eventually taking on her own as she went through the dance program at Leeside University. It was only natural to come back when she found herself living in Leeside again.

"Morning, Ellie. How are you this morning?" she chimes. Bellamy is probably the happiest person Eliana knows. Or at least that's the vibe she gives off. She's always so cheery and has a warm and welcoming smile. She's like the company mom, only she's twenty-three. She is truly an old soul, and it's impossible not to love her.

"I'm doing okay," Eliana answers. "Little car trouble this morning, but I managed to get here."

"Oh no. Do you think you'll need to take it to get fixed?"

Eliana raises a hand and crosses her fingers in front of her. "I hope not. I don't really have the funds for any major repairs right now."

"That's always the way, isn't it?" Bellamy replies, turning back to her computer.

"It appears that way," Eliana says more to herself than to Bellamy. Eliana waves half-heartedly at her before walking to the staff room at the back of the studio. She puts her duffle bag into her locker, removes her outdoor shoes, and slides on her dance slippers. She's got a class of toddlers this morning for their ballet lesson, followed by a couple of teen contemporary groups, and finishing up with a tween school jazz class. It's her busiest day of the week, and as much as she never saw herself as a child dance instructor, she loves coming in and seeing all their faces and the pride as they finally land their spin or jump for the first time.

Eliana would prefer to spend her days on the big stage, dancing her heart out, drenched in sweat and out of breath. However, thanks to an injury last year preventing her from her dream of dancing full-time, she now shares her love of the art form by teaching the next little stars. The same injury alongside an unsupportive boyfriend also meant she had to move back home to Leeside. No longer able to keep her apartment in the big city without the principal dancer's earnings and feeling alone in her relationship, Eliana moved back home a couple of months ago. It's not exactly where she saw her life heading when she moved to the big city, but she's still happy to be able to share her passion on a smaller scale if it means keeping dance in her life.

Growing up as a human in Leeside was interesting, to say the least. While she's heard the council has made great strides over the past few years to create stronger bonds between human and supernatural beings, it wasn't always that way. Some previous council members were quite combative and didn't think humans had a place in town. Thankfully, those members are no longer in power, and the community has been moving forward with greater inclusivity. From what her family has said, the annual community bonding event, Mixing Our Spirits, has been a great help. The council has strived to include human perspectives and considered them as they develop new initiatives to better the town. The way the human city council and the supernatural council have come together has been inspiring.

She loved living in Hollybrook and all the opportunities it gave her to pursue her dreams. However, even with Leeside's challenges and growing pains, if she can't be in Hollybrook, Eliana wouldn't want to live anywhere else. The community is so tight-knit. Everyone knows everyone and, with it, all of their business. As annoying as it can be, it's also comforting on some level.

Eliana checks the clock on the wall, noting she has a few extra minutes before her toddlers arrive. She opens the door to studio two, turns on the lights, and makes her way to the beam in front of one of the mirrors. Eliana starts by placing her hand on the bar, turning out her feet, and pushing down into a plié. She runs through a familiar series of movements, warming up her muscles, though they won't be used enough with this little group of children to warrant it. When she's done, feeling loose and ready, she brings herself to the corner of the studio and dances her way to the opposite corner, performing a series of jumps, turns, and extensions. While she was given the all clear for movement before she moved back home, the fear of going through that agony again keeps her from pushing herself too hard.

Brushing her hands along her tights, she attempts to wipe the nerves away. So when she gets these few spare minutes every now and again, she likes to run through old sequences, reminding her body of what it was once capable of. She'll likely pay for the leaps later, but for now, she'll allow her heart to continue to sing, relishing the exhilaration that comes with flying through the air.

After a few passes and breathing heavily from lack of regular practice, her concentration is broken when a series of little hands begin clapping behind her. Blushing, she turns and faces her tiny audience. "Thank you, friends. Are you ready for today's ballet lesson?" The children cheer, running to the side wall where they keep their bags.

Quickly falling into the rhythm of teaching, Eliana finds the class soars by. But there is no time for rest as her next class comes in right on the heels of her little toddlers. Soon enough, the morning passes with barely enough time for her to eat lunch before her afternoon sessions begin. The natural rhythm of the day continues as she works with each group.

With the day finally done, she collects her belongings from her locker and makes her way toward the door. Bellamy calls to her before she can step out. "Oh, Ellie, your brother called earlier. You were in class, and I didn't want to bother you."

"No worries. Did he say what he wanted?"

"No. He only asked if I could tell you to stop by on your way home."

Sighing internally, she forces a smile. "Thanks." It's not Bellamy's fault that Everest couldn't bother to text her. He knows she'd have her phone in the studio. She waves goodbye to Bellamy and rolls her eyes to herself as she exits the studio.

"He likely wanted to talk to Bels anyway. The fool keeps trying to ask her out and won't take no for an answer," she mumbles to herself.

Tossing her bag in the back seat, she climbs into her car,

puts the key in the ignition, and turns it, but the blasted thing doesn't start.

"Fuck me," she groans, leaning forward and resting her head on the steering wheel in frustration.

Taking out her phone, she brings up her brother's number and presses the dial button, saying, "Hi, Everest," when he answers.

CHAPTER 4

Eliana

A fter jump-starting her car, Everest told her she'd need a new battery sooner rather than later. She thanked him for his help, but she doesn't have the money for that right now. This means she's driving back to the studio today on nothing but the wings of hope that she can make it another couple weeks. But those wings are looking pretty bare about now.

"Not again. Come on," Eliana says with frustration, banging her hands on the steering wheel. Pushing her foot down on the brake, she turns the key in the ignition, only to be answered with an annoying whirring noise and then deafening silence.

"Fuck."

She rests her head on the steering wheel, tears building in her eyes. Wiping the tears away with the sleeve of her sweatshirt, she leans back and rests her head on the headrest. She's always hated that she cries when she's angry, frustrated, or stressed. She hates it even more that she's going to have to pay to have the car towed to a nearby shop and pay a mountain of money she can't afford to get it fixed.

Digging her phone out of her bag on the passenger seat, she unlocks it and opens up a search engine to look for a towing company. After calling and giving her information, they inform her that a driver would be there in the next forty minutes. She then searches for a nearby shop and finds Hellbent Motors. The name sounds familiar, but she can't figure out why. Either way, it's only a few miles away, so it will have to do. She gives the number a quick call and checks to make sure it's okay to bring her car in. With the go-ahead from the young guy on the other end of the line, Eliana makes her final call to her boss at Strike a Pose.

"Thank you for calling Strike a Pose; how may I direct your call?" Bellamy answers.

"Hey, Bels, it's Ellie. Can you get June for me?"

"Sure, one sec," Bellamy answers, placing the call on hold and starting the calm hold music. The softness of the tune challenges her current mood, and rather than being peaceful, it ignites further anger in her. She needs this money and can't afford to miss teaching a class, but now she's going to be stuck for at least an hour dealing with her stupid fucking car.

"Hi, Ellie."

"Hi, June. I'm sorry for the short notice. My car broke down on the way to the studio, and I'm not going to be able to make my two ballerina tots classes this morning. Would you or Sienna be able to cover for me while I get this disaster heap towed and taken care of?" Eliana tries to sound apologetic rather than angry, but she's not sure it comes through. If it sounds angry, June doesn't let on.

June pauses before answering, likely running through the schedule for the day to make sure the changes work. After a moment, she replies, "Yes. Yes, that should work. Sienna can take your first class, and I can do the second. Are you okay?"

The question is simple, but it deflates her. Tears build quickly again, and she fights against it, not wanting to unleash everything on her boss, who is asking out of necessity. "Yes. I'm okay. Thanks for asking," she replies, meaning every word of it. "I'm waiting for the tow truck. I'll let you know when I'm on my way."

"No worries. Thank you for letting me know, hun."

"Thanks for your understanding, June. See you in a bit." Eliana hangs up and sighs. She's parked on the side of the road, so she's safe. But now she's also hungry. With time to kill, she goes to the coffee shop across the street.

With food and tea in hand, she settles back into the car and waits for this stupid tow truck. The driver arrives right at the forty-minute mark. He hooks up her junker with ease and instructs her to get into the cab. After she awkwardly climbs in, he asks, "Where are we headed?"

Eliana double-checks her phone before replying, "Hellbent Motors. It's over on Roundtree."

He nods. "Yep. You sure you want to go there?"

"It's the closest, so it will have to do."

"Alright," he replies. His words are brief, but not untoward. As a relatively young woman, Eliana knows she can never be sure how these kinds of situations will go. She probably should have called Everest, but the last thing she wants is for him to know he was right. As protective as he can be, he's still her brother and will take any opportunity to tease her.

Thankfully, the ride to the shop is brief and the driver isn't overly chatty. Eliana hates making small talk with strangers as it is, but today in particular, she isn't in the mood for it. She needs her car fixed; that's all she cares about.

When they arrive, he backs her car into a spot out front and unhooks it before giving her an invoice for the service. She digs her wallet out and pays, and then the man hops in the truck and disappears as if he were merely a figment of her imagination. Maybe he is, and this is all just a twisted game her brain is playing on her.

Her head is down as she walks to the front door, placing her phone and wallet back in her bag. She pulls the door open, still too focused on trying to close her bag with one hand and keep it slung on her shoulder. The door chimes overhead, and a gruff voice sounds from somewhere in front of her, "Hi. I'll be right with you."

Her head pops up. She knows that voice. She hasn't heard it in some time, perhaps even years, but she knows it. She'd know it anywhere.

"Declan?" she asks, looking at the boy, no *man*, behind the counter.

"Yeah," he responds nonchalantly, clearly having not noticed her yet.

Fuck, he looks good.

CHAPTER 5

Declan

E *liana.*

His eyes meet hers, and it's like time stops. Fuck, he hasn't seen her in years. Despite being his best friend's little sister, she had moved away before he became friends with Everest. They've managed to run into each other the odd time at their family home, but it's always been in more of a passing than anything substantial. He places his hand on the desk to steady himself. The feel of the wood under his hand brings him back to reality. The one where Ellie stands in his shop.

"Eli... ana. What brings you here?" he says, sharper than intended, trying to swallow the strange urge to go to her, and the power rises to the surface of his skin. He doesn't mean for it to come out that way.

"Well, this is a mechanic's shop, and I have a car that needs repair."

"And you chose my shop?" he asks, eyes wandering down her body, making a mental note of the curve of her hips. Did she always look this fucking good in tights and oversized sweaters?

"I thought the name sounded familiar, but I didn't know this was your shop. I chose the closest one to where I broke down."

Still stunned and trying to process how she wound up at his shop, he can only say, "I see."

"Now that you're up to speed. I'm already late for work and would prefer not to spend longer here than needed. So can you take a look and let me know what the issue is and how much it'll cost?"

He shakes his head, clearing the way his brain has short-circuited.

She wants him to look at her car.

Yes.

He's a mechanic.

He needs to go and look at her car.

Finally coming back into himself, he switches into mechanic mode. She's a regular customer. He can do this.

He steps out from behind the desk, moving toward her, but she steps to the side, allowing him space to move past and keep distance between them. Eliana unlocks the door for him, and he pops the hood. He does a quick check and then asks her to try starting it. It whirrs sadly and then dies. He walks over to the driver's side where she opens the door, thankfully not whacking him with it. "It could be a starter or battery. I'll have to get it into a bay for a better look."

She flops her head back on the headrest. This is clearly not the answer she wanted. "How long will that take?"

"Probably a couple of hours."

She gives a resigned sigh. "Fine."

"Come back inside, and we can get you into the system," he responds, trying to sound positive despite the unusual nerves churning in his stomach. She follows him in and within a few minutes, she is all set up. "I'll give you a call when I have a confirmed answer, and you can decide from there."

"Fine," she practically grunts at him. She turns and walks toward the door, dialing a number into her cell as she does.

"I can give you a ride to work, you know, if you want," Declan calls after her, not knowing why these words fly out of his mouth.

"It's fine. I'm calling a cab."

"It will save you some money," he says. He recalls Everest always saying she's afraid to spend money, and given the potential cost of fixing her car, he can understand that she may want to save every penny she can.

She stops, hesitating, contemplating whether it's worth it.

"Fine," she evidently relents.

Declan leans over, picking up his keys from the side of the desk. He calls into the shop, letting one of the other guys know to bring her car in and that he'll be back shortly before leading her around the corner to where he's parked.

"No. Absolutely not," she says.

"It's what I drove to work today."

"I am not getting on the back of your motorcycle."

"Look, we can stand here and bicker, and you can eventually agree to get on, or you can agree now and save the energy," Declan says, picking up his helmet and sliding it on before swinging a leg over the top. He pulls the extra helmet he carries around out of the cubby at the back and hands it to her. Glaring at him with the most beautiful hazel eyes, she takes it and puts it on. She swings a leg over and settles behind him. Her arms wrap around his stomach, and he will deny it until the day he dies, but he swears butterflies soar in his stomach as she embraces him. He's spent years chasing this feeling. No one has ever been able to make him feel anything other than hollow. Now, his best friend's sister is here with her arms begrudgingly wrapped around him and his mind is busy spinning through all the ways he can try to keep her there. "Wanna tell me where we're going?"

"Strike a Pose dance studio."

"Which is where, exactly?"

"Get us to the corner of Frost and Hemlock, and I'll direct you from there," she says flatly.

Declan nods quickly before leaning the bike slightly to release the kickstand and pushing the start button. The bike roars to life beneath them, the familiar vibration calming his fluttering stomach.

CHAPTER 6
Eliana

With her arms wrapped around Declan's midsection, they ride through Leeside, where she has no choice but to inhale his oak and oil scent. It's masculine, whatever that means, and fills her nose, working itself into every crevice of her being. The few times she'd met Declan and been near him, she could never remember him smelling so *intoxicating*. The strip of long hair down the center of his head is braided down the back of his head, with the end of it peeking out of the bottom of the helmet. What she can see of the sandy-colored strands this close-up reminds her of the beaches she saw while traveling in her early twenties.

Burying her face into his back, she inhales deeply, feeling an innate urge to imprint him on her skin. To burn his presence onto her being, for fear that she may never experience being this close to him again. She pulls her hands together a little tighter, feeling the give of his soft stomach underneath. She can feel the strength within him, but the outer layer is soft. Comforting even. Despite every effort not to, her mind wanders, wondering what it would be like to rest her head on it. Would he be soft and welcoming like a comfy bed?

Tapping his shoulder, she signals for him to turn right. Her studio is up the street, and it quickly dawns on her that this ride is almost over. Which means she may not see him again, as she doesn't know if he'll be there when she picks up her car. Does she want to see him again? Her gut tells her yes. But why?

Because he's currently making your pulse sing.

But he's Everest's friend. His best friend. Her big brother's best friend isn't going to want to hang out with her.

You don't know unless you ask.

She groans internally.

"What was that?" Declan asks, turning off the ignition.

"Hmm?"

"You said something? Or you were about to say something?"

Shit. Apparently, that groan was more external than she intended.

An embarrassed flush rushes up her neck as she swings a leg over the seat, holding her bag in place on her back and disembarking while trying to hide her reaction. Turning to face him, her eyes meet his.

Fucking hell, his eyes are perfect. As she goes to thank him, his crystal blue eyes quickly flare with something. Fire? Anger? Annoyance. She's not one hundred percent sure. But whatever it is, it sends goosebumps from her fingers to her toes.

"Are you gonna need a ride home?" he asks.

She shakes her head, trying to clear it of the unseemly thoughts coursing through it. "Oh. No. I should be okay. I can catch a ride with one of the other instructors."

Eliana is pretty sure she sees Declan deflate a little. Does he want to pick her up? "Oh," he replies, sounding a little sadder than he did a moment ago.

Unsure of what to do now, she adjusts her bag on her shoulder and motions behind her with her thumb. "I, uh, gotta go. I'm already super late." She takes a few small steps back, awkwardly raising her hand, and waves. "Thanks again. And let me know what the car needs and the expected costs."

He slides his helmet back on, leaning forward as he prepares to start the bike again. "Will do."

"Bye, Declan."

"Bye, Eliana." And holy shit, if her name doesn't sound like a prayer to the heavens. Sent directly from his lips to whatever gods or goddesses he worships.

"Thanks for the ride, Bels. I really appreciate it," Eliana says, climbing out of Bellamy's car. Her phone vibrates in her hand as she leans down to talk through the open window.

"Unknown Number" dances on the screen when she glances at it before silencing the call.

"Not to worry, love. I'm happy I could help. I can pick you up in the morning if you'd like."

"That would be lovely, thank you. Declan said it should be ready to go tomorrow afternoon, so I'll cab over there and pick it up before heading home."

"Sounds good, Ellie. I'll see you tomorrow."

"Bye." Eliana waves as she watches Bellamy pull away from the apartment building's entrance. Bellamy honks the horn, sticking her hand out the window, and waves before shrinking into the distance.

As much as she hates asking for favors, preferring to do things on her own, she's thankful that she has coworkers like Bellamy who have also become friends. When Bellamy heard what happened with Eliana's car, she was the first to offer her assistance and refused to take no for an answer, even if it meant Bellamy had to drive out of her way to bring Eliana home.

Eliana rides the elevator up to the eleventh floor, then makes the short distance down the hallway. Unlocking the front door, she steps into her home and sighs deeply, letting the frustration from the day flow out and releasing the energy that has been wound tight inside her. Although she's been busy teaching most of the day, her thoughts refuse to stray from the cost of her car repairs and the tempting demon who was going to fix it.

Tossing her bag on the floor and kicking her shoes off, she walks down the hall to her kitchen, where she spends a few minutes reheating a couple of slices of pizza in the air fryer and pours herself a glass of soda. She makes her way to the sofa, placing her food and drink on the coffee table. On the side table rests the remote and her current crochet project—a baby blanket for her pregnant coworker, Aria. She picks up the hook and yarn, settling it onto her lap, and turns on the TV, finding this week's episode of *Haunted Shores*, her favorite ghost-hunter show that looks at abandoned seaside buildings. She leans forward, taking a sip of her drink and a bite of the pizza, before sitting back and picking up the hook and yarn. She slides the hook between the yarn, wraps the working strand around it, and pulls through, wrapping the yarn again and pulling through both loops. Slide. Wrap. Pull through. Before long, the rhythm of hooking, scooping, and pulling the yarn back through takes over as she counts stitches, making sure to increase and decrease as needed.

As she builds on her chevron blanket, stitch by stitch and row by row, Eliana's thoughts wander back to the sandy-haired demon she had her arms wrapped around that morning. She may often be lost in her thoughts, but she's not oblivious. That demon is *fine*. She'd obviously seen him before. It would be hard not to, with him being her brother's best friend and all. Letting her mind wander back, it has to have been at least a couple of years since the last time they crossed paths, and those years have treated him well. Like really well. His shoulders feel broader, and from what she could tell with her arms around his chest, he's filled out nicely.

She didn't expect to see him when she walked into that shop, and she truthfully didn't know Hellbent Motors was his. Thinking about it now, the name and owner combo makes sense (him being the son of a former demon lord in the underworld, and all) and she recognizes why it would have sounded familiar, likely having heard Everest mention it a time or two. Though, she does tend to tune him out when he gets to talking about cars.

But the way Declan said her name when he saw her nearly made her knees buckle.

Eliana always hated it when her friends had crushes on Everest when she was younger. It frustrated her that friends would arrange to hang out with her in hopes of actually seeing her annoying big brother. Thinking of Declan now, though, has her finally understanding the draw. She has no reason to go and hang out with her brother, but she can't deny the urge to call him up and see what he's doing. Spending more time with him would mean she has a greater chance of running into Declan, of course.

Looking at the clock, she sees it's already been an hour, a new episode of *Haunted Shores* has started, and her pizza is long gone. She doesn't even remember finishing it off. Aside from dance, crochet is one of the only things that brings her so much peace while allowing her to process her thoughts. She gets lost in the rhythm and counting. No one told her there was so much counting in crochet when she started, but the counting and repetitiveness in the patterns help her focus. Some days, when she's really into whatever it is she's making, be it a sweater, a blanket, or a scarf, the pattern is all she can think about, and she'll find herself repeating it to herself as she dances, turning it into a new count for her to follow.

As the ghost hunters hold up an infrared camera, looking for heat signatures, she looks at the clock again. It's only seven thirty. Certainly, not too late to call Everest. He's likely chilling at home. Maybe even lonely. She wouldn't want her brother to feel lonely, she rationalizes to herself.

She picks up her phone, unlocks it, and finds her brother's name in her contacts. Her thumb hovers over his name. Before she can second-guess herself, she taps on the screen and calls him.

"Hey. What's wrong?" Everest answers.

"Hello to you too, and nothing's wrong. Why would you think something is wrong?"

"Because you only ever call me when something's wrong."

Eliana scoffs. "I do not."

"You do, too. Also, what kind of sociopath calls someone up without a text first?"

Huffing out an exasperated breath, Eliana sidesteps the

bait, refusing to feed into his attempt to annoy her. "Hi Everest, how are you doing?"

He laughs, knowing what she's doing. Their relationship has been tenuous at times, mostly in their teenage years, but as they moved into their twenties, they found their groove and can now get along amicably. One thing she's always loved, though, was how he's been protective of her their entire lives. Always willing to go to battle for her. Keeping her safe. Heaven only knows how many boys he's scared off over the years, though he wasn't able to scare the last one off. Of course, all of that doesn't stop him from being a right pain in her ass when he wants to. "I'm great, lil' foot. What's up?"

"Nothing much. Was wondering what you're up to and if you wanted to go get a coffee or something?"

He pauses. "You wanna get coffee?"

"That would be why I asked, yes."

"With me?"

"Again, I did ask," she says, feeling tension building at the base of her neck. Maybe this wasn't such a good idea.

"Why?" he asks, clearly skeptical.

Sighing, she says, "Because I haven't seen you in a bit and thought it would be nice to hang out. But you'll have to come pick me up; my car is at the shop."

"Right, yeah, Declan said something about that."

She gives him a moment, waiting to see if he's going to agree to her suggestion. When he doesn't answer, she prods. "So? Do you wanna?"

"Sure. I guess. I still think you're up to something."

"I'm not," she practically whines.

"Alright. Alright. I'll be there shortly." He hangs up before she can say anything else.

CHAPTER 7

Declan

"Why are we going out for coffee so late?"

Everest, taking his eyes off the road, turns his head and glares at Declan. "Late? Dude, it's not even eight. Did you suddenly turn into an old man in the last twenty-four hours? Is it past your bedtime, old fella?" He turns his eyes back to the road, an annoying smirk sitting on his ugly face. He's so fucking proud of himself.

"You're such a dick."

Everest laughs. "And yet, here you are."

"Anyway..." Declan says, drawing out the word. "Do you plan to answer the question?"

"Do you?" The fucker laughs again. If they weren't traveling as fast as they were, Declan would be tempted to open the door and roll out. Hell, as it is, he's still tempted.

Everest looks over at him and must pick up on Declan's frustration as he answers, "The call you saw me end when you came back from the kitchen."

"Yeah."

"It was Ellie. She was being weird and asking to hang

out. So I agreed, and since you were already with me, I figured you could tag along."

Declan does his best not to visibly perk up at the mention of Eliana's name. "But you two never see each other."

"We see each other," Everest says before clarifying, "Just not often. As I said, she was being weird about it. So something's likely up. She probably needs money because of how much you're charging her to fix her car." He looks over at Declan again and smirks at him before facing the road again and turning down a side street.

Declan rubs the back of his neck with his hand, hating how uncomfortable that look from Everest made him feel. As if Declan already didn't feel bad enough. He tried to keep the cost as low as possible, giving her the wholesale cost where he could. But fixing the car was cheaper than replacing it altogether, and it's not like the shop doesn't need the money. That's always been a difficult part of him, balancing the need to charge what is needed to keep the shop up and running, while also trying to be cognizant of how expensive these things can be for people. He likes to think he strikes a good balance, but some days, it's definitely harder than others to charge what is necessary.

When Everest's truck pulls up in front of what Declan can only assume is Eliana's apartment building, she's already waiting outside. Declan has to cover his mouth and pretend to yawn to hide the sharp intake of breath as he takes her in. Even though it's a bit cooler tonight, she's dressed in an off-white sundress that stops mid-thigh, showing her deliciously toned legs, black Converse, and a jean jacket. Her blond curls are partially tied back, framing her face and sitting softly on her shoulders. She looks every bit as perfect as she did in his shop earlier.

Looking at Everest, Declan sees concern, but it quickly vanishes as Eliana jogs over to them.

"You gonna let her in or sit there staring at me? I know I'm pretty, and it's sometimes hard to look away, but this does work better if all three of us are in the vehicle," Everest says.

Shit. Well, at least he thinks I was staring at him. "Yeah. Sorry." Declan opens the door and hops out. Eliana climbs in and slides across the bench to the middle seat. Because, of course, Everest has to have an older truck that only has the front bench seat for three people. Declan follows Eliana in and closes the door behind him. He reaches for his seat belt and when he turns to clip it in, he nearly bonks heads with her.

"Shit. You go first," she says.

"No, after you," he replies, motioning like some Victorian gentleman giving a pass to a high society lady.

She nods, smiling at him, and then buckles herself in before facing forward. Declan clips himself in and does the same, trying to ignore the heat radiating up his left side from every point where their bodies touch as the truck jostles as Everest drives them into town.

"Everyone good with Taster's Delight?" Everest asks as he turns onto another street.

"Yeah, that's good," Eliana replies at the same time Declan says, "That works for me."

Everest snorts. "You two are so agreeable when together. Maybe the three of us should get together more often."

As much as the idea of spending more time with Eliana sounds exciting, Declan is afraid of what that might do to him. The current of heat flowing through him from simply having their knees, hips, and shoulders touching has him thinking of every disgusting thing he's ever seen come out of or inside of a car, hoping that it will keep his dick from standing at attention. As it is, it's barely working.

Everest parks the truck, and before he can even unbuckle himself, Declan is out of the vehicle and nearly five paces away, sucking in breath after breath in an attempt to calm his body. But then she climbs out, her dress riding up to expose her thighs, and he's fucking done for.

His brain instantly floods with images of his hands running up her legs, feeling how soft she'd be under his rough hands. Wondering what it would be like to kiss them. Lick them. Slide between them...

"Fuck."

Eliana jumps, and Everest turns to him, cocking an eyebrow. "You alright, man?" he asks.

Declan turns, putting his back to them and tilting his head back. He breathes out. "Yeah, I'm good. Forgot something I needed to do at work today."

"Ah. That sucks, but you'll be able to fix it tomorrow, I'm sure," she says kindly.

Everest comes to stand next to him, placing a hand on his shoulder. "What she said." He points to the store across the street. "Anyway, shall we go get some coffee?"

Declan swallows. "Yeah. Let's go."

CHAPTER 8

Eliana

"So what are you having, lil' foot?"

"You do realize I'm twenty-eight, and I haven't been into dinosaurs since I was like six, right?" Eliana says. She was never a fan of that nickname. It's not her fault that she fell in love with *The Land Before Time* when she was young. She became obsessed after seeing it for the first time and insisted on watching it every day after kindergarten for a year. She watched it so many times that the DVD was nearly burned out. Of course, that fascination meant that she was quickly labeled lil' foot after the main dinosaur, and the name has stuck. For her entire life.

"Yes, I know how old you are. Trust me. I've been keeping track of how long you've been a pain in my ass since the day you were born. In fact, it's been precisely..." his words fade off as he does some mental calculations, "10,345 days."

She rolls her eyes at him before walking around him to approach the counter. He snorts behind her, clearly amused with himself. They've always been like this: Eliana, the younger sister, trying to be friendly and get along, while Everest, the older brother, is always teasing her.

"I'll have a peppermint hot chocolate, please." She steps aside, letting the boys order, and moves to step back to pay, but Declan taps his card before she can get to it. "Thank you," she says softly. She barely makes eye contact with him, afraid that looking at him will make her cheeks appear more rosy than they already feel. Fuck, being in his proximity is making her insides warmer than her hot chocolate.

Her drink is the first to be ready. Picking it up, she moves to one of the tables along the far wall, trying to put a bit of space between her and the handsome demon.

Wait. Why is he here?

She tilts her head back, realizing her error in not asking if Everest was alone. They must have been together when she insisted Everest come out.

After a moment, they settle at the table with her, their drinks in hand. Everest takes the seat across from her, but fuck her when Declan sits next to her. His leg brushes hers as he settles, sending little sparks up her body. Wanting to keep her cool, she subtly shifts away, putting what little space she can between them. She catches his curious expression as he looks at the new gap between them.

Oblivious as always, Everest leans forward, putting on his serious face. "So, what kind of trouble are you in?"

Eliana rolls her eyes. "I'm not in any trouble."

"Bullshit. Something has to be up for you to be so insistent to see me."

"Nothing is wrong. Did you ever think I simply wanted to spend some time with my big brother?"

He laughs. Full-bellied, booming laughter.

"Really?" she asks.

Wiping tears from his eyes, he says, "Yes. You never

want to *casually* hang out. You've been home for two months, and I've barely seen you. And with your car in the shop, I figure there's something wrong." He shifts his eyes, narrowing them at Declan before returning his attention to Eliana, "Do you need money? Do you need help finding a new car? Is there a dead body in the trunk?" His gaze flicks to Declan again as Everest silently mouths something to her about not letting Declan know, and he'd help hide the body.

She laughs at him lightly before waving him off. *There's that protective mode he seems to like so much.* Even joking about hiding a fictional body shows the lengths he'd go to. Which is part of the reason she never told him about her ex.

Eliana sips her drink, trying to put some thoughts together while ignoring how Declan is watching her. It feels somewhere between curiosity and hunger, and she's avoiding looking over to see which one is more prominent. Instead, she puts her mug down and leans in, placing a hand on top of Everest's. He sits upright, his brow furrowing as if preparing himself for the bad news. "Ev. I love having you as a big brother, and I love so much that you care about my well-being—in your own roundabout, jackass sort of way— but I promise you, there is nothing wrong. The car is going to be fine. Declan has reassured me that it's a simple fix and I don't need money from you. I can also promise there are no dead bodies to worry about. I missed the past few family dinners and felt like I hadn't seen you in a while. That's it. I swear." She leans back, wrapping her hands around her drink, though it is much cooler now. She takes a sip, watching him digest what she said.

While she waits, she catches a movement from Declan out of the corner of her eye as he slides his phone back into his coat pocket with a look of frustration, creating a troubling crease between his brows that she'd love to smooth out with her thumb, easing out whatever concerns he may have.

Eventually, Everest swallows and nods, drawing her attention back to him. "Alright then." He sips his drink and says, "Did you hear about Mom's boss?"

With the moment between them over, he becomes his animated self again. When she shakes her head in response, he launches excitedly into a story about their mother's boss being caught stealing money and how it was a whole scene trying to get the woman out of the office. As the story unfolds, they all fall into fits of laughter, and it is right then, when she hears Declan's deep rumble, that it fills her body with life. It works its way to her heart, settling in as it finds its home as if it has always belonged there. It's something she hasn't felt in some time, and seeing the light that now dances across his features, she knows that she's going to need to hear this sound again. And soon.

They spent longer than she thought they would at the Taster's Delight, but she's not mad about it. Yes, seeing her brother was fun. But the highlight was watching how Declan's eyes crinkle when he laughs and how wisps of smoke periodically circle him when he's relaxed. Admittedly, she's not spent much time around demons or other magical creatures. But there's something about seeing him so at ease as magic floats around them. It adds an interesting contrast to the happy image, knowing that there's power under the surface, waiting to be set free.

"Thanks again for buying my drink," she says, standing with him outside of the truck while Everest scrolls on his phone in the cab.

"It's no problem." He looks down at the ground, shuffling his foot. "Anyway, your car should be ready

HOOKED ON A DEMON

tomorrow afternoon. I'll give you a call if anything changes."

"Thanks, Declan."

"Anytime. Have a good night, Eliana. It was nice to see you again."

The way he says her name makes her feel all warm and fuzzy, like a warm blanket fresh from the dryer. She hasn't dated since she ended things with her ex. Not that she thinks anyone would blame her if they knew the truth. She promised herself after she left Hollybrook that she would take time to be alone. To spend time discovering who she is or at least who she wants to be. But with how he's looking at her right now, there's a not-so-small part of her that wonders if Declan might be the one to help her find herself again.

She watches Declan while he climbs back to the truck, noting the way his broad shoulders shift with each step, and how his jeans hug his well-formed ass and thick thighs.

Thank you, football.

Everest is too busy looking at his phone to have noticed anything that may have passed between the two of them. Declan climbs back in the truck, barely having enough time to close the door before her brother yells out, "See ya, lil' foot!" and speeds away.

Shaking her head, wishing that stupid nickname would go away, Eliana turns and enters her apartment building.

CHAPTER 9

Declan

Collapsing onto the couch next to Buckley, Declan turns his phone back on. Charlotte, aka Charlie, wouldn't stop texting him while they were out with Eliana. He told Charlie no, he couldn't meet up tonight; she kept insisting, trying to convince him. Rather than continue to turn her down, he thought it was best to turn his phone off.

As the device comes back to life, he sets it down on his lap and waits for the incessant buzzing to stop. It takes a minute, but eventually it does. Looking down, he sees a whopping thirty-four missed messages from Charlie, plus four from Clarissa and two from Olivia.

He releases a deep sigh. Not even reading any of the messages from Charlie, he already knows that whatever was between them needs to come to an end. He was up-front the night they met, saying he wasn't looking for any kind of commitment. Now she's not only not listening to him, but sending an additional thirty-four messages. It's unhinged. He brings up their chat and types out his standard break-up text.

DECLAN

Charlie. I had a great time with you;
however, I am not looking for something
serious, and I cannot give you what you
need. You deserve someone better, and I
wish you the best of luck in your search.

After sending the message, he goes to her contact info, taps until he reaches the block option, clicks it, and watches the number disappear from his phone.

His head falls back, resting on the arm as Buckley crawls up his side and nestles between him and the back of the couch. Buckley's head lands decidedly on his chest, and Declan's hand finds the top of his furry friend's head. The one hundred and thirty-ish pound dog is like the most cuddly weighted blanket. As he absentmindedly pats the top of Buckley's head and plays with his ear, Declan finds himself closing his eyes and dozing off with thoughts of seeing Eliana tomorrow dancing in his head.

BANG!

BANG!

BANG!

Buckley roughly pushes himself up and bounds off Declan, barking like a fool as he charges to the door. Bleary-eyed, Declan rises from the couch, where he accidentally spent the night, and staggers to the door, rubbing his hand over his face and trying to get his eyes to focus.

"Bucks. Enough."

The barking stops.

Declan abruptly opens the door. "I don't want what you're selling."

"Well, it's good I'm not selling anything then." Her fisted hand falls to her side, but the sneer on her face tells him everything he needs to know.

Charlie.

Fuck.

"What are you doing here, Charlotte?"

"Really? That's what you have to say to me after that piece of shit text last night and then blocking my number. Or at least I assume you blocked it since none of my messages went through."

Declan crosses his arms and leans against the open door frame. Buckley sits next to him, channeling his most intimidating presence, which still doesn't come across any scarier than a teddy bear. "I said what I needed to last night."

"You didn't even give me a chance."

"How do you know where I live, anyway?"

"You aren't exactly unknown in this town, Declan." He rolls his eyes. "I deserve an explanation. You were fine with us the other night. What happened?"

"You don't want me to answer that."

Her hands rest on her hips, and she juts her foot out. He knows she's pissed, and whatever answer he gives, whether the truth or a lie, is not going to make her feel any better.

"Yes, I do. You sent me a chicken shit text, Declan. You said I deserve better, and I do. I deserve you telling me the truth to my face. I deserve at least that much respect."

Truth it is, then. Maybe if she hates him enough, she'll leave him alone. He didn't lie when he said she deserved better than him. He's not the kind of guy she wants. He's not boyfriend material.

"Charlie, you texted me thirty-four times last night. Thirty. Four. I was out with friends. I told you I wasn't available, and you refused to take that for an answer. Instead, you continually hounded me, trying to convince me to leave what I was doing, which wasn't even an option as I wasn't the one driving. Even if it was an option, I said no, and you refused to accept that boundary. Your response was beyond excessive and, frankly, tells me all I need to know about you." He watches her face start to pinch together as she tries to fight off the tears. But he needs her to see that what she did wasn't okay and that there is nothing else here, so he continues, "I also knew that once I tried to break things off, you wouldn't respond favorably which is why I blocked you. I didn't lie when I said I wasn't the right person for you. Yes, we had a good time, but it was one night. You need more than I am willing to offer. I have no interest in pursuing anything further with you, and the fact that you are standing here, in front of my house, after I said things were over, proves my point. I am sorry if you are hurt, but trust me when I say I am not sorry about trying to break things off the way I did. I wish you had listened."

Her mouth opens and closes, but no words escape. Declan takes that as the acceptance he needs. "I need to go and get Buckley his breakfast," Buckley gruffs in agreement beside him, "and then get ready for work. I hope you have the day you deserve. Goodbye, Charlotte."

With Buckley following him, Declan steps back and closes the door, leaving her on the front step. He leans against the door, listening carefully and hoping she will be smart and walk away. He hears a sniffle, her footsteps fall away, and her car starts. Only when he's sure she's gone does he move back into the house to start the morning routine with Buckley happily bouncing behind him.

Stepping out from under a hoisted car, he wipes his hands with the rag from his pocket and tosses it on the shelf beside the tool chest. His forearm slides across his forehead, wiping away the small beads of sweat that formed from a strangely difficult-to-remove oil filter, and then he takes a swig of water from his oversized bottle. It's one of those massive ones that holds a bazillion ounces and has times listed on the size to try and encourage him to drink. Petra got it for him last Christmas, and as much as he hates to admit it, seeing it go down and hit that little goal throughout the day is oddly satisfying.

As he puts the lid back on and picks up his rag again, one of his front staff comes through the door into the shop. "Hey, boss. Some blond lady is here for you."

Eliana. His heart does a little skip, and fuck him if he doesn't enjoy it. He clears his throat, hoping it will hide the excitement that's now rising in him. "Thanks. Tell her I'll be out in a minute."

"Will do."

"Oh, and Xavi, can you bring her car around? It's the silver Nissan."

"On it," Xavi responds before turning and leaving through the same door he entered. Declan watches him go to the key wall and then dash off again through the back door to retrieve her car.

He washes his hands in the sink, buying himself some time to try and settle the butterflies in his stomach as he reminds himself that she's a client. Who also happens to be his best friend's sister.

Taking a deep breath, he pushes himself through the door and steps into the reception area, where she stands looking out the window. The sunlight streaming in frames her like she's a goddess unleashed, making her glow. It highlights her curves perfectly, and he shakes his head, trying to clear it from the racing thoughts that certainly lead to filthy places.

She must hear his approach as she turns slightly and spots him, giving him what he hopes is a smile meant just for him. And if his heart skipped a beat when he heard she was here, well, seeing her smile at him has his heart doing a full-on jig.

He's so fucked, and he doesn't even care. Not if it means he gets to see her look like this.

"Hi, Declan."

He steps toward her. "Hi."

A silence falls between them and it's as if his brain has forgotten how to form words or what it is he needs to say. Her head tilts to the side, watching him curiously. It takes a moment before she finally says, "Is my car ready?" and gestures behind her with her thumb to the parking lot in front of the shop.

The question finally sparks the routine back into him, snapping him back into mechanic mode. "Yes. Sorry. Xavi should be bringing it out front any moment." As he finishes his statement, her car pulls out and parks in the spot next to the door. "There it is." He awkwardly points to it. "We can go and take a look first if you want."

"Sure. That sounds good."

Declan nods and steps to the side, allowing her space to move and reaches for the door. He pulls it open and gestures with his free hand for her to go through first. As she passes in front of him, his nose inhales the most wonderful scent— peppermint and a hint of something citrusy. He sniffs again lightly, not wanting to make what he's doing obvious. Grapefruit. Peppermint and grapefruit. His new favorite smells.

He follows behind her, trying to burn the scent into his

memory before settling beside her. "Alright, so we talked about the starter. We got that fixed, and the battery was nearing the end of its life anyway, so that was also replaced. Upon inspection, as you would have seen in the report, we noticed the tie-rods were toast, and it needed an oil change. So we took care of those, too. It was honestly a good thing it came in when it did. It should start with no problem now, and if there are any concerns over the next couple of days, please don't hesitate to reach out or bring it back."

Her face falls. "Wow. That was more than I was anticipating. I'm afraid to ask how much this will cost me."

"Well, let's head back inside, and we can go over the payment details."

"Okay," she says softly, the light she had when she first looked at him now gone.

Standing at the counter, he pulls up her receipt. Clicking a few keys, he watches as the number drops significantly before selecting print. He grabs the paper from the printer and places it in front of her.

Her eyes widened as they ran down the paper. She raises her eyes to look at him and back down, then back at him again. "Declan, I can't. You can't."

He smiles. "I can. And I did. Benefits of being the boss." He doesn't often do things like this for people, but giving her such a massive discount helps her out, so it's an easy decision."

"Well, thank you. I appreciate it so much."

"You're welcome. I'm glad I was able to help." He taps some buttons on the machine and passes the payment terminal over to her. Stapling the payment receipt to her printed one, he picks up a business card and writes his cell number on the back. "If anything goes wrong, or you have any questions, don't hesitate to text or call me."

He swears he sees a hint of a blush creep up her neck, but that can't be right. "Again, thank you so much, Declan."

His smile broadens, almost hurting his face it feels so big. "You're welcome, Eliana. Have a great rest of your day."

She smiles and picks up her papers with his card, then turns, walking out of his shop. His eyes follow the sway of her hips as she goes, and then he waves back as she pulls away. He's not sure why, but it feels like he lost something important.

He stands at the desk for a little bit after she leaves, perhaps hoping she'll return or that he'll come to his senses and go after her. But neither of those happen. Instead, he lets loose a sigh of resignation, returns to the shop, and continues the oil change he was working on when she showed up, thinking about how she smiled at him the whole time.

"Lach!" Declan bellows, walking in the door of his brother's place.

His older brother strides around a corner, entering the living room on the left. "What?" His face shows concern and a bit of annoyance as he adjusts his pants. Meaning he and his wife, Petra, were likely up to something and Declan interrupted.

"Nothing. Didn't know where you were and didn't want to walk around the house playing find the demon."

"Well, I was trying to play that... but you have some inconvenient timing."

"Gross."

"Well, next time, call first so I can tell you not to come over." Declan laughs. Despite the harsh tone, he knows his brother is only kidding. Or is mostly kidding. He's honestly surprised he hasn't walked in on Lachlan and Petra in a heated moment yet, especially given he rarely announces his visits. "You'll learn your lesson one day," Lachlan says as if reading Declan's mind.

They walk through the house, stopping in the kitchen for a couple of drinks, and then head to the back patio, where they settle into the chairs by the fire pit, which comes to life as they sit.

"Thanks, Petra," Declan yells in the general direction of the house. He didn't see her scamper off as they walked through, so she was either well-hidden or managed to escape from wherever they were canoodling before he got there.

Lachlan sips his beer and looks Declan over. "You appear to be in good health. You don't need money. But why do I get the feeling that you have come here for a reason today and not because you want to see my sexy ass?"

Sometimes, he hates how well Lachlan can read him. Yes, his older brother helped raise him, especially after their father died and their mother wasn't able to care for them appropriately. Lachlan stepped up and did what he could while trying to bring the underworld to some level of balance as he undertook a role he never wanted. He's done great work since then. After Petra joined the supernatural council, they continue to do wonders, creating all sorts of new programs to help the underworld citizens better themselves and see the possibilities that are out there. That crime and pain are not the only things they have.

"Getting right to it, huh?"

"You interrupted me about to fuck my wife senseless," Lachlan says, snickering when Declan dramatically cringes, "so yes. I'm getting right to it."

"Do you really need to say that?"

"Yes." Lachlan laughs.

"Ugh. You're the worst."

"Yet, here you are, still not telling me what's wrong. I can go back to—" Declan grabs Lachlan's arm, pulling him back into his chair, interrupting him. "No. Fine."

"I hate that this is somewhat related to what you're talking about." Lachlan raises an eyebrow while Declan continues. "Not like that. I don't need the birds and the bees talk," Declan laughs. "Trust me, I know what I'm doing in that camp. But I guess, how did you know it was time to settle down and stop all that fooling around?"

"Do you see my wife?"

Declan snorts. "Valid. But when did you know you wanted more than just the lay? The conquest?"

Lachlan laughs. "Again, have you seen my wife?"

Declan's head drops, his eyes staring into the ground as frustration builds and smoke begins to swirl around his feet. "Dude, you know what I mean."

"Oh, put the demon back in its cage. I'm just playing." Declan's smoke vanishes as quickly as it appeared, apparently listening to Lachlan's command before he could do it himself. "Look, I was never really like you. I didn't do all the messing around you have." He raises a hand to stop Declan's interjection. "Yes, I had some fun, but you know as well as I do that as soon as Petra came into my bar, there was no one else. I tried dating, but there was nothing really there. Before that, any escapades I was involved in were mostly half-hearted. I knew it wasn't what I wanted in the end, so why go through all that to end up hurt or hurt someone else? Ya know."

"Yeah. I guess. Like I enjoy it, I really do. But also, I'm getting tired of slinking out of women's bedrooms."

"Yeah, I can see that. Maybe it's time you take a step back and think about what you really want. Think beyond the pussy, if you will."

"Oh, goddess." Declan laughs. His brother has never been a philosophical one, but that has to be the worst thing he has ever said.

Lachlan leans over and claps his hand on Declan's shoulder. "If you're asking if it's time to settle down, it probably means you're ready to do so. Something to think about." Lachlan stands and begins walking back toward the house.

"Where are you going?" Declan asks.

"I'm going to finish fucking my wife. I'd get out of here if I were you."

Declan runs into the house behind his brother, puts his empty glass on the counter, and out the front door, hearing Lachlan's bellowing laugh following him all the way out.

CHAPTER 10
Eliana

"I've thought about what you asked me to last time," she says, crossing her legs onto the oversized cushion. "Oh?"

"I think part of what's been contributing to my sense of being lost, is that I don't necessarily feel anchored here anymore. I spent so many years needing to get out and to leave Leeside, and now I'm back here, essentially against my will," she holds her hand up, stopping the anticipated question, "and while I have family and a friend or two here, I still don't feel like it's where I'm meant to be. My days in the city were filled with action. I was constantly busy. I was an active member in the dance company. And I don't have that here. I need something to sink my teeth into."

"And how do you propose you find that *something to sink your teeth into?*"

"I don't quite know yet, but I think that's what I need. Some kind of task to feel connected and more purposeful."

"And what about your family?" Colson asks.

"What about them?"

"How do they help you to feel connected?

It's a good question. Eliana doesn't see them nearly as often as she feels she should. Friday night dinners used to be a regular occurrence before she moved away, and now, it's only when she has the time or the energy. However, she is planning to attend tonight's dinner. "Family is hard. I feel like I'm constantly lying to them. They still don't know everything that happened. But I don't want to focus on that right now."

"Okay. Then, I expect an update on the progress toward your goal at our next session," Colson replies as he makes a note on his pad.

She smiles, feeling, not for the first time, more renewed with a sense of motivation with a goal post in mind. "That I can probably do."

"But I do want to provide, maybe, a word of caution."

"Okay."

"You've said you felt lost, and now you've come up with a goal to work toward. I want you to be aware of how you're feeling now and be careful that this feeling doesn't become a crutch for you later. You can't spend your life constantly chasing goals as a way to avoid dealing with whatever else is going on inside."

Well, I didn't need to be called out like that.

"I understand and appreciate the warning," she replies, knowing she's come up with this plan for that exact reason.

Friday family dinners are a regular occurrence for the Oaks family. The invite is basically open, with Eliana and Everest showing up when they can. Their parents are really good about understanding that their work schedules are not consistent, and as such, that means they may not be able to stop in every week. As is the case with Eliana. She's only attended once since moving back, and it's likely been three or four weeks since her last attendance. As she pulls up to their childhood home, she feels a sense of calm wash over her.

She's missed these nights.

"Hello?" she calls into the house, closing the door behind her.

"Kitchen!" her mom's warm voice responds from deeper inside. Eliana kicks off her ankle boots and hangs her coat in the front closet before walking down the hall toward the center of the house.

"Hi, Mom." She opens her arms and gives Cora, her mother, a hug, breathing in her vanilla scent.

"Hello, darling. It's been too long," she says, releasing Eliana and holding her at arm's length, taking her in.

"It definitely has. Work's been so busy lately."

"Always is. You'd think people would want to spend time with their children on Friday nights."

Taking a glass from the cupboard, Eliana laughs. Her mother has a point. For some reason, the Friday evening classes are always the first to fill up. "Apparently, they'd rather spend time with me."

"Well, I can see why!"

"Really? I can't," Everest says, sliding in behind her and grabbing a glass as well.

Eliana rolls her eyes. She steps away, opens the fridge, picks up a container, and pours herself a glass of mango juice. She puts the container back and closes the door in Everest's face. "Oh, I'm sorry. Did you want something?" she says before sticking her tongue out at him.

"Oh, you two, give it a rest," Cora says, playfully tossing dishtowels at them. "Dinner is about ready, go set the table."

"Yes, Mom," Eliana and Everest answer in unison.

"So, how's the car?" Everest asks, placing plates around the table.

Eliana follows behind him, placing the cutlery and napkins down at each setting. "It's good. Started without a problem to come here."

"Good. Declan's a good guy and a great mechanic. I'm not happy that you're still driving that piece of junk, but I'm glad you wound up there."

"Hey, you leave my hunk of junk alone. It's been a great car to me, and I won't let her go before she's ready."

Everest stops, leans in, and with his voice low, says, "Lil' foot, she was ready about five years ago." She scoffs, and he jumps away before she can swat him. The audacity.

Crossing her arms across her chest, she glares at him in the way that little sisters do when trying to make a point. "Well, when you want to pay for a new car for me, let me know."

Laughing, he replies, "Yeah. I'll get right on that."

Before Eliana can say anything else, their mom and dad come into the dining room, hands full of delicious-smelling food. Their dad, Amos, puts the already sliced roast on the table while their mom places the mashed potatoes and roasted carrots. "Sit, sit," he says, gesturing to the table, "let's eat before it gets cold."

"Don't have to tell me twice," Everest responds, placing a napkin on his lap and sitting all in one swift movement.

Pretty soon, they settle into comfortable chatter while they eat. Amos asks Eliana about her day and what's going on at the studio while Everest tries to coerce their mother into agreeing with him that Eliana should get a newer and safer car. Despite his enthusiasm, Cora ends up agreeing with her, as Eliana is the one who needs to pay for it.

When dinner is done, and Everest and Eliana have washed and dried the dishes—with only a small bubble war in the process— they settle in the family room for their family game night. Everest, of course, chooses the worst game in history, Monopoly. Nothing spells family fun like cheating each other over with capitalism. But that's what they do.

They play, they joke, they bond. These nights, while becoming less common with all of them there, are some of her favorites. Some of her best memories have come from these nights. Being able to spend time together and feel that sense of connection. She loved growing up in this house and loves her family, as frustrating and persistent as some of them can be. As she looks around, she realizes how much she's missed all of this. Years away in Hollybrook, while pursuing her dreams, kept her from her family. At the time, she felt like the sacrifice was worth it for her success. Of course, now, she realizes that it wasn't likely the case. Hollybrook allowed her to live her biggest dream, but it also brought her her worst nightmare and forever changed the fiber of her being in so many ways.

Eliana is the first to go bankrupt in the game, and soon after, the game collapses completely as Everest buys up everyone's properties. Somehow, he always manages to win when they play this game, and now that she thinks about it, Eliana is pretty sure he has it rigged in some way. There's no way he's that good.

Putting her coat back on in the entryway, her hand slides into her pocket and wraps around the little business card from a certain demon mechanic. Not wanting Everest to question why she has it, especially not with Declan's personal number on it, she makes sure she pulls her hand out slowly so the card doesn't slip out, and then buttons the pocket closed, keeping it secret and safe.

Hugs and kisses are given, and then she and Everest are ushered out the door. Standing on the front step, he motions for her to go first. "I wanna make sure it starts properly."

"I thought you said Declan was a great mechanic."

"He is. But your car is a disaster, so I wouldn't put it past the junk heap to stop working in protest."

Eliana lets out a frustrated groan. "Fine. But look, I know you mean well underneath all that snark, but can you give me a bit of a break?"

He casts his eyes down for a moment, seeming to think over her request. "Fine. I want what's best for you, Ellie. I always have. I don't know what I'd do if something happened to you. Your moving away was hard. I kept away because I knew you didn't need your big brother hovering over you, but it was still hard. I worried, like I do now with that piece of junk. I just ask that you call me if you need help, okay?"

The moment of sincerity nearly breaks her. She wants to tell him everything that happened in Hollybrook, but it doesn't feel important now. Instead, she simply responds, "I will. Love you, Ev."

"Love you too, lil' foot."

She climbs into her car, hoping that it won't prove her brother right. Thankfully, it starts without issue.

It's been two days since her family dinner. She's spent a good chunk of those same two days staring at the number scrawled on that silly business card.

She spins the card on the counter, watching the numbers

blur. When it stops, she runs her thumb along the writing, feeling the indent from the pen and marveling at the slant of the text.

The curve of the eights, in particular, makes her toes tingle. Never in her life has she found a number sexy, but the thought of his hand making the mark and how his hand moves… it's hot.

"What's wrong with you?" she asks herself. Pushing herself away from the counter, she grabs a glass from the cupboard and fills it with cold water from the filtered jug in the fridge. As she turns to close the fridge door, her phone chimes. Picking it up from the counter, she glances quickly at the card still sitting there, calling out to her.

KAIA

Good morning bestie!

Was thinking of doing a little brunchie-brunch today. You interested?

ELIANA

Brunchie-brunch? Really?

Yes. It's a delicious meal between breakfast and lunch. Often with mimosas.

I know what brunch is 😌

I was questioning your phrasing lol

Brunchie-brunch is perfect. It's fun, it's clear. It's the best.

Anyway, you in?

Where? What time?

Krumb-Krushers

10:30?

Oooh. Krumb-Krushers is great.
She checks the time on her phone. Meeting for 10:30 doesn't give her a ton of time, but she also hasn't seen her bestie in what feels like forever. And she does have the day off… so a mimosa or two wouldn't be a horrible thing. Her phone chimes in her hand again, drawing her attention back to the conversation.

Way to leave a girl hanging…

You do know I like to keep you in suspense

Don't I know it.

So what do you say? Will you go on a brunchie-brunch date with me?

Alright, yes! But only if you stop calling it brunchie-brunch.

I'll try, but I can't make any promises.

That will have to do, I guess.

I'll see you soon!

Arriving at the restaurant, Eliana takes a quick glance in the window, trying to see if Kaia is here yet, and uses the opportunity to check her reflection. She tucks a stray hair behind her ear and sees a hand inside waving at her. She raises a hand and wiggles her fingers back at Kaia, then reaches over and pulls open the door.

The bell chimes overhead, and as she steps into the building, she's overtaken by the smell of fresh bread, bacon, and coffee. She must be hungrier than she thought because the mix of scents is heavenly and causes her mouth to water.

As she steps toward the table, she notices that Kaia isn't alone. She didn't say anything about it being a group gathering, and the fact that it won't be the two of them for a girl's date saddens her a bit, but she puts on a smile anyway, not wanting to upset anyone at the table.

"Ellie!" Kaia jumps up, stepping quickly around the table, and hugs her. "I'm so happy to see you."

Laughing, Eliana replies, "I can tell. It hasn't been that long. Though I do appreciate the enthusiasm."

"Oh, shush. I'm happy to see my friend." Moving back to her seat, Kaia extends her hand and waves it at the open chair, "Sit. Sit."

Eliana removes her coat, hanging it on the back of the chair, and does as instructed.

"Ellie, this is Charlie and Wendall," Kaia says, gesturing to the other ladies at the table, who each extend a hand and shake Eliana's. "I know Charlie from my old job at the bank, and Wendall is her friend. We happened to come in at the same time and got to chatting, so we grabbed a table together." Kaia looks at her, secretly asking with her expression if this is okay. Of course, it's a little late now, but Eliana is nothing if not a people pleaser, so she nods slightly and sees the sense of relief cross her friend's eyes.

"So wonderful to meet you both. How long did you two work together?" Eliana asks Charlie.

"A couple of years. It was my first job after getting my degree in business administration from Leeside University.

Kaia took me under her wing, showing me all the things I needed to know when working in the field." She laughs. "I always felt like I was bugging her with all my questions, but she was so gracious, never hesitating to help me when I needed. We ended up hanging out outside of work and became actual friends."

Kaia smiles at her as she takes a sip of her water. "She's being modest. Charlie was one of the best employees we had. Not seeing her every day and being able to gossip about all things Leeside was probably the hardest part of leaving that job."

"But you needed it. You weren't going to get the growth you wanted if you stayed there any longer."

She nods in agreement. "True. Anyway, I was so happy to run into you that I couldn't miss the chance to have a meal together."

Eliana looks over at Wendall, who appears bored with the conversation. Not that Eliana blames her, it feels a little odd watching the two of them. Looking at Kaia again, Eliana can see a little flush in her cheeks. Perhaps there's more to that friendship than Charlie is saying. Trying to bring the conversation away from whatever may exist between Charlie and Kaia, Eliana turns to Wendall, asking, "What about you? How did you and Charlie meet?"

Wendall's face lights up, as if the tiny question is the best gift in the world. "We are actually childhood best friends. We met in kindergarten and, according to our parents, became instantly attached at the hip. We had to have playdates every weekend, much to our parents' grumbling."

"Aww, that's cute," Eliana says. "Kaia and I met as children, too. We were like five or six, I think. We shared a deep love of princesses and turtles. Like you, we've been kind of inseparable since. Though we never lived together."

She laughs. "As much as we love each other, I don't think that would have gone well."

Kaia laughs along with her. "Yeah, that would have been a quick way to end our friendship." Charlie and Wendall join in the giggles, and Wendall shares some moments of tension they had as roommates, including when Charlie's ex-boyfriend was found sleepwalking naked around the apartment, which causes the group to break out into another fit of laughter.

As the laughter wanes, a waiter arrives at their table and takes their orders. The conversation continues easily between the four of them, and Eliana could easily see the group getting together more often.

"Oh, I have to tell you about this horrible hookup I had recently."

Eliana catches Kaia's eyes light up, and Wendall's eyes roll. Clearly, Wendall has already heard all about it, but Kaia's practically salivating at the juicy story ahead. Eliana sides a little more with Kaia, her interest piqued because, well, dating horror stories can be fun as hell.

"Ooooo, spill it," Kaia says eagerly.

Charlie laughs, takes a bite of her eggs, and starts. "Okay. So I met this guy at a club. It was the typical kind of meeting. We locked eyes, and he came over and started dancing with me; we got drinks, went back on the dance floor, and, well, things were clearly heating up. We started making out on the floor, and it was like no one else was there. We didn't care. Hands were roaming, tongues were flying, and his ridiculously big dick was trying to bruise me through my dress."

"Off to a good start," Eliana interjects.

"Right? Anyway, one thing leads to another, and we go back to my place, fuck all night, and like this guy is *good*.

Really good. I have never been eaten out like that. I swear, he devoured me like I was his last meal."

Wendall coughs beside her, trying to hide a giggle, and Eliana catches the side glances from the patrons nearby. Charlie doesn't give a shit and continues, "Anyway, it was wild and hot. Honestly might have been the best sex I've ever had."

Eliana sees Kaia's eyes widen again, this time from surprise. "That's something! Also, I'm kind of jealous," Kaia laughs. "I could use a good lay right about now."

"Can't we all," Eliana says mostly under her breath, causing the group to erupt into laughter again. To be honest, since her ex, the interest in sex hasn't been there. That is, until she saw Declan. He's certainly ignited parts of her again.

"So what's the bad part? Because that all sounds like a dream," Kaia asks.

"Well, when I woke up, he was gone. He skipped out without saying goodbye." Eliana's face tightens in sympathetic frustration. That's never a good feeling. Not that she can speak from experience, never having had a one-night stand. "I get that it was likely a one-time thing. But like that was especially asshole-ish. We had exchanged numbers at some point, so I texted him the other night to try and meet up again for another round. He brushed me off and then tried to say that I deserved someone better. But he was a complete dick about it."

"That's rough," Eliana says at the same time Kaia says, "What a dick."

The couple next to them glares at them, and Eliana nudges Kaia's arm with her elbow. "Sorry," Kaia says with a sheepish look.

"Look, it's for the best," Wendall interjects.

"Yeah, I guess." Charlie agrees, picking up a piece of toast. "But like, the way he devoured me..." She sighs. "I would have liked at least one more go."

Wendall pats Charlie's arm in fake sympathy, saying, "I know," with a not-so-subtle smirk.

As the meal ends, Eliana feels a sense of joy at how the gathering unfolded. Did she want to give up what feels like precious girl time with Kaia? No, but as they walk out the door and say their final goodbyes, she can honestly say she's pleased to have met them. So much so that she exchanges numbers with Charlie and Wendell, and they agree to meet up again soon.

Kaia hooks her arm into Eliana's while they walk back to Eliana's car. She leans her head on Eliana's shoulder and sighs. "Thanks for that."

"For what?" Eliana asks.

"For going along with it. I know the plan was for the two of us, but Charlie was a good work friend, and I couldn't pass up having a chance to catch up."

"I'll admit I was a little bummed to see you sitting with them when I first entered, but they were really nice and I'm happy to have met them. I hope we can do something again in the future."

She can feel her smile through her coat. "Well, I'm happy to hear that. I like being able to bring different parts of my life together."

"Do you want a ride home?" Eliana asks, stopping beside her car and pulling her keys out of her pocket.

"Nah, it's okay. It's only a couple of blocks, and it's quite nice out today."

True. It's oddly warm for fall in Leeside. "Okay. Well, let's not wait over a week to see each other again, please."

"Yes, Mom."

Eliana gasps, dramatically holding her hand to her chest, feigning offense.

"Oh, please. You know you are the one who makes sure everyone is taken care of. Total mom."

With her voice laced with fake disgust, Eliana replies, "Still. No need to say it out loud."

Kaia's head falls back as she laughs. Once she's composed herself, she pretends to wipe away a tear before looking back at Eliana. "You're the best kind of mom, though. You let me stay out late and don't pressure me to have kids."

"True. No one needs that."

"Preach."

Eliana snorts and then pulls Kaia into a hug. "This was great. Text me later and let me know when you're available to do something later in the week." Kaia's arms wrap around her, squeezing her tightly.

"Will do."

Climbing into her car, she waves as she pulls away, grateful for a friend like Kaia who keeps her on her toes, even if she thinks she's a mom.

CHAPTER 11

Eliana

"Alright, team, we need to start putting together plans for our end-of-season showcase," June says from the front of the staff room.

Staff meetings are usually held once a month, but June called this one early. Knowing that the staff wouldn't be happy about having to stay after hours so soon after the last staff meeting, June was kind enough to send out an order form for the Bittersweet Acorn and ensured everyone had dinner. Which is why, as Eliana looks around, everyone is enjoying themselves. Nothing makes dancers happier than a free meal. June may have accidentally set a precedent for future meetings.

"So, our showcase is taking place in six weeks, and to say we are behind on planning would be a bit of an understatement. We will want a dance number for each class to present, as well as decorations, sponsors, and treats for the attendees. I am open to all of your ideas."

Eliana takes a bite of a fry and raises her hand. Though long out of school, the rule of raising your hand and waiting to be called on is so deeply ingrained that she doesn't think she'll ever feel comfortable openly speaking out. June looks at her and nods, giving her the floor.

She swallows. "I have lots of ideas, but before I let them run amok, I'm curious, do we have a general theme we want to build toward?" Eliana asks.

"Good question. What do you all think? Do we want an overarching theme?" June asks, putting it back to the team. She's always been good about ensuring her team feels included and valued as contributors. It's one of the reasons Eliana came to work at Strike a Pose when she moved back.

Different team members start calling out answers.

"Holiday."

"Dance of the night. Little moody and suspenseful."

"Under the sea. Mermaids, jellyfish, sharks…"

Bellamy groans beside her and whispers, "Under the sea is so overdone." Eliana nods in agreement as the suggestions continue.

"Dancing through the decades."

"Hollywood."

"Masquerade."

The room ooohs at the final suggestion. "A masquerade theme could be fun and leaves lots of room to play with it," Bellamy says. "Think of how dramatic it could be with the older ballet classes, while the younger children could be more playful. I think that's a great idea."

Other staff murmur their agreement, and June calls for a staff vote. "Alright, hands up if you think we should do a masquerade theme?"

All but one hand rises.

June turns her body to face the only staff member who is not in agreement. "What's your concern, Lola?"

Eliana sees Lola shift in her seat, uncomfortable with everyone's attention on her. "I… I…" she visibly swallows.

Zoe, sitting next to her, places her hand on Lola's shoulder in silent support. Lola looks at her, nods, takes a breath, and tries again. "I worry that it will be a bit too mature for my younger children. When I think of a masquerade, I think of how they are associated with mystery and sometimes desire, and that doesn't feel right for my little friends."

"Thank you for sharing. Bellamy, could you explain how you see it working for the younger dancers?"

Bels sits up straighter, ready to dive in. "Absolutely. I think for our younger friends, it could be more of an exploration of character. The mask represents something new they can be. It can be playful and fun, with a more lighthearted tone. Think of trick or treating on Halloween. That's essentially a socially acceptable masquerade—it's bubbly and fun for young children. Think of a more playful Swan Lake but with masks."

Lola nods along and thinks about it for a moment before saying, "Okay. I may need some help figuring out something that will work with my littles, but I'm willing to give it a try."

June claps her hands excitedly. "Wonderful!" Eliana raises her hand again. "Yes, Ellie?"

"What kind of budget are we looking at for decorations and costumes?"

"That's a great question. There are obviously some funds set aside from the annual budget, but if we can arrange a sponsor or two to help boost that, it would be great. Sponsors could also help make the event larger in general and potentially help draw in some new students."

"Do you have potential sponsors in mind that you'd like us to reach out to?" Bellamy asks.

"I do not. I am open to any collaboration, as long as it's a suitable match. Family-friendly, of course, and they need to be a favorable business in the community."

Elliana gazes around the room, noting the small side conversations and people trying to figure out who they could approach, but there's only one person she has in mind. A certain sandy-haired demon whose number is practically burning a hole into her kitchen counter.

June calls for their attention again. "Reach out to who you think would be a good fit. Ideally, we'd like to have two or three sponsors for the event, but we'll gladly take more. I trust your judgment. If you make an agreement, please ensure that you notify me of the details and how they wish to be included. If there are no other questions or concerns, we can call this meeting to a close, and you all can go home!"

June comes to her as she is packing up her belongings before heading out. "Eliana, I would like you to be the overseer for all of this. I've seen your growth as a leader over the many years I've known you. I've seen you grow from student to instructor, and even though you've only been back with us a short time, I think your experience working with larger shows would be a great asset. I also think you have a great ability to connect with people and are well-loved by our families, and I would love for you to have a more active role in the process."

Words appear to be escaping Eliana. She never thought something like this would be an option, let alone that she'd even been considered for the role. But this is one of the other reasons she came back to Strike a Pose—trust. June has known Eliana most of her life, and that history is hard to replace. "I don't know what to say." *Other than this is exactly the opportunity I was hoping for when I had my last appointment with Colson.*

"Thank you is always a good start," June teases.

"Yes, absolutely, thank you. So what would my role entail?"

"I'll still handle the big details, but I think you would be a good point of contact. Think of yourself as a liaison. I would also have you on site to help manage or oversee the construction of the set pieces and overall design."

She still doesn't know what to say, but June trusting her like this feels like a big deal. "I would love to."

"Excellent. We can chat more tomorrow."

She nods and thanks her again because what else can she do when she's been handed a great opportunity?

Eliana looks around the room and sees side conversations continuing, overhearing wonderful suggestions for sponsors, such as the Bittersweet Acorn, The Dandelion Inn, and Taster's Delight. But the more she thinks about it, the more she believes Hellbent Motors would be a perfect fit. It's family-oriented with a focus on keeping families safe, well-known in the community, and tangentially connected to the supernatural council, which is never a bad thing. So what better partnership than with a dance studio that caters to a mix of humans and magical creatures and that teaches the power of dance to connect?

Yes, it's a perfect pairing.

Now, if only she could build up the courage to call him.

CHAPTER 12
Declan

"Why are we going out again?" Declan asks, knowing full well why Everest wants to go out tonight. Personally, Declan would rather stay at home with Buckley. Usually, he's down for the bar nights and the game of cat and mouse. The will she, won't she. But ever since Eliana walked into his shop, he's wanted nothing to do with any other woman. Of course, he can't tell Everest that. Instead, he plugs along playing up the fact that it's been a long week, and he's tired, all the while hoping that Everest will get distracted by some woman and Declan can go home.

Declan slides onto a stool along the bar at the Bittersweet Acorn, which happens to be owned by his older brother, Lachlan. He signals to Daisy, his sister-in-law's best friend and bartender, that he'd like a beer and settles in for the night while Everest starts making the rounds.

It doesn't take long for Declan to finish his drink, and as he tips the glass back to get the last drops, Everest emerges from the crowded dance floor with two women hooked onto his arms. One for each of them.

Turning to face them, he leans back, placing an elbow on the bar top, and spreads his legs, trying to make himself look bigger and, with any luck, uninterested. Unfortunately for him, one of the women, a vampire he's pretty sure, steps forward and slides herself between his legs before leaning forward, putting a hand around the outside of her mouth, speaking into his ear.

"Hi. I'm Becky."

He turns his head to speak into her ear. "I'm Declan."

"Nice to meet you, Declan. Your friend there," she says, turning and pointing behind her before facing him again, "said you were cute, but I think he underplayed you a bit."

"Really? Why's that?"

"Because you are gorgeous. I swear all the other women's eyes have been on you since the moment you stepped foot in here."

Declan laughs. She turns her body slightly and sits back, resting her ass on top of his thigh.

Everest did well. He picked out a girl who fits his usual taste. She's curvy, blond, and has either a phenomenal set of tits on her or a bra that is doing the goddess's work. Either way, she's stunning. But even so, his mind is still wandering back to the way Eliana looked in those tights and how the light hit her hair as she stood by the shop window.

He rests a hand on his leg, careful not to touch her backside. "You're probably right, but it's not for the reason you think," he responds.

"Oh?"

"My brother is the owner." He watches as the realization hits. What that statement means, and all the weight that goes with it. People aren't watching him because he's hot. No, they are watching him because they know who he is by association, and with that comes some level of power and influence. They watch because they know he could ruin their night or make their entire year if he wanted. Human or supernatural alike, being close to members of the supernatural council means you have an influence, too, and that breeds all kinds of feelings. "You must not be from around here," he says with an amused laugh.

"No. We're from out of town, but we know about the council. They've done great work over the past couple of years."

"Agreed. Much needed work."

She smiles. "Also agreed." She pauses, appearing to muster some courage before saying, "Look. I know we've just met, but would you want to go somewhere a little quieter?" Her cheeks flush, and the embarrassment is adorable on her, but he knows that if he says yes, she'll want more than he's interested in giving.

He takes a deep breath. "Becky, you seem wonderful, but I don't think that's a good idea."

She practically deflates in his lap. Making a move on someone, or asking them out, is never easy, and regardless of how much you prepare yourself for the possibility of a 'no,' the rejection still stings.

Leaning forward, he speaks softly into her ear. "If we had met last week, I would have jumped at the chance to get to know you. You are stunning, and I'm sure there is someone out here who would be more than happy to spend some time with you tonight."

Smiling, she stands, brushing her hands down her thick thighs and smoothing out her dress. She turns to him again, leaning forward, giving him a great look down her top and what he'll be missing out on, and says, "Whomever she is, I hope she knows how lucky she is." Righting herself again, she turns and walks over to her friend, whose hand is running up Everest's thigh.

Her friend, clearly feeling pretty good, watches another woman walk by and, as the music dies, yells to Becky as she approaches, "Oh my goddess, Becky. Look at that woman's ass! It's huge!" Becky and others around them giggle.

Declan leans back on the bar, holding a new beer in his hand thanks to Daisy, and Everest gazes over at him, quirking an eyebrow up, silently checking in. Declan raises his beer in salute, his sign that yeah, he's good, and takes a sip.

That was all Everest needed, as a moment later, Declan sees him raising a hand and waving goodbye as he leaves the Acorn with both Becky and her friend in his arms.

While he may not have wanted to be out tonight, Declan hangs around a little longer, chatting to Daisy when she gets a moment.

"Your buddy left you, huh?" she laughs.

His forearms rest on the bar top as he leans forward to answer. "Fucker dropped me like a dirty sock."

"Can't say I blame him. That woman who was all over you was hot as Hades. Thought for sure you were leaving with her."

Everest probably figured the same thing. He can't think of any time he's ever seen Everest leave with two women. That will be an adventure for him for sure. One which Declan knows he'll hear all about in the morning.

"Can't deny she was beautiful. Just wasn't feeling it tonight," he replies.

She looks him over. Her gaze assessing him, searching for the hole in his statement. She doesn't need to look hard to find it as she smirks at him knowingly. "Who is she?"

"Who's who?"

"The girl you're hot for. The one who made you think twice about going home with the blond."

She hands him a glass of water, and he sips before he answers. "Don't know what you're talking about."

"Bullshit," she scoffs. "Anyway, the Lach-monster should be in shortly to close out the night if you want to stick around."

He loves his brother, but if Daisy saw through him so easily, there's no way he's sticking around to be scrutinized by Lachlan. His shadows can sniff out secrets better than a hellhound. "Nah, I'm good. I should be heading home. Buckley needs to do his late-night business and such."

"Uh-huh," Daisy replies, unconvinced.

He downs the rest of his water and stands, pushing away from the bar. "Shut up," he says, laughter in his tone.

"Do you need a cab since your buddy left?"

"Nah, I'm gonna walk. Thanks, though."

"No problem. I assume you don't want me to tell Lach you were here?"

"That would be preferred."

She nods. That's one of the great things about Daisy. She knows when to keep things close. "Alright, have a good night, Declan."

"Thanks, Daisy," he says, raising his hand behind him as he walks out the door.

CHAPTER 13

Declan

BARK! BARK! BARK!
Declan jogs through the house, reassuring Buckley as he goes. "Alright, Bucks. Good job!" Patting the big oaf's head, he looks through the small side window, only to be met with Everest's eager face on the other side.

"Let me in, jackass."

"No. I don't want any of your cookies."

"But they're delicious."

"How delicious?" Declan asks.

"Magical. Like the best you've ever had."

Declan laughs, flipping the lock on the door. "If you don't have cookies, I'm going to be really disappointed." He opens the door, and Everest's stupid face greets him. Declan looks to Everest's open arms and empty hands. Alas, no cookies. "Nope. No cookies. No entry."

"How about I give you an IOU?"

He looks at his friend, arms outstretched as if waiting for a hug. The playful look on Everest's face starts to falter as Declan makes him wait a bit too long, getting to where he questions if he should really be here. "Alright, fine. Come in. But I expect double cookies next time."

Everest jumps in place and claps like an excited child, exclaiming, "Yay!" They laugh together, their deep voices carrying into the entryway and down the hall as Declan steps aside to let him in.

"Honestly, surprised to see you today. I figured you'd be sleeping all day after what I can only assume was a night without any rest."

Despite not being able to see his face with his back to Everest while he makes coffee, he can feel the unbridled excitement emanating from his friend. The energy Everest has brought into the room is bursting with a saucy story of sexual escapades. As much as Declan could handle not having to hear all the sweaty details, he knows Everest is champing at the bit, eager to share. So he asks the one question he knows will set it all off. "How was it?"

Everest sucks in a deep breath, and then he's like a burst damn. Details, mimicking positions, all the different places they finished throughout his house. It all comes flooding out.

"Seriously, you missed out on a wild ride, man," Everest says, rounding out his story. "Becky was a phenom, and Lydia, well, I think she may be a goddess because I saw the fucking light man. I've never come so hard in my life."

Rolling his eyes, Declan shifts positions on the sofa, which they moved to somewhere around when Everest recounted how Becky ate out Lydia while he fucked Becky in the kitchen.

"I wasn't feeling it. But I'm glad it was a good time for you."

"What's gotten into you?"

"What do you mean?"

"Dec, Becky was a bombshell. You never turn down that kind of opportunity."

Looking down at his hands, Declan repeats what he told Daisy. "I was tired, and Buckley needed me home." He leans forward, picking up his coffee cup as Everest side-eyes him. Thankfully, Everest doesn't push any further because Declan isn't sure he will be able to form the right words to tell Everest that he went home alone because he couldn't get the image of his best friend's little sister out of his head. He doesn't need to know that he was thinking about what Eliana would look like sitting on his lap the way Becky did, or how he pictured peeling her workout pants off her glorious ass painfully slow, teasing her sensitive flesh along the way. No, Everest definitely doesn't need to know any of that.

Declan puts his cup back on the table, subtly readjusting himself in the process so as to hide the growing bulge in his pants. The last thing he needs is Everest noticing Declan's raging hard-on while recounting a missed portion of the night's threesome encounter.

As Everest drones on, Declan's mind wanders back to Eliana. He makes necessary sounds of agreement when needed. Everest has always been overly open and his stories are full of embellishment, which is fine as Declan's used to it now. He's happy Everest trusts him enough to share so openly, and that their relationship allows for this. There's this weird idea that guys can't share deeper thoughts or feelings, but he and Everest have never subscribed to that. Which is also why keeping his bubbling interest in Eliana is so challenging.

With that thought, he reaches for his phone in his pocket and checks for any messages or missed calls for what feels like the thousandth time today. And he's only been up for a few hours.

"So, anyway, do you wanna go grab some lunch?"

Shit. Everest must have finished his story while he zoned out. Everest looks at him quizzically as if he's been waiting too long for a response. Declan nods before answering a simple, "Sure."

It doesn't take long for Declan to get changed. He pats Buckley on the head as he leaves. Then he's back in Everest's truck and on his way into town.

Everest parallel parks and turns the truck off before hopping out. Declan looks up at the sign beside him and smiles. Nip & Nibbles has become a favorite of his. They were a food truck vendor at this big event Daisy and Sloan put on a year or so ago, and were apparently such a big hit that it led to the owner being able to open a brick-and-mortar location as well. Lachlan and Petra were raving about it after, and so Declan, fearing he was missing out, came with Everest and one of their other buddies—who Declan spots already at a table when he opens the door— for lunch one day, and now it's become a regular spot for them.

They both wave to the owner, Sulma, who stands on a stool in front of the counter looking into the open kitchen, and then slide into seats on either side of Tai. "Hey man, how you doing?" Everest asks, picking up the menu in front of him.

"Not bad. Not bad. How about you guys?"

Everest's eyes rove over the food options, and without looking up, he says, "I'm good. But I think Declan may be getting sick."

Concern fills Tai's features. "Dude! And you came to lunch?"

Everest laughs. "Sick of getting laid."

Both Tai and Declan groan at Everest's dumb joke. Declan, attempting to sidestep that comment and avoid the potential ribbing from Tai as well, answers for himself, "I'm good. Shop has had me busy. Everest dragged me out last night and is all butthurt that I didn't want to join him in a four-some so he was left to a threesome. Please don't ask him anything about it or you'll never get him to shut up."

Everest snorts. "It's true. TLDR: it was amazing. Becky..." he says before Declan cuts him off, saying, "Anyways... what are you thinking of ordering?"

Tai and Everest laugh at him, but thankfully, Everest takes the hint and returns his attention to the menu.

As they look through deciding what they want to order, Tai leans back, picking up his drink with purpose. "So uh, Ev. I hear your sister is back in town." Declan has a feeling he knows where this is going, and he's interested to see Everest's reaction. If he remembers the stories correctly, Tai had a crush on Eliana when they were younger, but nothing ever happened, and then she moved away.

Everest closes his menu. "Yeah, so?"

"Wondering how she's doing these days?" Tai asks, trying to be casual about it, but it's clear to everyone at the table what he means.

Everest leans forward, fisting his fork and poking the tines into the table. "She's single as far as I know, if that's what you're asking. And before you go further, the answer is no. She will never date a friend of mine." He looks at Tai, then at Declan. "And I mean never. If either one of you even thinks about it... well, I will end you."

Tai opens his mouth to say something back, but Declan's hand claps him on the shoulder and shakes his head.

"The last guy she dated before she moved away was

such a douche. Just didn't give two shits about what she had to say or what she was interested in. I tried telling her she deserved better, but she wouldn't listen. She was heartbroken when he ended things," he explains with a smirk.

"Wait? Did you have something to do with that?" Tai asks incredulously.

"As far as she knows? No. And it will stay that way," Everest responds, staring them both down. "But I may have threatened to cut his balls off if he ever spoke to her again after I saw him yelling at her one time." He laughs as if it's a funny memory now. "She's my little sister, man. Gotta keep her safe."

Declan swallows and wipes the sweat that's formed on his brow. *Well fuck.*

The waitstaff shows up a moment later and breaks the hovering tension at the table. After they order, the table fills with chatter as normal, and the rest of the meal passes smoothly. It's not until they are walking out, Everest a couple of feet ahead, that Tai turns to Declan. "Look, I know it's not really my place to say anything, but I've heard some rumors going around about you."

Declan sighs. "What's being said?"

"I've honestly tried not to pay attention to it. But some chick named Charlotte has been going around talking about how you sleep with women and then sneak out like one of your brother's shadows."

Fuck. Declan runs a hand over his braided hair, frustration building inside. The last thing he needs is this. He should have known she wasn't going to go away easily.

"Thanks, Tai," he says, placing his hand on Tai's shoulder and squeezing it. "I appreciate it."

Tai looks down, almost sheepish. "I know you two," he

says, nodding his head toward Everest, "like to have your fun, but if I can be honest with you, don't you feel like it's time to grow up a bit? You're in your thirties now, dude. When are you going to leave these games behind?"

Declan stills, Tai's words hitting a spot he wasn't expecting. Not knowing how to respond, he simply nods, taking his hand back. "Thanks again, Tai," he says as he waves goodbye before climbing into Everest's truck, where he waits for him. Tai's hand rises in a wave before they pull away.

"What's with the serious face?" Everest asks.

"Just thinking about that burger. Fuck, it was good," Declan lies.

CHAPTER 14

Eliana

Pick it up and call him.
    Or text him.
    Or send a fucking carrier pigeon.
Do something.

The internal battle rages as Eliana stares at her phone, trying to convince herself to pick it up and use the number she has long memorized. Her back rests against the front of the fridge for a moment before she slides down, phone in hand, and sits on the floor.

Holding it in her lap, she unlocks it and taps the call app. She enters the numbers burned in her brain and hovers her thumb over the dial button.

DO IT ALREADY!

Tightly squeezing her eyes shut, she lets her thumb lower and tap the screen. Within what feels like nanoseconds, the call goes through, and it starts to ring.

Heat floods her system, and sweat beads on her brow. Her palms are sticky and clammy, and she's certain there is a giant sweat stain forming in her pits. "Oh shit. Oh shit.

Fuck. Fuck. Fuck," she says, scrambling to a standing position while pressing the speaker phone button.

"Good afternoon to you, too, Eliana."

FUCK! He answered. It feels as though all her nerve endings are firing at the same time while a thousand bugs crawl over her body. Goddess, why is she such a mess? She wasn't ready to call him, and now he's answered. Waiting for her to say something. Shit! She has to say something. *Anything.*

"Huh." She clears her throat. "Hi. Sorry."

"Hi, Eliana."

Goddess, he needs to stop saying her name like that. *Eliana.* She nearly swoons thinking about it. "Hi," she manages to breathe out.

"I think we've covered that." He laughs. It's different from the other night. Easier. Smoother. Yet, it still fills her soul. Finding its home.

"Right. Yes."

He laughs softly again. "What can I do for you?"

"Right. Umm… See… Mydancestudioisputtingo-nashowcaseandweneedsponsorsandIwaswonderingify-ourautoshopwouldliketosponsorus," she says, so fast that it all sounds like one long word.

"Sorry, I didn't catch that. Must be a bad connection."

Yeah, in her brain.

"Can you repeat that?" Declan asks.

She takes a deep breath, settling her nerves enough to be able to speak at a more normal pace. "My dance studio is putting on a showcase, and we need sponsors. I was wondering if your auto shop would like to sponsor us?"

He may only pause for a second, but to Eliana, it feels like years. Was she completely out of line? Did she overstep?

Oh gosh, what if he hates children dancing and finds them creepy?

"Sure. That'd be great," he says, pulling her from her spiral.

"Really?"

"Yeah. We're always looking for ways to support the community, and if you're involved, it has to be a great opportunity."

Heat floods her skin again. Only this time, it makes her cheeks rosy with blush. "Thank you. Thank you. Thank you. I have to talk to my boss first, but I can stop by the shop with any paperwork for you."

"Sounds good."

Eliana beams. "Thanks, Declan. We'll talk soon."

"Absolutely." Right as she's about to hang up, she hears him say, "Oh, and Eliana…"

"Yes?" There he goes, saying her name again…

"Next time, don't wait so long to call a guy." He disconnects the call before she can say anything, but her brain immediately hones in on the *next time*.

Running her hands down her hips, Eliana smooths out the sides of her blush dress and hopefully her nerves along with it. June was thrilled with the idea of Hellbent Motors being a sponsor and couldn't wait to hand the paperwork over. Taking a deep breath, she reaches the door of Hellbent Motors and pulls it open, the bell overhead signaling her arrival.

When she enters, her eyes instantly find Declan seated behind the counter. He looks up and smiles. Fuck, that tiny action makes her insides do a flip.

"Hi, Eliana," he says, standing and leaning his exposed tattooed forearms on the desk's upper ledge. He's not an overly muscular-looking guy. This is not to say he's not strong; he's just not as muscular as his brother. Declan's broad chest and strong arms, likely from hauling car parts around all day, look so welcoming, and she can't stop herself from wondering what it would be like to be held against him. Now that she gets a chance to really look at him, she notes how large a man he is. He's well over six feet, making her feel tiny, and he's so powerful in presence and stature. He's sturdy without being overbearing or threatening, at least to her. She knows he used to play football with Everest, and she can see why. He would be a force to be reckoned with on the field.

She sees a muscle tendon twitch under the skin on his forearm, and hot damn, that small action is sexy as hell. If she's being honest, he pulls off that big grizzly bear persona a little too well. Especially with the added stubble he's sporting.

"Hi," she says. *Do I always sound this breathy?* Shaking her head, getting rid of that thought before it has a chance to fully take hold, she steps toward him.

"Hi," he responds softly, his eyes dipping down briefly before coming back up again.

When her eyes meet his, it's like a charge goes off in her brain, setting off a series of fireworks that send shockwaves down to her toes. She swallows, hopefully not too loudly, and says, "I… I brought the paperwork for you." She places the envelope in her hands on the desk and slides it toward him.

"Wonderful. Thanks."

"It's not much, a couple of pages for you to sign off on. My boss, June, says it's more of a formality than anything else. Something to ensure that we're both on the same page regarding expectations."

"And what are my expectations?" he says, flicking his eyes to hers. She's sure there's a bit of hidden meaning behind those words.

"Nothing significant. She said there's a line in there for you to fill out what you want to contribute, and how you want your contribution recognized. But otherwise, you're signing off as a way to recognize that you are supporting a children's dance group and that you agree to a family-friendly collaboration."

A small smirk emerges, making his cheek display the most adorable dimple she needs to actively stop herself from putting her finger in.

"Sounds good." He scribbles a couple of things on the paper, signs where it's needed, and places the papers back in the envelope. "How's the car running?"

"Oh. Good as new. Or, well, not new, but good. No problems," she stammers like an idiot. Why does she suddenly forget how to speak when it involves him?

Laughing gently, he replies, "That's good. If there are any issues, don't be afraid to let me know."

"Okay." He hands the envelope back. His fingers graze hers so briefly that if she were to blink, she would have missed it. Yet the sensation lingers. The heat. The spark. It's there, hovering over the tips of her fingers. Unsure what to do with that, she knows she needs to get out of there before she does something dumb.

Envelope in hand, she steps back and walks toward the door, turning back after a few steps to say, "Thanks, Declan. It really means a lot."

"Anytime." He sits back down, shuffles a paper or two,

and barely loud enough for her to hear, he says, "And, you look great in that dress, by the way."

Struggling to find her voice, she manages a soft "Thank you" before opening the door and walking out, feeling the flames from his gaze lingering on her.

CHAPTER 15

Declan

"Hello, welcome to Strike a Pose. How can I help you?"

"Hi. I'm Declan Grace," he says as the receptionist tucks a strand of hair behind her ear, and a faint pink blush dots her cheeks. "I'm here to meet with June."

"I'll let her know you're here."

"Thanks." He turns around and sits in one of the chairs off to the side. The receptionist bounces off to the back somewhere and returns a moment later. "June will be with you in a moment. I'm Bellamy, by the way."

"Hi, Bellamy. Nice to meet you."

A little giggle escapes her, and she covers her mouth out of embarrassment, but he smiles back at her, trying to appear friendly but not flirtatious.

Before he has time to pull his phone out of his pocket to start mindlessly scrolling, an older woman emerges from the back wearing dark dress pants, a dark green turtleneck, and a gray cardigan. She brings the glasses that hang around her neck to her face and puts them on, then looks over at him. "Declan?"

He stands, instantly extending his hand to shake hers. "Yes. Hi, you must be June."

"I am. So nice to meet you, and thank you for stopping by. Why don't we go back to my office to chat?"

"Yes, ma'am."

June turns and leads him down a hallway before turning into the room at the very end. As he turns in, he glances into the room across the hall. With the large couch along one wall and the fridge and counter along the back. Staff room. Unfortunately, he doesn't see Eliana.

"Please, sit," June says, stepping behind her desk and gesturing to the seat across from her. As he sits, his mind briefly wanders to wonder how many hard conversations have been had with someone sitting here. As the owner of Hellbent Motors, he knows how many he's had, each one vividly burned into his own mind.

"So, first, I want to thank you so much for your generous offer. We didn't have any extravagant plans for set design, but with your sponsorship and volunteering, we can do so much more than we initially planned."

"It's my pleasure. As an organization, one of our primary values is community support, so I'm thrilled to contribute to what I'm sure will be a great night for the children and families. The staff at the shop are all eager to start building, too," he says, and it's not a lie. When he told them yesterday about the offer he included alongside his sponsorship funds, they were practically vibrating with the opportunity to help.

"That's so good to hear," she says before handing him a sheet of paper with a long list of materials and a to-do list.

"I know this looks like a lot, and it probably is, but with your generous offer, and with the presumed skillset you and your staff will bring, I figured I could be a bit ambitious. The plan for the night is a masquerade theme, and so with that, we wanted to build a sort of ballroom backdrop. Maybe some staircases, structures to hang lush curtains from, etc. Eliana will be able to fill in any other details for you."

Looking at the list, he agrees she definitely chose to be ambitious. But with his team, he knows it shouldn't be a problem. "And where will this be hosted? Can I see the space so I know the physical limits we are working with?"

"Absolutely. We've booked the main auditorium at the Stanley Theater. I have a class to teach shortly, but..." she says, pausing to look at the schedule for the day, "I can have Eliana walk over with you, as she should be in any minute." Her eyes catch something behind him. "Wait, there she is. Eliana!"

A slightly rustling sound behind him makes his insides flutter.

"Yes, June?" He turns around. "Oh. Declan. Hi." Her cheeks instantly pink with that gorgeous blush of hers.

"Hi." He smiles, letting his eyes flow down her body, hungrily taking in how her tights highlight every delicious curve.

"Ellie, could you take Mr. Grace here down to the auditorium for the showcase? He and his team will be helping to build our sets, and he would like to see the space before they get to work."

Eliana's eyes find his. Is that a bit of trepidation he sees in them? Or desire? Whatever it is, it's gone before he has a chance to work it out. "Yeah, sure," she answers, her voice slightly shaky.

June claps her hands together like it's a job well done. "Wonderful. Well, off you go then."

Declan stands, extending his hand to shake hers again. "I think this is going to be a great partnership," he says before letting his gaze wander back to Eliana, who still stands in the doorway.

"Me too. I can't wait to see what you all do."

With that, Declan turns, stepping away from the desk and toward the whole reason he agreed to do this in the first place—Eliana.

It doesn't take long for them to arrive at the theater, and surprisingly, there are no issues getting inside. June wouldn't have sent them here if they couldn't get in, but in his mind, there wouldn't be anyone here, and a trip over would be for naught. Thankfully, that isn't the case.

Stepping inside, he's taken aback by the coziness of it all. He's never been inside, so this is all new to him. Having grown up mainly in the underworld, he didn't have the opportunity to see productions here as a child, and frankly, as an adult, he can't say he frequents theaters for anything other than the odd movie. He catches Eliana watching him as he marvels at the venue.

His eyes scan the surroundings, taking in the mood and aesthetic of the space. The walls are a deep red with an abstract black and gold tiled floor. There are plush black and red chairs that sit off to the side, and drapery hanging over entryways that make it feel like you're about to see something magical.

"Thank you so much, Walter," she says to the man who now walks toward them.

He extends his arms, wrapping her in a hug, and the demon inside Declan does not approve. He growls internally, ordering Walter to take his hands off.

In the rapidly growing frustration, small tendrils of smoke swirl from his fingertips. Declan turns, steps away, and clenches his eyes tight. He breathes in deeply, centering himself and shoving his demon back down in his box in the process. When he turns back around, Walter and Eliana are staring at him with quizzical looks. "Sorry, thought I was going to sneeze and didn't want to get it all over you if I did," Declan says smoothly, hoping they buy it.

"Much appreciated," Walter says, though his tone is questionable. "I'm Walter Graves." His hand extends, and he steps toward Declan, who closes the distance.

Declan's free hand lands on Walter's shoulder in that special bro-handshake-way, as he clasps Walter's extended hand. "Declan Grace. Nice to meet you, sir."

Walter laughs, letting go of Declan's hand. "Sir? I don't know the last time someone called me, sir. Walter is fine."

"Well, nice to meet you, Walter."

"Same." He turns to Eliana. "The room is all yours, take your time. Give me a holler when you're ready to head out so I can lock up behind you."

"Will do. Thank you again," she says to Walter's already disappearing form. Turning back to Declan, she casts her eyes away, as if she's afraid to make eye contact with him. "He's a funny man."

"Hmm. Seems it."

"Shall we go in?"

"That is the reason we're here," he says, winking at her. *Oh, Hades. Did I wink at her?*

She lets out a little giggle, and it's the most adorable sound. Light and happy—like the early morning birds chirping with the sun as it comes up. The demon within him practically bounces inside, wanting to come to the surface to see her. To be near her. But he shoves him back down.

"Let's go then," she says, smiling at him before she leads them into the auditorium.

CHAPTER 16
Eliana

E liana pauses inside the door and allows Declan to walk ahead of her. She's seen this space a hundred times before, dancing here as a young child and many times as an adult before she moved away. It's one of her favorite stages, if she's being honest. Most people think she'd love the big stages. The ones that celebrities and the public pay buckets of money to see the big names perform on. And before moving back home, she'd agree with them. But she's always loved this stage. It feels more personal and more intimate to be in a venue like this. The ability to see most people's faces is unmatched.

"This space is..." he pauses, his voice full of awe, "fantastic. Seriously, it's beautiful," he finishes as he turns back around and faces her, stressing the word *beautiful* as his gaze takes her in.

Eliana looks away, unable to handle the look he's giving her. It tells her stories of longing. Desire. Potential. It's too much. *It's inappropriate*, she chastises internally, reminding herself that he's her brother's best friend, and they are here on business.

He can't keep looking at her like that. "You can't keep looking at me like that," she says, more to herself than to him.

"Like what?" he asks, stepping up to her.

Her cheeks warm. "I didn't mean for you to hear that."

"But now you need to tell me," he says playfully, rocking back onto his heels. "Like what?"

Despite the pull she feels to look up and drown in those crystal blues of his, she keeps her gaze down, focusing instead on the pattern of the carpet in the aisle.

His hand hesitates between them for a moment before he places his curved index finger under her chin and gently lifts her face to look at him. "Like what?" he asks again, his voice turning husky.

Her eyes find him, and it's over. She has no more resolve to withstand him. "Like you want me. Like you want to devour me."

He gives her the tiniest of smirks, and it's the sexiest fucking thing she's ever seen. "Maybe I do."

Heat floods her body, and her knees go weak. If she were prone to swooning, now would be the perfect time to do it because holy Hecate, he is looking at her like he wants to do so many naughty things to her.

"We can't," she whispers, barely able to find breath under the weight of his heated gaze.

"Says who?"

"Everest."

She catches the shift in his expression at the mention of her brother's name. It's gone as quickly as it appeared, but it was there—that slight recognition of the barrier between them. He sidesteps it, saying, "I'm pretty sure he's never told me no. At least not explicitly. So I don't see the problem."

He finally removes his finger from under her chin and gently clasps her hand.

"Declan." *Why does his name feel so good on my tongue?* "Ev would never be okay with it. You know him. I know him."

"So he doesn't need to know. As of right now, there's nothing to know. We can see where this goes for now and keep it between us. Assuming, of course, that you are interested in exploring whatever this is between us."

"I do. I mean, I am. I don't know why, but I'm drawn to you. You set me aflutter like no one else ever has, and I find myself flustered around you."

"I've noticed." He laughs.

"But I don't know if I can lie to my brother."

"I wouldn't call it a lie, more omitting the truth… again for the time being. To give us time to figure out if there's something here."

"And how do you suggest we 'figure things out'?"

He steps into her space, wrapping their clasped hands behind her back and pulling her into him. Her head tilts back so she can still look into those precious blues. "Well, we could go on dates. Spend time together. I'll be here quite a bit, too."

"June did ask me to be an overseer of the project."

"Perfect. So there's a valid reason for why you'd be here, checking me out."

"True," she responds, ignoring his purposeful slip but knowing full well she'd definitely be checking him out. Her eyes dip down his lips, plump, perfect, and so close. "But you and Everest hang out a lot. How do we avoid running into him if we go on dates?"

"I can tell him I'm busy with work, or Buckley, my dog, misses me. Whatever it is, I'll figure it out. What do you say? Will you go out with me, Eliana Oaks?"

She runs everything he's said through her mind again. Can they do this? Can they actually be together and manage to hide it from Everest? Does she want to?

She looks back up at him, looking deep into his eyes, and feels his chest pause as he awaits her answer. "Okay, I'll go out with you."

Before she can second-guess it, his lips are crashing onto hers, and it's everything she had imagined it would be.

CHAPTER 17

Declan

S cents of peppermint and grapefruit fill his nose, making his brain go haywire as he realizes what he did. No, what he's doing.

He's kissing Eliana.

She said okay, which to him meant he was free to do what he'd been thinking about all morning. She wasn't wrong when she said he was looking at her like he wanted to do things to her. With her. For her. It's all he's been able to think about since she walked into his shop with her broken-down car. Everything he's done since has been because of her. Rejecting Becky. Trying to stay home more, despite Everest's objections, so he didn't risk doing something stupid. Even turning down Charlie when they went for coffee.·

All of it is for her.

Eliana had barely looked at him and he knew he didn't want anyone else.

Which is such a strange thought. He'd never considered her in that way when they'd crossed paths before. Maybe because he's been too tied up in his freedom and the excitement of another conquest. Or maybe it was because she was a few years younger, so he only saw her as Everest's little sister. Whatever the reason, he realizes he was so wrong. So very fucking wrong. His lips on hers tell him that with great certainty.

His free hand cups the side of her face briefly before sliding to the back of her neck, tilting her head back further, giving him better access. Releasing her hand from behind her back, his other hand joins the one on the back of her neck. She pushes her body against his as her hands work their way up his back.

Her mouth opens slowly, giving him opportunity to deepen the kiss, their tongues meeting tentatively at first, testing this new development. She pushes her hips into him, and he groans into her mouth. She swallows the sound hungrily while her hands find his hair, tangling her fingers into his braided mohawk, and pulls.

He groans again and nips her bottom lip. "Oaks," he says, his voice low. Strained. *More*, his demon demands. And fuck if he doesn't agree. He needs her. Needs more.

His tongue traces her lips, and she nips him back. He tastes her again as she tugs on his hair, sending waves of heat through him. His cock is already hard and throbbing in his jeans. She grinds her hips into him, pushing against his cock, making him ache for more. He pulls away, putting a little space between their bodies, and rests his forehead on hers. "Oaks. If you keep doing that…"

"What? What are you going to do?"

He sighs. "Nothing. Because as much as I want to, I will not have our first time being in the aisle of a theater where little kids are going to perform."

She laughs before lifting her face to his again and kissing his lips gently. Eliana brings her arms down and places her hands on his chest before reluctantly pushing herself out of his grasp, leaving him feeling adrift as he tries to find his sense of balance in a space without her in his arms, where she belongs.

Swiping a finger across her deliciously swollen lips, her gaze roams his body from head to toe, pausing briefly as she takes in the bulge in his pants.

"Like what you see?" he says, adjusting himself.

Her eyes flare with heat, and he knows she does, but she looks away, blushing. Fucking Hades, she's gorgeous when she's playing shy. She didn't hesitate even once when he placed his mouth on hers. And that little challenge a second ago? Oh, she's bolder than she likes to let on.

"We should get going," she says, her eyes still on his crotch.

Leaving this moment is the last thing he wants to do, but he knows she's right. He needs to get to the shop, and she needs to get back to the studio. "Lead the way."

She turns, walking back down the aisle with her eyes on her phone, giving him the most glorious view of her ass in dance tights.

Mine, his demon growls.

Couldn't agree more, buddy.

Back at the shop, all Declan can think of is how Eliana's body felt pressed against his. He's had more than one of his mechanics snap their fingers in front of his face to get his attention back to what they were talking about. Everything about that kiss was perfect. The taste of her lips. How she smelled. The way her fingers wove into his hair as she took

HOOKED ON A DEMON

as much as she gave. Every bit of it was better than he ever could have anticipated.

He certainly hadn't planned to make out with her in the middle of the theater, but he's definitely not complaining. Knowing that she is overseeing their work isn't bad either. As he said, it helps to provide an excuse for why they will be seen together if anyone asks.

The biggest issue, of course, is going to be Everest. Fucking Everest. The best friend he's ever had. The one who has been with him for years now, by his side, cheering him on. He even helped set up Hellbent Motors before it opened. They spent days together painting, installing racks, and organizing tool kits. Declan was the one who suggested keeping whatever it is he and Eliana are doing a secret from Everest, but it doesn't mean he feels good about it. He's never had a secret from Everest, and with something this big, Declan knows there's no way this won't come back to bite him in the ass.

At the same time, if he can continue to feel even a fraction with Eliana that he felt with her today, whatever blowup Everest will have will have been worth it. Or at least that's what he hopes. Now, he has to figure out how to keep the fact that he's dating his best friend's little sister from his best friend, who also happens to be the guy he hangs out with most nights and who has a nasty habit of stopping by unannounced.

Declan runs his hand over his face, letting the frustration of the situation he got himself in wash over him for a minute before he stuffs the feeling away. It can be a problem for future-Declan to figure out.

"You ready, boss?" Sebastian asks, snapping Declan's thoughts back to what he needs to focus on.

"Yeah. Let's go."

As part of sponsoring the showcase, Declan offered to cover the cost of the materials they needed to build the stage sets. June was more than happy with that offer, as lumber and fabric can escalate costs rapidly. She gave him a list to help, and while Declan doesn't intend to go wild with the materials, he is thankful that Hellbent Motors is doing well enough to cover the cost easily. Thus, the task this afternoon is to go shopping with Sebastian and get their required pieces delivered to the theater.

"You got a list, boss?"

"Yes," Declan replies, handing over the piece of paper to him. "And I've told you, you don't need to call me boss all the time."

"Okay, boss."

Declan laughs, Sebastian not even noticing what he did. Instead, Sebastian's eyes are laser-focused on the paper, likely memorizing it or mentally placing it in the best shopping order. He's still a kid, really, at only twenty-one, but he's probably one of Declan's best guys. Sebastian is great when it comes to attention to detail and has a memory like no one else. He can be a bit awkward with customers, but he tries hard and is always eager to help or learn more.

They climb into Declan's truck and make their way to the local hardware and lumber store. It's not a far drive (it never is in Leeside), but he and Sebastian chat a bit on the way. Declan is forever amazed at how Sebastian's brain works and how it picks out different problems or patterns. Along the way, the kid shares about his own experience at the theater when he was young, and when he looks back at the list again, he shares that they'll likely need more of the materials than what's listed.

"No problem. Put in what you think we'll need," Declan says, pulling into a parking spot.

With the numbers corrected and Sebastian's perfected shopping order, they zoom through the store, tossing whatever they need in the cart and then ordering their lumber. It takes a little less than an hour, and they are on their way back to the shop. As they get out, Sebastian stops and turns to Declan. "Everything alright?" Declan asks.

"Yeah, boss. Wanted to say thank you for taking me. I want to be a business owner like you someday, and I appreciate being able to do things like this. It shows me how I can be a good business owner."

The sentiment takes Declan off guard. That's not at all what he expected, and fuck if it doesn't make him tear up a little. It's hard to know if he's making a difference, but for Sebastian to say that. It means so much.

"Thanks, Sebastian. That means a lot." Declan rubs his eye, ridding it of the tear that has escaped. "Anytime you wanna talk business, say so."

"Thanks, boss." Sebastian then turns on his heel and darts back into the shop, ready for whatever task is next.

CHAPTER 18

Eliana

"Kaia, his hands were on me. Like on me," she flops onto her couch, placing her phone on speaker before laying it on her stomach. "And the way he slid his hand onto the back of my neck... goosebumps."

"Holy Hecate, that's so hot."

"Right!"

"So what now?"

That's a good question. They agreed to figure things out, but Declan hasn't reached out to her yet. Granted, she hasn't messaged him either.

"I don't know. It's only been twenty-four hours," Eliana says. So it's not unreasonable that they haven't talked yet. But that fucking kiss has been on replay in her mind ever since. Well, that and the size of the bulge in his pants. "I don't know," she repeats, deflating a little from the high of retelling Kaia about her super hot encounter with the demon daddy. Well, not literal daddy... as far as she knows. "Oh, goddess. What if he has kids?"

Kaia laughs. "Where in the flying monkeys did that come from?"

"Right, sorry. You're not privy to the thoughts in my head." Eliana laughs. "I thought of him as a hot demon daddy, but then had a verbal freakout that he is a literal daddy. He's not a daddy, right?"

"I mean, if the rumors are true…" her friend replies, leaving the words hanging in the air between them.

Eliana jolts herself into a seated position, catching her phone before it hits the floor. "What rumors?" she nearly screams.

"I'm kidding!" Kaia exclaims, laughing at Eliana's expense. "I have heard rumors, but it has nothing to do with him being a father."

Eliana picks at a fluff in her pants. "What rumors have you heard?" she says, hoping she comes across as more curious than desperate.

"Someone has a crush."

"Shut up. What have you heard?"

"Some rumors are going around about him being a bit of a playboy and a jackass when he ends things. If he even does. Apparently, he's a fan of leaving before his partner wakes up and then refuses to respond to follow-up messages. Really, general douche canoe stuff."

"Oh." *That sounds like the guy Charlie was talking about at brunch. Could Declan be who she was referring to?*

"But I'm sure it's not true," Kaia says quickly, trying to soften the blow. "People in this town like to talk, and we know how jealous they can be. Especially when it concerns someone connected to the council."

"True," Eliana replies, though she doesn't believe it. Rumors only become rumors because there is at least some truth to them. The question is how much truth there is to what's being said about Declan.

"I know that's not what you wanted to hear, and who knows how much of it is true, but protect yourself, Ellie. The demon may be hot, but it doesn't mean he's good for you."

"I know, and I will."

"And if he hurts you, I have plenty of connections who owe me some favors," she says, laughing dangerously.

"Thanks." Eliana knows Kaia comes from a good place, and they always have each other's backs. "Anyways, I gotta go get ready for work. Dinner on Friday?"

"Absolutely. Love ya!"

"Love you too!"

Eliana disconnects the call, and as much as she knows Kaia means well, she can't help but feel a sense of foreboding.

The smell of sawdust and the sound of tools banging and whirring greet her as she enters the theater. The staff of Hellbent Motors is hard at work and has been quick to start the building process. Which is probably good, given the showcase is now about a month away.

It doesn't take long for her gaze to find Declan. A very shirtless, glistening in sweat, Declan. His back is broad, the muscles underneath his skin flexing and moving with each shift in position he makes. When he stands, the sweat shines on his bare skin like a beacon. For her tongue.

Swallowing, she pushes down the urge to lick her way up the corded muscles in his arms and steps toward them. She's only here for a daily check-in. That June asked her to do. Because his team is being kind and building their sets, that's the only reason she's here. Her presence has nothing to do with the hot demon who notices her approach and flashes her the brightest smile.

Her stomach flips with his eyes on her. She tucks her hair behind her ear and looks away, unable to handle what a look from him does to her. There must be a draft in the building, causing goosebumps to go up her arms. That's the most reasonable explanation.

"Good afternoon, Miss Oaks," Declan says, facing her. A light fuzz across his bare chest looks soft, and Eliana forces her hand to stay at her side despite an insatiable need to run her fingers through it.

His stomach is softer than that of other guys she's dated. He's not ripped, with stacks of abs. Instead, he's like a cozy teddy bear, with some squish and give. Honestly, he looks like he'd be the perfect cuddle buddy.

A flush moves up her neck, her hand moving up to try and cover it, hoping to disguise that her mind was wandering to places it shouldn't be. However, it doesn't appear as though she has hidden much. Declan smirks at her knowingly before alternatively flexing his pecs and making them dance.

"Good afternoon, Mr. Grace. It looks like you all already have a great start on the sets," she says, trying not to smile.

"Yeah, it ain't been so bad. Nice to get out of the shop, really," says one of his staff members, who she believes is named Humphrey. Declan introduced everyone to her yesterday, but the names are still a bit fuzzy.

"Well, thank you all the same. We really do appreciate you volunteering your time. I hope the shop isn't suffering because of your efforts here," she replies, looking up at Declan.

"Nah, we're good. The shop has enough staff that we can swap in and out as necessary."

"That's good."

He has watched her every step and continues to do so as she moves closer to the stage and to the stairs leading up. His gaze is like a caress of her skin, taking in whatever he can. "That. It. Is," he says. Eliana catches the double meaning of his words and blushes again. She's going to have to get that under control if they are going to try and do this dating thing. Or fooling around. Or whatever it is they agreed to.

It's been two days since the make-out session, and they still haven't discussed it. Or made plans to see each other again. In trying not to appear needy, she's maybe played it a bit too easy, and instead of messaging him to arrange something, she's anxiously sat back, waiting to hear from him.

It's been torture.

Standing on the stage, she finally raises her eyes and meets his. And the way he's looking at her now... pure heat. It warms her insides in the most delicious of ways.

But if he's so hot for her that his look could set fire to this entire building, why hasn't he reached out? Is this part of his game? To tease and taunt and leave her guessing? Is that a game she's willing to play?

Declan works his way toward her, stepping over tools, feet, and cords as he does. The rest of his crew return to whatever task they are doing, ignoring the hulking demon as he traverses the short distance to where she stands.

"You alright there, Oaks?" he asks. He glances over his shoulder, making sure no one is watching, before bringing his hand up to brush her arm lightly.

Why is it so hot when he calls me by my last name?

"Yeah. I'm... good," she replies, hoping it comes out more confident than she feels. His touch is brief, but it makes her toes tingle with anticipation as she wonders what it feels like elsewhere.

He leans in, and she can smell the musk of hard work on him. It's delectable. Her hand moves as if of its own volition, linking her pinky finger with his as it rests at his side. Casting her eyes to his face, she catches a slight quirk of his mouth. The subtlest of movements as the right side of his perfect lips picks up, creating a wonderful dimple that she wishes she could put her other pinky into. Her eyes meet his, and his gaze dips briefly to her lips before locking with hers again. The entire interaction lasts mere seconds but feels like an eternity to Eliana; all the while, she hopes the others in the room continue to pay them no mind. If they continue to do this, this secret they have surely won't be a secret much longer.

"Would you like to get together tomorrow night?" he asks, breaking Eliana out of the haze she has fallen into. Any prior concerns she had about him not texting her vanish.

An eager smile fights to cross her lips, but she fights it back. As well as the urge to jump up and down, shouting her acceptance. Instead, as calmly as possible, she replies, "That would be nice."

"Great. I can come pick you up at seven?"

"That's perfect." She can't fight the smile any longer. Squeezing her pinky finger on his, she hopes it conveys her excitement.

He squeezes hers back before letting go and winking at her. "I can't wait." He steps back, putting distance between them, leaving her feeling unsteady. "I've gotta get back, but thank you for stopping by and checking in, Miss Oaks," he says more loudly.

"It's looking great! I can't wait to see the final product," Eliana responds, both playing along with the little act he's instigating and wanting to make sure the others know their efforts are appreciated.

She walks off the stage, waving to the crew as she does, and heads back to the dance studio for her next class. However, she has no idea how she's going to teach when Declan has now filled her mind with the anticipation of tomorrow.

CHAPTER 19
Eliana

"Alright, friends, make sure you practice your first position, rond de jambe, and plié movements. The more you practice the easier and more natural it becomes. Thanks for a great lesson!"

"Bye, Miss Oaks," her students call out as they file out of the studio. Well, all except one. One of her little friends comes over, dragging the toes of her ballet flats on the floor as she does. Eliana squats down, bringing herself down to the child's level. "How can I help you, Calista?"

"Miss. Miss Oaks…" Eliana waits patiently for her little friend to gather the courage she needs to speak. "Can you show me the round of jam again?"

She holds in the giggle that wants to come loose at *round of jam*, instead reassuringly responding, "Absolutely." Eliana stands, putting her hand out for Calista to take. "First, we want to start at the bar. Stand with it at your side and place your left hand on top." Calista stands in front of Eliana and follows her directions. "Do you remember first position?"

"Yes," Calista says before turning her feet out and bringing her feet together.

117

"Good. Straighten your back."

She does.

"Good. Now, with your right leg, you're going to put it out in front of you and point your toes." She watches Calista perform the movement. "Wonderful. Now sweep your foot around to the back like you're making half a circle. When you get to the back, you bring your foot forward again and return to first position."

Eliana moves to stand in front of Calista. She demonstrates the movement, then steps away from the bar to watch as Calista repeats it. "You try."

Calista holds herself up straight, sweeps her leg around perfectly, and returns to the starting position as if she were a professional and had been doing it all her life. "Perfect! Do you want to try again to make sure you remember?"

Calista beams. "Yes!"

"Go ahead." Eliana gestures with her hand, signaling for Calista to go, and then claps enthusiastically when Calista is done. Seeing her little stars master these moves never fails to fill her heart.

"You ready, Callie?" her mom says from the doorway.

"Yes, Mom! Thank you, Miss Oaks."

"Anytime," Eliana calls out as she watches Calista run to her mom.

With that being her last class of the day, Elliana quickly sweeps the room before turning the studio lights off. She gathers her things from her locker in the staff room and says goodnight to Bellamy on her way out. Perhaps, unfortunately, she can't go straight home. Instead, it's off to see Dr. Colson for an evening therapy session.

On the drive over, she works through what she would like to talk about, but knows that they both allow the conversation to go wherever it needs to. She's avoided talking about Declan so far, but she can't leave that much longer.

She pulls into the parking lot at Colson's building, parks, and then makes her way inside, finding his office like it's second nature. Which it practically is, at this point. She tries to keep her appointments pretty regular. Or at least as regular as her work allows. Everything for the showcase is starting to ramp up, so that may get in the way for a bit, but she does what she can to stay consistent with Colson because it helps her keep it together.

"Come on in. Have a seat," Dr. Colson says, holding the door for her. "How have you been this week?"

"I've been good."

He sits opposite her, picks up his pad and pen, and poises them on his knee, as usual. "Just good?"

It's funny the little routines they both have fallen into. She sits on the small couch, sliding her feet out of her ankle boots, and brings them onto the cushion beside her. She leans onto the arm and picks at the fluffs on the hem of her sweater. "I've met someone." She flicks her eyes up at him, looking for a response, but he gives nothing away, which is probably a good thing given his profession. Can't have your therapist making faces at every big revelation and all that.

"And how does that make you feel?"

"Scared. Anxious. Uncertain. Content."

"Why those feelings? Why scared first?" he asks, making notes.

It's a good question. She hadn't considered the order of her response; she listed how they came to her. "My last relationship wasn't a good one. So scared seemed to fit."

"What happened in your last relationship that makes you scared of this one?"

She picks at the fluff on her leggings, running her hands

over her thighs as she thinks. Eliana hasn't shared the details of what happened with Sam with anyone other than Kaia, and Kaia's like a steel trap with personal information, so no one else knows. Not even Everest. "Things with Sam didn't end well. Frankly, they didn't *go* well either. We were together for two years, and he was possessive and controlling. By the time I ended things, he had alienated me from almost all of my friends. The only one I had managed to keep in contact with was Kaia, and even then, that was spotty. He didn't know I was still talking to her, but she helped me find a way out. When I left, I deleted his number and left everything I had worked towards behind. "

"So why are you scared about this new relationship?"

"Because it's new. Because I'm worried it will end up the same way things did with Sam." Saying all of this aloud is hard. She's got some distance between her now and the ending, or rather, fleeing, of that relationship, so that she can talk about it. But the pain of admitting how he chipped away at who she was is still there. It's a rumble of anger under her skin, reminding her of how being with Sam forever changed her.

"Has this new person done anything to make you think they are similar to Sam?"

She tilts her head back, resting it on the back of the couch, looking up at the ceiling as she thinks through every interaction with Declan so far. "Nothing immediately stands out. Though, to be fair, we haven't actually gone out yet. You know, just the two of us. But what if..." She trails off. Colson waits for her to finish her thought. "But what if he's hiding it? What if he's stealthy about it, like Sam was? Making me become a shell of myself, one tiny piece at a time."

"What if he's not?"

She sighs, bringing her head back down to look at him. "It's possible. He is friends with my brother, but I don't know whether that's a good sense of judgment or not."

Colson huffs a small laugh, and it feels like a triumph. "So if it's possible that he's not like Sam, don't you think it's worth at least giving this man a shot? Let him show you how he's different."

"I mean. I guess that makes sense. But how can I trust that he won't do the same thing?"

"That's a great question," he responds, leaning forward to rest his forearms on his knees—another one of his preferred poses. "Unfortunately, I don't think there is any way to truly know."

She laughs without humor. "Thanks. That's uplifting." She catches the smile he gives her in return. He's objectively attractive, but he does nothing for her.

"What I mean is that we never truly know someone's intentions, but if there is nothing causing your warning system to go off—and given your history, I think it's safe to say it would—then I think it's okay to give him a chance to show himself to you. You've been through a lot and experienced trauma, so it's natural that you would be hesitant. However, your experience also means that you are more in tune with yourself and the behaviors of your partner. So he'd have to be really good at being manipulative to get it past you at this point. It's okay for you to seek out happiness. Comfort. Even intimacy. Be open with him when you're ready so he knows where you're coming from."

The fact that Colson is so good at his job is sometimes annoying, but Eliana knows he has a valid point. Declan has been nothing but kind to her and has been the complete opposite of Sam. "Okay. But if he turns out to be a complete jerk, I'll never come back here," she says sarcastically.

"I will give up my license if that happens," he replies, laughing.

CHAPTER 20
Declan

Stepping out of the shower, he grabs a fresh towel from the shelf and wraps it around his waist, tucking the end in to keep it in place. He picks up a second towel, running it over his hair before tossing it in the basket waiting outside the washer as he passes the laundry room on the way to his bedroom.

He hasn't been able to get Eliana out of his head all day. The way she hooked her finger into his yesterday was such a small gesture, yet the contact made him long for more. The way she looked at him… Hades, it was enough to drive him crazy with need. And the little pout of her lip as she held back a smile, fucking hell, he wanted to reach out and run his thumb along it. To feel how soft it is under his rough skin.

He may have suggested this arrangement between them, but he didn't realize how hard it would be to keep his hands off her in public spaces. It's why he allowed himself the small graze of her arm. He wanted to touch her. No, he *needed* it. To feel her against him, even in the smallest of ways.

As he dresses, he tries to think of a time when he's had such a pull toward a woman, and his mind comes up blank. Of course, he loves the carnal aspects of being with a woman, but this is… different. It's as if his entire being needs to be with her.

Eliana is all he can think about while at work, and when they are at the theater, he can't wait for her to pop in for her daily checks. There's absolutely no reason for her to be checking in on their progress every day. Everyone knows it. But it doesn't stop her, and if it means he gets to see her, even if for only a few moments, he will happily play along.

Pulling a dark green Henley over his head, his phone vibrates on his dresser.

EVEREST

Hey Smoke-show. Wanna hang tonight?

Fuck.

Declan knew that he'd need to find reasons to blow off Everest at some point, but if he's honest, he was hoping it wouldn't be for a bit. That there would be some help from the fates for the first little while, allowing him and Eliana to get together without having to lie to his best friend.

Yes, he told her he'd deal with Everest, but he hasn't quite figured out what that means or what it looks like yet. He needs to see where this thing with Eliana goes, but how does he lie to his best friend? The friend who's been there for him after he blew out his knee and needed surgery. The friend who helped him with getting Hellbent Motors set up. The friend who would literally jump through fire for him.

Declan runs his hand through his hair, lets out a groan of frustration, and then quickly braids it back. Picking up his phone, he does his best to settle the roil of guilt in his stomach and responds, potentially lighting the ember to burn his friendship to the ground.

DECLAN

SmokeShow? Really?

Three dots instantly appear.

EVEREST

Would you prefer Daddy?

Fuck no.

Damn. I was so looking forward to a new Daddy

Anyway...

Up for a hangout?

Here it goes...

I can't tonight.

Why not?

Tired and need a night in.

Work's been busy, ya know.

I'm cool with chillin at your place. I'll grab some beer.

Fuck. How do I tell him no?

Declan paces, knowing he needs to end this now before Everest even thinks about hopping in his truck.

> I think it's best if I chill on my own tonight. Buckley needs some time with me. He's been feeling neglected all week.

> And I think I may be getting sick, so I'm feeling a night in by myself.

Please buy it. Please buy it.

Three dots appear, then disappear. It takes a moment for the response to come through, and as he reads it, he knows Everest isn't happy.

> Okay.

It's only a single word, but that's so not Everest. Everest never shuts up. And the period at the end? Ugh.

> Maybe sometime this weekend.

> Sure.

Rather than try and make his friend feel better, and ultimately make it worse, Declan leaves it alone. He's never been one to say no to Everest, but Tai was right, it's time for Declan to grow up. He's been tired of the bar scene and games for a while, and ever since Eliana literally walked into his life, he's had no interest in those shenanigans anymore. But it's all Everest seems to want to do.

So yeah, he lied to his best friend. But he's been lying to himself much longer, and it's time he allowed himself to feel that happiness he's been avoiding for so long. And what is the first step to try to achieve that? Take Eliana out.

126

Pulling up to her apartment, his chest is tight as nerves run through him and dance around his insides like a little gnome building a new burrow. The energy within has him feeling restless and raring to go, but his brain tells him he needs to approach slowly. She's not just any woman to him, and he doesn't want her to feel as such.

It's been so long since he has properly dated that there's a part of him that doesn't know if he even remembers how to do this without the goal to be getting into someone's bed at the end of the night.

Swallowing, he does his best to calm the chaos inside of his body, then opens the door and steps out of his truck. He's only ever been outside of her building, so he doesn't even know what apartment is hers, and because he didn't think to ask, as he steps into the vestibule, he hopes her name is listed on the board.

His eyes scan the list of tenants and thankfully find Oaks, E about midway down the list. He pushes the button the board dials whatever number is programmed into it. A moment later, her angelic voice fills the space.

"Hello?"

Fighting a smile, he replies, "Hi. It's Declan. Do you want to let me up? Or you can come down. Whatever works for you. I'm easy." The words tumble out of him like a stream of consciousness, and without any sense of control from his brain... if he had one.

Oh, my fucking Hades. Shut up! His demon chastises.

She laughs at his flustered words, and it's a sound that hits him in the center of his chest, like a spell cast only for him. "You can come up. I need a couple more minutes. Apartment 1108."

"See you in a few." A loud buzzer sounds, and the

second door unlocks, allowing him to find his way to his princess in the tower.

The elevator ride up to the eleventh floor feels excruciatingly long. As he lets his smoke unfurl from his body, he's thankful he's alone in the enclosed space. It doesn't take long for the vessel to fill with smoke so thick he can't see his own hand in front of his face, but the release of his power loosens the tension inside his body. His shoulders relax, and the butterflies in his stomach finally settle. As the elevator slows, he pulls the smoke back in, making it look as if nothing happened to whoever may enter after him.

Her apartment is only a couple down from the elevator, and as his fist meets the door, his heart beats in time. *Mine. Mine. Mine.*

"Come in," she calls from inside.

Reaching for the handle, he knows that there's no turning back after this. Sure, they've kissed. And yeah, it was fucking great. So great he can't stop thinking about it, in fact. But this, stepping into her space before taking her out on a date. It changes things. Their relationship, whatever it was before, will not be the same. And his relationship with Everest changes, too, as Declan now has to find a way to keep this thing with Eliana a secret from him.

He takes a quick breath, his hand pausing mid-turn, checking with himself that this is what he wants. That he's prepared for whatever may come of this.

His hand completes the turn on the door handle, and he steps inside. A decision made.

CHAPTER 21
Eliana

Her breath stops the moment he walks through the door. Goddamn he is gorgeous. The dark jeans he wears hug his powerful thighs. He turns around, closing the door behind him, and... yep, the jeans also make his ass look spectacular. The years of playing football have definitely helped to hone what was likely already close to perfection.

Her eyes dart up his body when he turns to face her again, her cheeks heating slightly, knowing she was caught checking him out. His dark green Henley is snug against his broad chest, and his arms look like they are ready to burst from the sleeves. He may not be sporting a six-pack, but Declan looks like he was sculpted by Hecate herself and sent here to tempt her.

When she finally meets his gaze, it's heated. Apparently, he was checking her out, too. By the look on his face, it's safe to assume that she passed with flying colors.

"You like?" Eliana asks, doing a quick spin to show off her outfit.

She spent too long choosing the right clothes for tonight.

Not knowing where they were going meant she had to choose something comfortable and something more 'date-like' than her standard dance outfits. Her black skirt ends mid-thigh and pairs beautifully with the heeled boots that go up her calves. Given the cooler weather, she chose to pair it with a chunky, almost sheer, cream sweater that allows the black lacy bra underneath to peek through. She slides the posts of oversized silver hoops in her ears before sliding a gloss applicator across her lips to finish her look.

Declan clears his throat as if he's trying to force words to push through. "You look spectacular," he finally manages.

She picks up her clutch from the side table and steps toward him, not missing the way his eyes lock in on her legs. She may be heavier than she was as a professional stage dancer, but years of training mean that they are still powerful and, in her opinion, her best feature. "Thank you."

Eliana gets her coat from the front closet, and Declan gently takes it from her hands, holding it out for her to slide her arms into. As she does, she catches a whiff of his oaky scent. It's cleaner than previously noticed, not mixed with oil or sweat this time, but equally delicious. His fingers graze her neck as he pulls her hair out from under her coat, leaving goosebumps pebbled on her skin. When she turns around, he softly grasps her lapels and pulls her toward him. His lips find hers easily, as if they have done this a thousand times.

This kiss isn't like the one in the theater. It's not hungry. No, it's soft, gentle, even. It's the kind of kiss typically shared between long-time lovers. Yet, it still sends fireworks through her body, heating her from the inside out. This kiss may be gentle, but the power she can feel humming under his skin lets her know there's more, and he's simply holding back for her sake. "I've been waiting to do that all day," he says, resting his forehead against hers.

Heat rises up her neck as she blushes at the thought that he's been thinking of her all day. "Well, I'm happy you don't have to wait any longer."

"Me too," he growls. "But we should go before I do something stupid like bend you over that table and show you what else I've been thinking about."

Eliana's eyes flare as a mix of molten heat and surprise floods her body. *Yes, please.*

He steps back, only putting enough distance between them so he can open the door. Once out in the hall, he intertwines his fingers with hers, and they head off into the night.

It doesn't take long for them to arrive at their destination, and despite how content she's been merely riding through town with Declan, particularly with his hand on her thigh as he drives, seeing their venue for tonight is the icing on an already delicious demon-shaped cake.

"Welcome to Dusty's Drive-in, how many tonight?"

"Two for the *Haunting of Many* and *We Walk Alone*, please."

The attendant prints off their tickets and hands them to Declan. "Here you are. You'll be at screen three. Follow the left fork all the way down."

"Thanks."

"Have a great night, and enjoy the show," the attendant says before Declan pulls away.

"It has been so long since I've been to a drive-in movie," Eliana says, nearly bouncing in her seat with excitement. "I used to love coming here as a kid. I honestly didn't think they were still open."

Following the path as directed, Declan brings them to

screen three and parks in one of the back few rows, ensuring that there's room for smaller vehicles to be in front without their view being blocked. "It did close for a couple of years, but then someone bought it and has brought it back to life. It's been a huge hit since," he says, turning the truck off. "Shall we go and get some snacks before it starts?"

"Absolutely," Eliana replies, climbing out of the truck. "Oooh. I wonder if they still have the chocolate drops they had when I was a kid. Mixing them and gummy bears with popcorn was my favorite." Declan meets her at the back of his truck, an amused smile gracing his perfect lips. "What?"

"You're cute. That's all."

"I'm cute?"

"Yeah," he replies, lacing his hand with hers again. "I wasn't sure what you'd think about coming here, but clearly, I made the right choice. You are as happy as a kid in a candy store, and we haven't even made it into the *actual* candy store."

"You made a great choice," Eliana says, pushing herself onto her tip-toes and kissing his cheek softly. "The movie could be complete shit, and I would still be happy."

He laughs, throwing his head back. The sound is magical. It's deep and resonant, like the laughter has to work itself out of a deep cave. She hopes that's not the case. That his laughter hides so far down that it rarely makes its presence known. His laugh is like a song meant for her, and she'd be immensely sad if she never heard it again.

The walk to the concession building is short, but their hands stay clasped the entire way, and throughout the process of picking out goodies. Her eyes light up when she spots the chocolate drops, and Declan insists she get enough so that she can have some at home, which she happily obliges. Once they've collected the veritable mountain of snack food, they make their way back to his truck, where Eliana spreads out their selection of candy, popcorn, chocolates, and nachos along the dash as if it were a mobile charcuterie board.

Looking at their haul, a fleeting moment of embarrassment works its way through her brain. Years of being told what's appropriate to eat and not to eat as a dancer, has her brain wired to believe that indulging like this means she needs to train harder to keep the weight off. But as fast as the thought is there, she pushes it away, stuffing it back into that judgmental box she tries her best to ignore. She's spent too long working through these stupid rules to have it ruin this night for her.

"I think you had the right idea with the extra bottles of water," she says. "But you have to ration. No pee breaks during the movie."

"Ration liquids. Got it." The corner of his mouth quirks up a touch, showing he's amused.

"Same with the snacks. You can't go so hard on them that there's nothing left before the end."

"Don't stuff my face too fast. Good tip."

Somehow, she manages to tear her eyes away from his mouth and looks back at the feast before them. "I mean, there's lots here, but we need to be strategic about it."

He laughs gently. "I never thought watching a movie could be so… intense."

"Hey! Snacks are a vital part of the movie-watching experience, and I will not have us run out."

His eyes dip to her lips and then down her body. "Come here," he says, putting an arm along the back of the seats, opening himself up for her.

She kicks off her boots, not wanting to dirty the seat, and slides over so she's got her back resting against his side.

He leans forward, picking up the popcorn, chocolate drops, and gummy bears, and places them on the edge of the seat. "Is there a certain ratio we are concerned about, or is it a dump-and-mix situation?"

"Chocolate first, mix, then bears. You want the chocolate to melt enough that it starts to coat some of the popcorn."

Declan does as instructed and then passes the popcorn container to her, which she places in her lap. She grabs a small handful, ensuring a satisfactory mix of all the pieces, and pops it into her mouth. The saltiness of the popcorn pairs perfectly with the semi-melted chocolate, providing a great creamy hit, and the gummy bears finish it off with their chewy sweetness. "It's perfect," she says, grabbing another handful.

His arm reaches around her as he grabs his own, and she can't help but feel like this, right here, is where she's meant to be. It feels easy and free, like a home she never knew she needed.

As the previews start, Eliana snuggles into what she feels is the spot on his chest designed specifically for her. His arm wraps around her, pulling her in tighter, before he kisses the top of her head softly, and she sighs contentedly, wishing they could stay here, in this moment, forever.

CHAPTER 22
Declan

Hades, save me. Why does she have to smell so good?

Declan's index finger swirls figure-eights on the small patch of exposed skin on her hip. She's so soft under his rough hands. Her pale complexion contrasts with the dark ink of the tattoos that run down his forearm and onto his hand, making him itch to see his hand splayed across her naked flesh.

As he gazes down at her curled-up form, her head on his lap, and her breathing deeper as she sleeps, he feels a pull in his chest. It's a new sensation for him and one he's not quite willing to explore yet, but he knows there's something different about her. Well, he's known that since she walked into his shop. Since he began to question if he was ready to settle down. But whatever this is between them, even so early and new, he doesn't want it to end. Not anytime soon, anyway.

The credits roll, signaling the end of the second film, and he honestly has no idea what happened, having been too wrapped up in thoughts of Eliana and how he would love to have her head in his lap for other reasons. Imagining how her mouth feels around his currently hard cock.

The engine on the truck next to them roars to life, startling Declan and waking Eliana. She jolts up, pushing her mussed-up hair away from her face, looking around, momentarily confused. "Oh goddess, I fell asleep. On our date. I'm so sorry. I'm the worst date ever," she fires off, frantically searching for her boots.

Even in the dim light, he can see a flush of embarrassment rush up her neck. His hand lands on her thigh, and he squeezes gently. "Oaks. It's okay; kind of sweet actually."

She eyes him skeptically. "Falling asleep on you during a date is sweet?"

"Yeah. You felt comfortable enough to fully relax. I think that's a good thing." His hand slides up her thigh, then rests on her lower back, not ready to stop touching her yet.

"You're only saying that so I don't feel bad about ruining our date."

"You didn't ruin a thing. Even your little snores were adorable," he says, lightly teasing her.

She leans forward, burying her face in her hands. Her body heats with what he assumes is mortification as she grumbles through her hands, the sound muffled, "Fucking Hades. I snored?"

"A little," he says, taking note of how she's started to pick up the supernatural turn of phrases. It's cute that she's been around him enough that those little things have worked their way into her vernacular.

"End me now. Please. Better yet, I can walk home." She sits up, puts her hand on the door handle, and makes to open it. His hand lunges forward, gripping her wrist. Her head spins, eyes casting down to his hand and then up to his eyes. When she speaks, all hint of emotion is gone. "Please, let me go." Her voice is cold. Distant.

He releases her wrist as if she's scorched him. He knows he's fucked up, but he doesn't understand how. "I'm sorry. I didn't mean to scare you. Or hurt you. I... I just don't want you to leave."

She leans back in the seat. Her arms crossed over her chest. "It's okay," she says flatly. "Can you take me home now?"

Hurt settles in his bones as he starts the engine. "Yeah. Not a problem," he says, resisting the urge to try and fix this. To make right whatever he did to upset her.

The ride back to her apartment is silent. Awkward. Unsettled. He parks in front of her building, and as he turns to her to apologize again, she opens the door. As she gets out, she says, "Thanks for the date. Sorry again that I fell asleep."

"Eliana, can we talk about whatever happened back there?"

She closes the door and stands next to it, her face in the open window. "We can. We will."

"Okay. What—" he begins to ask before she cuts him off, "Not tonight."

She turns and walks into the lobby of her building, leaving him confused and worried that he has ruined everything with her before it can truly begin.

Declan doesn't sleep. Tossing and turning in bed, the complete change in her demeanor upon grabbing her wrist has him torn up inside. He needs to talk to her. To figure out why it upset her so much, so that he can make sure he never does it again.

He's had his fun, sleeping with different women. And he's definitely one to admit that he has lived up to the playboy moniker, but he's always prided himself on being a *respectable* playboy. Well, to the extent that a playboy who sneaks out before their partner wakes up can be. He would never do anything to hurt a woman intentionally, and the way Eliana reacted at the drive-in makes him think that someone has hurt her in the past.

Wisps of smoke billow out of him at the mere thought of some other person harming her. Someone causing her pain. He closes his eyes, resting one arm across his them while the other reaches out toward the fluffy weight at his side and begins stroking Buckley's ear. The softness of his fur, the weight of his head as he moves it and plops it sleepily on top of Declan's thigh, and the resigned huff Buckley gives off in the process helps to ease the flare of anger inside Declan's body. He senses the smoke that rapidly fired out of him begin to recede, and after a moment, it has completely dissipated.

Leaving one hand on Buckley's head as he continues to pet the beast absent-mindedly, his other arm flops to his side. His eyes open, and as he stares into the darkness, he knows he won't be sleeping at all tonight.

Deciding to text her, as it's too late to call, he picks up his phone from the nightstand and single-handedly types.

DECLAN

Hey Oaks.

> I know you're likely sleeping, and I know you said we'd talk about what happened later, but I wanted to say I'm sorry again. I shouldn't have grabbed you like that, and I can see how upset you were. I would never intentionally do something to hurt you or cause you harm.

> I'm sorry. I don't want this to be the end of us.

Hitting send on the final message, he stares at the screen, re-reading what he said, hoping she can see that he means it and that he wants to give this another try.

As he stares at the screen, three precious dots appear.

Then disappear.

And reappear.

When he's all but given up that a message will actually come through, it does. It's not big. Or elaborate. But it's enough to let him know it's not the end.

ELIANA

Thank you. I'm sorry, too.

I'll see you tomorrow at the theater 💋

CHAPTER 23
Declan

I t feels like it takes all day before Eliana walks through the theater door. When she does, she looks as gorgeous as always in her dark tights and oversized lavender sweater. Her work bag is slung over her shoulder and sways ever so slightly with each step.

"Hey, Eliana!" a few of the guys call out as they notice her walking toward the stage. Declan continues to nail together the two pieces of tree-shaped plywood he's working with, but keeps an eye on her as she makes her way toward them.

She smiles briefly, not quite reaching her eyes, and says hello back, asking them questions about what they're working on and how their nights were as she passes. They've really come to like her, and Declan's sure they look forward to her visits as much as he does. Or almost as much.

Kneeling down, her boots come into his frame of vision before the rest of her. When she stops beside him, he allows himself the opportunity to take her in; his gaze roves her body slowly, one painfully beautiful inch at a time. When his eyes finally meet hers, he sees a heaviness there. Tired. Or weary. With maybe a dash of forgiveness—and that's all he needs. If there's even a sliver of forgiveness available for him, he'll take it and work his demon-magic with it.

"Can we talk?" she asks softly as if she's unsure of his answer.

Standing, perhaps a bit too enthusiastically, as she steps back, putting space between them. "Absolutely." He steps to the side and holds his hand out, signaling for her to lead the way. She steps forward, leading them to one of the empty offices backstage.

She enters the office first, turning to lean against the front of the desk, her plump ass resting on the edge with her feet crossed in front of her.

"Do I need to close the door?" Declan asks.

"Nah. We should be okay. I only wanted to have a bit of privacy away from the rest of your staff."

Declan nods. Not knowing what to do with himself, he leans against the door frame, arms crossed across his chest. His stance feels intimidating, which he doesn't intend, but he can't think of anything else to do with his hands, and keeping them still prevents him from touching her.

Eliana looks at him, and it's like he's stuck in a riptide, hoping to find the surface but unsure if he will be pulled back out again. His eyes dip to her lips, where she's pulled the bottom one between her teeth and is agonizingly chewing on it. He tucks his hands further under his arms to keep himself from reaching out and pulling the delicate flesh from the vise grip she has it in. Watching her be so concerned about what she wants to say has him aching to run his thumb along her bottom lip and reassure her that everything is okay.

It takes her a moment before she finally releases her lip, leaving red marks along its edge. "I want to start by saying that I'm sorry for shutting you out last night. I'm not sorry about getting upset, but I should have stayed to talk."

"It's okay."

"It's not, but if we are going to continue figuring out whatever this," she says, gesturing between them, "is, then you need to know some things."

His arms fall to his sides as he fights the urge to close the distance between them. He doesn't know what's going to come out of her pretty mouth next, but he has a feeling it can't be good.

"No one other than Kaia and my therapist knows about this, and even then, they don't know the whole story." Something flashes in her eyes, but before he can make sense of it, it's gone. "So please keep it to yourself. I don't need Everest knowing and going all *big brother*, okay?"

"Absolutely," he says, involuntarily stepping forward and placing his hands on the back of the chair that sits between them.

"You know I moved away from Leeside to go to school and dance professionally." He nods. "While I lived in Hollybrook, I met someone. His name was Sam." His hands tighten on the back of the chair, turning his knuckles white, his gut telling him that whatever she's going to say will not be good. "Things started off well with Sam. We were like any other couple when we first started out. Things were hot and heavy, and we spent so much time together. To anyone looking in, it stayed like that. But it didn't take long for him to start putting little rules in place. Sam would get angry at me for staying out late or going out for a drink with my dancer friends after a Friday evening show. He didn't like it when I left in the morning before he got up, so I had to wait for him, even if it meant I would get in trouble from production. He must have watched me enter my passcode as he began to police my phone. Deleting text messages. I'm not entirely sure, but I also think he synced his with mine somehow, and so even if he wasn't checking it from my phone, he could still see every message that came through. He eventually poisoned me against my own friends and made me believe they didn't want what was best for me. They were only talking to me to get a piece of my fame, and so on. I soon found myself isolated, with only him as my 'person.' I didn't really clue into any of this until it was too late, and I was too deep. He never hit me, but he grabbed me a few times to prevent me from leaving during an argument."

Of course. That's why she shut down. Smoke seeps from Declan, swirling around him in thick waves as he takes this all on. She may have moved away, but if Everest had ever caught wind that she was experiencing this, there's no telling what he would have done. And without a doubt, Declan would have been at his side. Through gritted teeth, Declan says, "Where is he now?"

She laughs humorlessly. "That does not matter."

"It very well fucking does."

She pulls her bottom lip between her teeth again before pushing herself off the desk and stepping toward him. Her hand lands softly on top of his, and his grip instantly loosens on the chair. She takes his hand, linking their fingers. "Declan." Their eyes meet, and all the fury inside him melts away. Not because he's not enraged at her ex, because he most certainly is, but because he doesn't want her to see that side of him. She will only ever get softness from him. "Declan. I appreciate the sentiment, but I left him in the past, and that is where he will stay. What he's up to now is of no concern to me. I didn't tell you this to anger you or to seek revenge, but so that you would understand why I reacted the way I did. I had been talking about Sam recently with my therapist, and the way you grabbed my wrist—" Declan starts to speak, trying to apologize, but she holds a hand up to stop him. "It's okay. You didn't know. I know that. But yes, the way you grabbed me sent me back to that place. So, I shut down to protect myself. Again, I'm not sorry for getting upset, but I am sorry for shutting you out. I don't want to do that."

"I don't want you to either," he practically whispers. She smiles, and though he can still see the pain behind her eyes, the smile is there, too. She doesn't hate him.

She brings their hands down to hang in between them.

"Can I hug you?" he asks tentatively.

She nods. "I'd like that."

He brings their clasped hands behind her back and pulls her toward him. His other arm reaches around, engulfing her in the biggest hug he can muster, wishing he could erase her experience with Sam from her history. As her head tilts to rest on his chest, he places his chin on top, breathing her in and vowing that she will never face anything like that again.

CHAPTER 24

Eliana

T elling Declan about Sam was easier than she thought it would be. To herself, she sounded distant while she spoke about it all, but that made it easier. To remove the emotion from it, at least for her, means that she can't still be hurt by it. Dr. Colson would say she's lying to herself and that her reaction to the way he took her wrist meant that she's still very much impacted by those events.

After she and Declan finish talking, he asks if he can take her out again, to which she happily agrees. They part ways shortly after, him going back to work on the tree he was building and her stopping by the studio to drop off some supplies she needs for her classes tomorrow. The theater isn't far from her work, and she's happy to have the time alone to process their conversation.

Upon hearing the short version of her experience with Sam, it was clear that Declan immediately wanted to set the world ablaze. As she plays over his reaction in her mind, she comes to the realization that she has never had someone respond that way for her. To want to tear the world apart on her behalf. It was... hot.

Her relationship with Sam wasn't always like she told Declan, of course. They did have happy moments, but those are all tainted to her now, buried under memories of his control. After seeing Declan's reaction, she's sure that if he knew it all, he would cross the Earth to find Sam and make sure he never hurt another living being again.

Maybe that's not such a bad thing. She stops herself before she goes too far down that train of thought. Yes, Sam wasn't great to her. Far from it, if she's being honest. Yet, despite all that, she doesn't wish him harm. Just growth. With any luck, she'll never have to see him again anyway.

Eliana drops what she needs in her locker and manages to escape without getting caught by June or anyone else—practically a miracle. She drives herself into downtown, or what is classified as Leeside's downtown, and parks on the street outside of Taster's Delight.

Stepping inside, she's enveloped by the scent of freshly ground coffee beans and delicious pastries, causing her mouth to water in anticipation. When it's her turn, she orders her chai latte and a cardamom ginger biscuit. She finds a table in the corner and pulls out her crochet hook and yarn from her bag, setting them up on the table. With earbuds in and a new audiobook to listen to, she relaxes into the space, letting the world melt away as she gets lost in a world of dragons.

The door to Dr. Colson's office opens. Eliana rises from the chair in the hall, gathering her things, and then follows him in.

"Good afternoon. How's your day going?" he asks.

It's always the same—a standard greeting and question about her day, or week. It seems innocuous, but the routine start to each session helps to set her at ease. Especially when she knows she has some heavy shit to talk about that day.

Sitting on the couch, she kicks her shoes off and pulls her socked feet up beside her. "My day has been good. I was off today, so I spent a bit of time by myself at Taster's Delight, listening to a book and working on a new blanket."

"That sounds like a wonderful day."

"It was."

"But?" he prompts.

She pulls at the hem of her sleeve, pausing as she calls on the courage to start what she wants to say next. As always, Colson waits patiently, allowing her to find her words. "I also stopped by and saw the man I've been seeing."

"Why does saying that cause you to hesitate?"

She swallows. "Because we went out on a date the other night and I had a moment."

"A moment? Can you elaborate?"

"We went to the drive-in and I fell asleep." She laughs, remembering her mortification when she woke up. How she wished she had the power to open the earth right then and there to swallow her whole. "After some light teasing, I motioned to get out of the truck, and he grabbed my wrist. I shut down."

Her eyes flick up, catching Colson nodding as he makes notes. "Was that something that happened with your ex, Sam?"

She nods. "Yes."

"Why don't you tell me about it?"

She hesitates for a moment before breaking into the

same recount of her relationship with Sam that she told Declan. Some of it Colson already knows, and he makes the appropriate noises as she shares about her past again. When she shares about his more physical reactions, Colson goes quiet. When he finally says something again, it's not what she expects. "How did Sam react when you became injured?"

"He never physically hurt me. At least nothing beyond a small bruise."

"That's still physical harm, but we can delve more into that and how you still seem to want to protect or minimize his actions another day. What I meant was, how did he react when you were injured at work—on stage—and needed surgery and presumably care?"

"When it happened, he was out of town for work. When we were finally able to talk a couple of days later, he told me he was too busy and couldn't come back. I understood how important his work was to him and how hard he'd been trying for a promotion. So I told him it was okay."

"That must have been very challenging for you to be alone, fresh out of surgery."

Her gaze turns to the window, watching the leaves sway in the breeze. "I did okay," she says, her voice sounding distant, even to herself. Maintaining her distance and not dwelling on how she felt helps her to keep it together. She'd break if she let herself truly think about and revisit those first few days after losing her career. "I hired a nurse. They came to the apartment for the first couple of days post-surgery to check on me and make sure I was managing."

"And how did you feel?"

Turning her head to look back at Colson, she breathes deeply, trying to make it appear that she's steadying her emotions before she speaks. "I was hurt, obviously. But I understood he couldn't leave. So I did what I do best and managed."

"And that wasn't hard? To be on your own, in pain, facing the reality of your career, something you had worked so long to achieve, crashing down around you?" he probes.

Eliana wants to tell him to back off. To stop trying to get her to admit what she hasn't admitted to anyone. But she doesn't. Instead, she tells him what he wants her to say. "It was devastating. I had worked for years to get where I was and finally achieve my dream. I was a principal dancer in a professional production, and I loved every aspect of my work. So yes, to have it all crumble around me because of a shitty landing was quite literally life-altering." Her voice rises, the anger she's fought so hard to keep at bay breaking through the box she's kept it in. "I mean, I came back to the town that I thought I had outgrown and left in the past. It's embarrassing. So yeah, it's been fucking hard," she says, crossing her arms across her chest as she sits back roughly.

"From the sounds of it, you've had some significant life changes, left an abusive relationship, and are now entering into a new situation with someone else. Which, to me, shows that while your body has physically healed from your surgeries, mentally, you are still dealing with the fresh scab. There's so much regrowth that needs to happen, yet."

Eliana scoffs. "So what, I'm not mentally well enough to be in a relationship?"

Colson leans forward, placing his pad and pen on the desk beside him. Taking his glasses off, he huffs a breath on the lenses before cleaning them with the bottom of his sweater as he says, "No. Not at all. I think you're perfectly capable of having a healthy relationship, but your reaction to how he touched you makes sense, and the fact that you're here talking about it and talking to him shows that you're making progress. What I think you need to remember is that your body has a memory too, and you need to give it, and your mind, time to…" he pauses, *"recalibrate.* As I said, we'll return to your defense of Sam and the grace you've shown him, but you must recognize it was an abusive relationship and that managing its effects will take time. You also need to prepare yourself for the fact that certain things may always trigger you and bring you back to that space with Sam. And that's okay. What matters is that you don't stay there."

Your body has a memory, too. That statement, out of everything Colson said, sticks with her. There is no way that Declan could have known that grasping her wrist would have had the impact on her as it did. *She* didn't even know it would make her shut down like that. But the instant it happened, it was as if she were back there with Sam.

"Unfortunately, we are out of time today. But we can pick up here at our next session."

"Okay," Eliana replies, her voice feeling small as she's still stuck on that statement. *Your body has a memory, too.*

"Eliana," Colson says, calling her attention to him. Her eyes meet his, and she's greeted with compassion and empathy. "You did great today. It was a heavy talk, and you shared openly. Thank you. I don't take for granted how hard this can be."

She smiles briefly at him, not really knowing what to say, before gathering her things, sliding her shoes back on, and leaving his office.

"Your body has a memory, too," she says under her breath as she gets into her car. *Well, shit. What else does it remember that she's tucked away?*

CHAPTER 25

Declan

Buckley bounds down the hall, a big bear of black fur bouncing as he runs to meet Declan at the front door. It's been a long day. The extra hours at the theater mean that poor Buckley has spent more time on his own lately than Declan would prefer.

"Hi, bubba," Declan says, leaning down to ruffle Buckley's fur. The beast's head tilts, and his sizeable pink tongue lolls out of his mouth happily as his tail thumps loudly against the wall. "Let me shower quickly, then we can go outside and play for a bit," he says, as if Buckley understands reason.

Declan tosses his keys on the counter before making his way to the ensuite and hopping in the shower. Feeling clean again, he dresses and heads outside with Buckley. The giant ball of fur gallops around the yard, chasing after and catching the ball each time Declan throws it, bringing it back again and again. As Declan tosses the ball for what feels like the hundredth time, he hears the sliding door close behind him.

Buckley charges toward the new guest, their arrival more important than the slobber-covered tennis ball.

"Ooomph."

Declan turns to see Everest on his ass, Buckley standing over him with his paws on Everest's chest, holding him in place while licking his friend's face with fervor.

"Care. To. Call. Off. Your. Hound?" Everest says in between licks, turning his head to avoid accidentally making out with the dog.

"Depends. What's your purpose?"

"Dec!"

Declan laughs, amused at the image before him. "Alright. Fine," he says between laughs. "Buckley, off."

Buckley looks at Declan pleadingly as he climbs off Everest before flopping on the deck only far enough that he can quickly return to Everest if given permission again.

Everest pushes himself up on an elbow, turning his body to prepare himself to stand up. His other hand juts out and points at Declan, "Not cool." His tone says he's annoyed, but the smirk on his face confirms he's as amused as Declan.

"I love that oaf of a dog of yours, but man, it doesn't matter how prepared you are when those paws hit your chest; there's no staying upright," Everest says, laughing and doing his best to brush the dirty paw prints from his chest.

Declan gestures toward Everest. "Sorry about that, by the way."

"No worries. It will wash. And if it doesn't, well, I'll send you my cleaner's bill."

Declan huffs his amusement, knowing full well that Everest would absolutely send him a cleaning bill. "What brings you by?"

Everest brings his hand to his chest and leans back dramatically, feigning insult. "Does a best friend need a reason to stop by? Do I need to announce my intent to visit ahead of time?"

Yes, because I may be here with your sister and don't want you walking in on something… Should we ever get to that point.

"A best friend? No. You? Yes."

Everest scoffs. "Rude!"

"But true," Declan laughs, bouncing out of reach of Everest's playful punch to his arm.

"You know, I could go anywhere else and get this kind of treatment—" he raises a hand to stop Declan's next verbal spar, "but I choose to come here, to spend time with my supposed *best friend*. But I see how it is," he pouts, turning away, making to leave.

Declan quickly slings his arms around Everest's stomach, hugging him from behind. "I'm sorry, *best friend*. Won't you please forgive me for my heinous treatment of you?"

"That's better," Everest replies, perking up. "Now get off me!" His hands pull at Declan's in an effort to pull them apart to be freed from his grasp.

"Never!"

Everest squirms and manages to break free, putting distance between them, and holds his hands out in front of him, ready to karate chop Declan should he get within reach. Declan waves him off and laughs as he moves over to the cushioned wicker sofa and sits. Keeping his hands out ready to defend if needed, Everest moves to the other couch across from Declan and takes a seat.

Declan's smoke unfurls from him, venturing into the house. It returns a moment later with two beers held aloft, depositing one in front of each of them before retracting back into Declan.

"I always love when you do shit like that."

"It is a fun party trick. Also helps when I'm being super

lazy," Declan replies, popping the cap and taking a swig. "So what actually brings you here?"

Everest takes a sip before answering. "I haven't seen you in a while. Seems like you've been super busy lately with the stuff for Ellie's dance thing."

"Yeah, between that and stuff at the shop, it's been a busy couple of weeks. But we're nearing the end of the prep for the showcase, so it should slow down soon. Which I'm sure Bucks will be happy about." Hearing his name, Buckley raises his head. When no treats are offered, he dramatically drops it and goes back to sleep.

"I get that. How has everything been with Ellie's dance group thing, anyway?"

"It honestly hasn't been too bad. The shop helpers have been loving it. We've got a good crew, and Eliana has been great. She checks in on us every day and has been a wonderful guide through the project."

Everest narrows his eyes at Declan as if trying to determine if he said something out of place. After a moment, his features soften, and he relaxes back into the couch, laying his arm along the back while his feet go up on the small table between them.

"Yeah, she's had a rough go after that surgery of hers. She's so stubborn, though. Did you know she didn't tell any of us what was going on until well after it happened? She insisted she had everything under control and made Mom promise that she wouldn't go out to help her."

Eliana may have told him about Sam, but he didn't know about this. That she didn't get help. Or at least not from her own family, who would have been more than happy to assist her in her time of need. The strength it must have taken to go through all that with everything that was going on with Sam at the same time.

"Mom wanted to go so badly. Dad and I had to keep telling her not to. That if Eliana felt she needed help, she would have asked."

"Absolutely," Declan says, doing his best to agree with Everest despite knowing there were likely some other factors involved in her not wanting her mom there. Like a certain asshat named Sam. Which, reminds him, where was Sam during all of that? Declan wonders. The anger from the conversation with Eliana begins to rise, and he has to fight his demon and power to keep them in check. The last thing he needs is a shift for no reason while sitting here drinking a beer with his buddy.

"Anyway, she seems happy to be back at the studio, and it's nice to have her home."

"She is, and I bet."

Everest tilts his head back, chugging the rest of his beer. Placing the empty bottle on the table, he looks to Declan expectantly. "Let's go out."

Declan starts to protest, but Everest interjects, "Nothing wild. Let's go to the Acorn. I'll text Tai and Joley, and we can go for a couple of beers. Well, a couple more. What do ya say?" Everest cocks his head, pouts his lips, and bats his eyes. The picture of desperation.

Fuck.

"Fine," Declan groans. "But! Don't try and pawn some girl off on me."

"Why? Have you taken up a new pledge of celibacy?" Everest teases.

Yes. But only because I can't get your sister off my mind.

"No. Not feeling it lately."

Everest sighs dramatically, "Fiiiiinee," agreeing to Declan's condition. "Alright, you go get changed, and I'll text the guys. Be ready to go in ten!"

"Yes, Mom!" Declan teases before heading into the house to do as instructed.

"Welcome to Karaoke Night!" Daisy exclaims from the stage. "Tonight is all about letting loose and showing everyone those pipes you've been hiding. So scroll through the list of songs available here—" she says, conjuring a QR code in the air for patrons to scan, "and then click the link at the bottom to sign up with your choice. We'll get started in about ten minutes, which gives you enough time to order a few more shots of liquid courage," she finishes, winking at the crowd.

People clap, and excited chatter picks up as she walks off stage. Declan watches her briefly as she walks across the floor, stopping and quickly kissing the brunette sitting at the bar before going behind the counter and serving drinks. He's come to know Sloan over the last year or so during holiday get-togethers or casual hangouts at Lachlan's. She seems nice enough, and Daisy is clearly happy with her. If she wasn't, he knows Petra would most certainly use those infamous Premier Witch powers to dissolve Sloan's ass into a pile of goop.

"So what song do you wanna sing tonight?" Everest asks. "I was thinking of some romantic duet. Really show the ladies how soft and sensitive we are."

Declan laughs, but Everest's tone suggests that he's legitimately suggesting they sing something together. "No." Declan stares him down. He is not doing that. He refuses to embarrass himself that way. Besides, this was supposed to be a chill night, which, judging by Everest's now wandering eye, he's completely forgotten about as he tries to land the attention of some curvy redhead across the bar. He turns to Tai and Joley next to him, hoping for their support. Instead, he finds traitors.

"You two are first up!" Tai says, laughing like the dick that he is. "We figured with Declan's range and Everest's good looks that the song by Wicked Crew would be a perfect fit." Joley is in hysterics beside Tai, and as he leans back in his chair, balancing on the back two legs, one of Declan's little tendrils of smoke happens to slip out and push him over. Tai bursts out into further laughter. Declan and Everest join him, and even though he's red-faced with embarrassment, Joley joins in as well. He raises his hand, and Declan meets it for a high-five as Joley says, "Worth it."

Daisy appears on stage, with much encouragement from the crowd. When the whistling and hollering finally settle down, she brings the microphone up to her lips. "Alright, our first song is 'Careless in Love' by Wicked Crew, to be sung by the one and only Declan and Everest." The smirk on her face says she knows this is going to be a train wreck and that she's here for the ride anyway. "Let's give them a round of applause!"

The crowd claps loudly, and people nearby shout excitedly. Declan looks to both Tai and Joley as he and Everest stand. Letting his demon rise to the surface, he allows his eyes to flash gold while staring his traitorous friends down. "You both are on my shit list," he playfully growls before calming the demon within and walking away. As he makes his way to the stage, he hears Tai say in a mock scared tone, "Oh no, the big bad demon boy is mad at us. Whatever will we do?"

Declan picks up the mic and says, "Daisy, can you be sure to add Tai and Joley next? Pick something good for them, okay?"

She laughs as she slides back behind the bar and gives him a thumbs-up. She and Sloan put their heads together as the song starts up.

Everest and Declan turn to face each other, looking at each other like long-lost lovers in a storm. Everest's hand extends out, reaching Declan, but he steps back, keeping the distance and imaginary tension between them as the song builds. When the course breaks, they turn in unison to face the crowd, who roar back at them, egging them on. Everest falls to his knees in despair, and he pleads for Declan's forgiveness through the lyrics. Declan closes his eyes, mentally praying for Hades to save him from this spectacle. As the song shifts to a message of love, the protagonists, having worked through their challenges and swearing a never-ending devotion to each other, Declan opens his eyes, and they instantly land on her. *Eliana.*

CHAPTER 26

Eliana

T he last thing she expects to see when she walks into the Acorn is her brother and Declan belting out a ballad to each other. Everest is in his glory, soaking up the attention of everyone watching, but Declan's gaze tells her he only cares about one person in the room. Her.

His eyes track her across the room as the server guides her and Kaia to a table. She places her phone and wallet on the table and watches the show before them unfold.

The volume in the room rises as other patrons eat out of Everest's hand while he mimes falling in love with Declan. As the last round of the chorus starts, the room erupts, raucously singing along with her boys on stage. *Her* boys. The thought causes her to pause before she sits. The server says something to them, but with the crowd singing along, it's impossible to make out any of it. Not that it matters. Her brain is too busy short-circuiting, stuck on the idea of Declan being hers. She rarely wants to claim Everest, but Declan... That came out of nowhere. They've barely been on a date, and yet her brain is already laying claim to the demon. She's going to have to have a chat with her subconscious later.

The boys finish their song to exuberant applause and whoops of celebration, and Everest leaps off the stage. He high-fives anyone he can on his way to Eliana's table, with Declan following close behind.

"Ellie. What are you doing out? You don't go out," he says, raising his hand out to Kaia for a high-five. When she doesn't reciprocate, he runs his through his hair instead. Declan snorts behind him, and Kaia picks up the menu from the center of the table, not giving Everest the time of day.

Feeling her phone vibrate on the table, she flips it over and glances at the screen. "Nice to see you too, Ev," she replies, silencing yet another call from an unknown number.

Plopping down on the open seat beside her, Everest throws his arm along the back of her chair. As a server walks by, he circles a finger in the air, signaling a round of shots for the table. "Oh, don't be like that. You know I'm teasing you," Everest says.

"What are you two doing out tonight?" Eliana asks. "Looking for another heart to break?"

"Always," Everest laughs. "But this guy has gotten old and says he *doesn't want to,*" Everest says, adding a mocking lilt to the last few words.

"Or, maybe he's trying to be respectful of women," Eliana counters, quickly catching Declan's gaze before turning her attention back to Everest.

"Unlikely," Everest and Kaia say in unison. Eliana turns her head, glaring at her friend while Kaia laughs along with Everest. Hell must have suddenly frozen over if these two agree on something.

"Anyway," Declan says, sidestepping the conversation,

"Tai and Joley are up next, and we should get back to our table."

"Oh, they're fine. We can watch them make a fool of themselves from here; Hades knows they won't be anywhere near as good as we were. I mean, they don't have our chemistry," Everest says, reaching dramatically for Declan, who now sits on Eliana's opposite side. Declan laughs and bats her brother's hands away. Despite the crowd's murmur, that resonant sound of his sticks to her. Coating her in a warmth she didn't know she needed.

Tai and Joley take the stage, and Everest is right—they aren't as good as he and Declan were. But while everyone is watching the stage, Eliana can't keep her gaze away from Declan. He catches her watching and smiles, crinkling the skin at the corner of his eyes—utter perfection. When he winks at her, her stomach flutters, and it's like she's the only one in the world.

He glances at Everest, checking to ensure his attention is still on their friends, and then his hand finds hers on her lap. It's quick, as they can't risk Everest seeing, but as his thumb brushes the back of her hand, she wishes nothing more than for them to be alone. Before she can think of linking her fingers with his, he pulls back and mouths *tomorrow* at her. She nods in return, feeling the butterflies in her stomach once again.

Tomorrow.

Anticipation has been building inside her all day. Shortly after she got home last night, Declan messaged, asking about her work schedule. After some back and forth, they worked out that she would meet him at his place around seven. She'd be lying if she said she hadn't been counting the hours since.

It's times like these when she wished she had magical powers so that maybe it would help relieve some of the tension raging through her body. At least, she assumes that's a benefit of magic, that releasing it helps regulate the body. Now that she thinks about it, she's never asked any of the magical beings she's known and been friends with. To be honest, she really doesn't know much at all about how it all works. Just that it does.

As she does another series of pirouettes while she plays between classes, she makes a mental note to ask Declan about it in—she looks at the clock—three hours and twelve minutes. She has three classes left for the day and then will need to run home quickly to shower and change. Declan suggested dinner at his place, and it sounded perfect. She gets bored cooking for herself all the time, so the thought of someone else potentially cooking for her or the two of them creating something together is heavenly.

Her first class, a group of five and six-year-olds, passes quickly as they begin to focus on their number for the showcase. Their excitement to learn their roles is palpable. Her second class, a teen ballet group, is a little more frustrating. The mix of attitudes and questioning of her expertise is a challenge on a good day, but some days, their snarky little comments get under her skin.

Eliana may be back at Strike a Pose because of her injury, but she knows she is a talented dancer. Or was. Well, she *is*, but sometimes it's hard to think of herself as a professional still. It's something Dr. Colson has been helping her work on, among all of the other things. Seeing herself as valid even though her path now looks different. But it's still a work in progress. And some days, those comments from the teens challenge that progress.

She says goodbye to Bellamy and June as she leaves and drives home as quickly as her car will allow. After a brief shower, shave, and primp, she's ready to go again. Not knowing if she'll be drinking tonight, Eliana calls a cab, and after only a few minutes wait, climbs inside and is on her way over to Declan's. Despite being only ten minutes late, Declan, along with a large black dog, is pacing at the door when she arrives.

"Are you okay?" she asks, stepping through the door he holds open. She slides her coat off and holds it in her arms.

"I've been better." Declan snaps his fingers, and the dog walks over to a bed in the corner and lies down.

"Did something happen? Is it no longer a good night?" She turns, making to put her coat back on and leave through the still-open door, hoping she can flag the cab down again.

"Where are you going?" he asks.

Pausing inside the doorway, she glances at his confused expression and back at the door. "It doesn't seem like it's a good time for you. I thought you wanted me to leave."

He steps toward her, putting a hand out to grasp her arm, but stops short of touching her. "No. No. I was worried." She steps into his outstretched hand, making contact. Even through her coat, his touch heats her skin. His eyes dip down to his hand on her arm, then back to her eyes. "I didn't know if you had broken down or if maybe your shithead ex showed up and..." He pauses. "My brain and demon instantly jumped to the worst thing."

Her hand finds his and holds it as she steps aside, allowing him to finally close the door. Her free hand moves up, cupping the side of his face. "Declan, I'm okay."

"I know. I see that." The large dog comes out from the corner and headbutts her leg and then his hand. "This is Buckley by the way."

"Hi, Buckley," Eliana says before leaning over to pet his head. She smiles up at Declan. "It's adorable that you were so concerned, but this is Leeside. The worst thing to happen here was when a flock of geese held up traffic for half an hour."

He leans his cheek against her hand before turning his head and kissing her palm. "You're right."

"I know." She winks. "I know all of this—" she motions to the general space around them, "is new, but you'll have to trust that if something is wrong, I'll let you know. And also, don't be prepared to burn the world down at a moment's notice."

"Okay," he replies, helping her take her coat off again and hanging it in the front closet. "But, I can't promise not to be concerned about you. You've already been through so much. I can't stand the thought of anything else happening to you."

"I appreciate it, but you can't protect me from everything."

"I know. How about I'll do my best not to turn into an overprotective demon?"

"I'll accept that."

"Good." He pauses. "Can I hold you?" She nods, and before she can open her arms, he wraps his around her, pulling Eliana into him. Her body presses into his; their curves perfectly shaped for each other. Her hands splay on his chest, and he practically growls into the crook of her neck as he breathes her in. "I've missed being around you. Well, only you."

Goosebumps move down her neck while he runs his

nose up the side of it before nipping her earlobe. Giggling, she playfully pushes him away, trying to escape his hold. "Seriously, do you know how hard it was to keep my hands off you last night? Everest practically begged me to go out. I didn't expect you to show up, and then when he made us sit with you…" His words trail off as he punctuates each of the rest of his thought with kisses on her neck, chin, nose, and tentatively ending with her lips, "It. Was. Pure. Torture."

Her body melts into his, her hands roaming up his shoulders and wrapping around the back of his neck. His tongue slides along the end of her lips, tasting and teasing. When her lips part, he takes the invitation and nips them. The quick pinch of pressure sends fireworks throughout her, making her toes tingle and her nipples harden. Tilting her head, she opens her mouth further, allowing him in and meeting his tongue with hers. The kiss shifts from a slow, steady connection filled with longing to a more heated endeavor, hinting at their unspoken desires.

She's still barely in the door, and they've already worked through his alpha-esque concern to now realizing they are finally alone and what that could entail. When he pulls away and begins kissing down her neck again, his hands roam her body before firmly gripping her ass and she moans into his ear. His hands slide down the back of her thighs, and she has enough time to clasp her hands together before she's lifted off her feet and her legs wrap around his broad, strong back. Their lips crash together again, her hands gripping the braid on the back of his head, angling it so she can get deeper.

Declan somehow manages to walk them through the house to the living room, where he finds the couch and sits, unwrapping her legs from his midsection so she can straddle him more comfortably before he leans back completely.

Once positioned, his large hands find her ass again, pulling her into him.

She'd have to be oblivious not to notice the rather sizeable bulge now poking at her core. A part of her is curious about what exactly he's packing in those pants of his, but also this—making out like they are teenagers—is hot as fuck. It's been so long since she's had a good session of fooling around. There's no pressure here. No concern about what it all means. It's all exploration and learning each other.

Eliana wouldn't consider herself a prude by any means, but after years in a relationship with a person who worked so hard to diminish her, she's not in a rush to leap into that more intimate stage again, at least not until she feels she can trust whoever she's with. But this, his fingertips digging into her ass, the hunger to devour her bubbling at the surface as he kisses down her neck and onto her chest, the deep inhale he takes when he pauses with his face nestled between her breasts—it feels nice. Safe even.

Her hands wrap behind his head, as one of his hands comes up, pulling the top of her shirt aside to give him better access to the top of her breast. His other hand continues to massage her ass cheek as she grinds into him, feeling the pressure build between her legs. She may not be ready to sleep with him yet, but that doesn't mean she isn't ready for a fully clothed orgasm or two. Before it gets to that point, though, she knows she needs to make sure they are on the same page.

Placing her hands on his shoulder, she pushes back, putting a tiny bit of distance between them. Gazing up at her, his eyes flash demon gold before returning to their normal blue, but they remain heated. "I want to make sure that you're okay with it not going further than this right now?"

A growl rumbles in his chest. "Are you serious?"

She pushes herself a little further away, afraid that she's said something she shouldn't have or that she misread him. He was so protective and worried about her that she thought for sure he'd be okay with waiting. But then again... he is friends with Everest, and she knows how her brother is. Plus, add in the rumors about Declan and his escapades, and it's not hard to believe he'd be upset if he's not getting laid. "I'm sorry. Maybe this isn't a good idea. We should stop." She tries to push away again so that she can climb off his lap, but his hold on her is too strong.

He swallows, holding his eyes shut tight briefly as if trying to collect himself. "No. I'm sorry. I didn't mean for that to come out as it did. My demon is... eager... shall we say, and I'm trying my best to keep him at bay."

"Oh," Eliana replies, keeping her hands on his chest and leaning back, prepared to get up.

Placing a hand lightly on her chin, he angles her face down so their eyes connect. "I need you to understand that I will *never* force you to do anything that you aren't ready for. We can go as fast or as slow as you want. *You* are in control here, and *you* dictate the speed at which we move forward."

He didn't say anything tantalizing, and yet, she feels a heat rush up her neck. "Oh. Okay." Her eyes dip to his lips before going back to those crystal blue pools of wonder. "I... I need to be sure. I can't do the fling thing."

"That's okay. I don't want to do the fling thing with you, either." His voice deepens, and the rumble in his chest that she feels under her hands lights up her insides. "But know this, Eliana. When you're ready, I plan to make you come as many times as I can so that you never forget how perfect you are." She swallows. "Until then, I'm happy to do this, or snuggle, or even sit on opposite ends of the couch like we are teenagers being supervised."

"Thank you."

"You don't need to thank me for being a decent person," he says, lightly stroking her arm with the tips of his fingers.

"No. But I appreciate it nonetheless."

His other hand slides up to the back of her neck, pulling her face to his. Their lips meet softly this time. Naturally. As if she's coming home after a long day. It fills the little hole in her chest a little more, reassuring her that whatever this is between them could be something worthwhile.

"If that's all, shall we make dinner?" he asks.

"That sounds like a wonderful idea," she says as her stomach grumbles loudly in agreement, causing them both to laugh.

"Alright. Let's go feed the beast!"

He kisses her again before she climbs off his lap. His fingers interlace with his as they walk into the kitchen to make dinner together, Buckley following close behind, as if it's something they do every night.

CHAPTER 27
Declan

Her eyes sparkle in the light. The flecks of green in the hazel base call his attention, drawing him in. He could fall into them on a whim and die a lucky man.

"So what are we making?" she asks, leaning against the counter, crossing her arms over her chest, causing his eyes to dip to her pushed-up and plump breasts. When his gaze flicks back up to her face, she's smirking back at him.

"Well," he says, stepping into her space, caging her in, and casually reaching behind her with one arm to pick up the cloth-covered basket with dough. "I thought we could make pizza," he says, his voice low, into her ear. As he draws back, he doesn't miss the fact that her smirk has been replaced with a heated expression. Her eyes watch him with desire as her cheeks take on a flushed hue.

He steps back again, placing the basket on the counter behind him before taking the flour out of a bottom cupboard nearby. Pushing his sleeves up, he catches her throat bob as she swallows. He may have agreed to move at

169

whatever pace she's comfortable with, but that doesn't mean he can't taunt her in subtle ways. He's seen how she watches him when they've been at the theater. Or how her eyes traveled his body before they went to the drive-in. Declan may need to be patient, as agonizing as it may be, to hold off touching her in ways he only dreams about, but if she expects him to hold back on the flirting... well, they will both be in for some trouble.

Declan senses her eyes following his every move, and it seems to take her a moment to regain some sense of composure before asking what she can do. "If you could chop up some veggies, that'd be great. There are mushrooms, peppers, onions, and olives in the fridge. Take out whatever you like."

She nods in response and starts digging through the fridge. "Do you have any basil?"

"I do. Bottom drawer," he says, sprinkling flour on the clean counter. "It should be in a little clear package."

"Yep, got it. And where would I find a cutting board?"

"In the little cupboard next to the stove." He listens as she opens the door and pulls out what she needs before getting to work. They fall into a comfortable silence as he stretches out and shapes the dough, and she washes and slices the toppings. When the dough is ready, he takes the sauce he made earlier out of the fridge and begins building the pizzas.

"Can I ask you something?" she says, sprinkling cheese over sauced dough.

He kisses the top of her head. "You can ask me anything."

"How does being a demon... work? Like what causes the power? Do you need to practice using it?"

He laughs lightly, finding her series of questions adorable. To be honest, he hasn't even had to think about it since he was a young child. It's a natural part of him. But to her, someone who hasn't ever experienced it or likely been with someone who has supernatural abilities, it must seem so otherworldly. "I did need to practice, yes. Lachlan helped a lot with that when I was younger. Our father was absent, to put it mildly, and our mother struggled. We both have a good relationship with her now, but it took time to get there. So Lach truly was my father figure growing up. Well, as much as he could be. When we are young and growing into our powers, it's no different than being a teenager and having your hormones all over the place. The exception is that we can cause a lot more damage if we throw a tantrum," he laughs, memories of fights with Lachlan and them using their power against each other flashing through his mind. "As for how it all works, no one really knows, as far as I am aware. It's something we're born into, but there's no real understanding of how or why it chooses the beings it does or what leads to the power manifesting the way it does. We know that it is attached to bloodlines. Or at least, that's all I've ever learned about it. I think there's a fear in the community that if information were to spread about how supernaturals are created, situations would arise where humans are forcibly turned into supernaturals. So it's all kept pretty hush-hush."

"That makes sense." She shivers. "I've heard some stories from my parents about what was going on with Grog and with the Hale family as well. That seems terrifying enough."

"Yeah, we were challenged as a community when Grog was trying to ruin Petra and prevent her from taking power.

Losing Gladys was rough for her, and having him be at the helm of all of that was even worse. But she, along with Lachlan, Ecia, and the changes they have made in the council, has done wonders. It's like a breath of air when we were all struggling to breathe."

With the pizza ready, he slides it onto the preheated stone and puts it in the oven, setting a timer for five minutes to remove the parchment paper. They lean on opposite sides of the counter. His eyes travel her form before meeting hers and continuing. "It's kind of hard for me to think about what it feels like to be a demon because it's all I've ever known. It's something there inside me. All the time."

"Does it hurt?"

He tilts his head up, looking at the ceiling as he thinks about his response. "Only when he's demanding a shift and I try to force against it. But I so rarely do a full shift these days that it's a non-issue, really."

"Why?"

Another thing he hasn't had to think about in some time. "I think at this point, I'm just comfortable in my human form. My father was a crime lord in the underworld. He made Lach an enforcer. Once our father died, Lach refused to use his demon form for some time, unhappy with what it represented. Wanting to be like Lach meant that I did the same. Now it's just second nature."

"What causes the shifts?"

"Usually extreme emotions. Typically, anger for me. Something has to enrage me so much that I lose that aspect of control."

"What do you look like? As a demon, I mean."

He smiles at her, letting the expression reach his eyes, hoping that he shows how much he appreciates her curiosity. "Bigger. Taller and broader. My skin toughens as a means of protection. Horns grow out of here and here," he says, touching spots on his forehead, "and my eyes turn to demon gold."

"Do you ever shift… at other times?" His gaze shifts to hers, where heat greets him.

"That's a dangerous question, Miss Oaks." Her cheeks flush. "But yes. I have done partial shifts when engaged in activities."

She licks her lips, drawing his eyes to them. *Fucking Hades.* "And what's that like?"

He steps toward her, raising his hand to tuck her hair behind her ear. Leaning in, a rumble starts in his chest. Her hand lands softly on his pec, and her breath hitches as she feels the vibrations. Whispering, he says, "like the best orgasm you've ever had. Toe-curling, star-seeing, ecstasy." A small whimper escapes her as he presses his body against hers and kisses the crook of her neck. As he's about to lick the hollow at the base, that perfect little spot he's been eyeballing all night, the oven timer goes off, breaking him from his desire-laden stupor.

They manage to make it through the rest of dinner with calmer flirting and relaxed, if sexually charged, conversation. As Eliana helps him clean up, placing the dishes in the dishwasher, the sound of a vehicle door slamming and Buckley letting out a bark calls their attention. Their heads abruptly turn toward each other, her face reflecting Declan's sense of alarm back at him.

"Honey! I'm home!" Everest calls, closing the front door behind him.

Eliana springs into action, sliding the back door open and exiting into the yard. The door closes softly, and she disappears from view seconds before Everest turns the corner and enters the kitchen.

"Aww, man. I missed dinner," Everest mock pouts. "Any leftovers?" He opens the fridge, not waiting for Declan to respond, which is probably for the best, as he's still too busy wrapping his mind around the fact that he and Eliana were literally seconds away from getting caught. Not that they were doing anything untoward, but Everest would certainly have had questions about why his little sister was there. Alone. With Declan.

Everest pulls out the container with a couple of slices of leftover pizza, pops the lid, and takes a slice out. Biting a chunk off the end, he lightly tosses the container on the counter and, with a mouth still partially full, groans and says, "Man, your pizza is the best. Forget running a mechanic business; you need to open a pizza shop."

Declan laughs uncomfortably. Eliana's coat is still in the closet, and her boots are at the front door—thank Hades that Everest isn't the most observant person in the world. Regardless, he needs to get them to her somehow without his uninvited guest knowing about it.

It doesn't take long before Everest is trying to cajole him into going out for another chill night out. As Declan thinks of excuse after excuse to try and get out of it, Everest grunts in frustration and excuses himself to go to the bathroom. As soon as he's out of sight, Declan calls on his power and uses his smoke tendrils to grab Eliana's effects as he throws open the front door, nearly running into her.

Her hands are running up and down her arms as she bounces in place, trying to keep warm in the cool night air. His heart cracks at the sight, and he pulls her into himself, giving whatever warmth he can as the tendrils of smoke place her coat on and help her into her boots. Buckley gruffs behind him, but he doesn't care. They only have a moment before Everest is back. With her fully dressed, he cups her face in his hands and kisses her roughly. The feel of her lips on his is heaven.

Footsteps sound behind him, ending the kiss long before he wants to. In a hushed voice, he says, "I'm so sorry. I didn't expect him to come over tonight. I'll call you tomorrow." She nods, her expression a mix of panic and sorrow. Before either one of them can say goodbye, Declan turns, closing the door on what should have been a wonderful date and time to get to know each other better.

"See, Bucks, there is no one there," he says, quickly covering up the real reason for his being at the door.

Everest ruffles the fur on Buckley's head. "Silly pupper."

Exasperated, Declan follows Everest and Buckley back into the kitchen where Everest finishes off the other two slices of pizza and makes another plea to go out. When Declan denies him again, Everest finally relents and makes his way to the living room, where he flops down on the couch, remote in hand, and begins scrolling through the various streaming options, trying to find something to watch.

"I'm actually kind of tired," Declan says, feigning a yawn that he hopes is convincing enough.

"You know, if I didn't know you better, I'd think you're trying to get rid of me." Everest laughs, evidently thinking that's an absurd idea. If he only knew what he interrupted.

"Nah. It's been a busy couple of weeks."

"Well, then it's a perfect time to lie back and watch the newest Axel Jacks movie," Everest replies, pushing play.

"Alright." Declan loves his friend and would do anything for him, but he can't risk Everest finding out about this thing between him and Eliana. So, for now, he'll do what he wants. He pats the cushion beside him, calling Buckley up. The fur monster hops up, curls into a ball, and, within moments, begins snoring. Declan, legitimately feeling tired after the events of the night, slides down and lays his head on Buckley's hips, using him as a pillow, watching the newest action flick with his best friend—both furry and human—beside him.

CHAPTER 28

Eliana

"**M**y brother almost caught me with the guy I'm seeing."

"And why is that a problem? Can he not know that you're dating someone?" Dr. Colson asks partway into their next session.

"He can..."

"But?"

"The issue is more *who* the someone is," Eliana hedges.

"And who is the someone?" he prompts.

"His best friend."

"Ah. Again, I ask, why is that a problem? Do you not think your brother would be happy to see you happy?" Colson responds.

"Why is it a problem that I'm dating my brother's best friend?" Eliana asks, incredulous.

Dr. Colson flips the page of his notebook and writes a new line of text before answering a simple and undignified "Yes."

"Aside from him being my *brother's best friend*," she stresses, adding extra emphasis on Declan's relationship with

Everest, "he knows the guy. They go out together all the time. He knows the type of guy he is. Or maybe he was. I don't know; we haven't really talked about his dating history." She feels herself getting flustered at the thought of Declan dating someone else. They haven't had that conversation yet. Or at least not entirely. She shared her history with Sam, but it was different. It was something he needed to know. "Either way, I assume he wouldn't approve of it for that reason alone."

"And what kind of guy is he?"

"With me? He's kind. Gentle." Her fingers touch her lips as if pulling up the memory of the other night on Declan's couch, how his stubble felt against her skin, and the hunger that guided him. They could have consumed each other right then, and there had she allowed it. Recalling what he said about waiting until she's ready, she adds, "he's also patient, funny, and interested in me and what I have to say. He listens, which is new for me. To have it feel as though the person I'm with actually cares and wants to hear what I have to say."

Colson leans forward, resting his arms on the chair, looking intently at her. "That sounds like someone you should be with. I think your brother would be happy you have found someone who makes you feel that way."

Unable to bear his gaze any longer, she simply replies, "Yeah."

"Have you told your family about Sam yet?"

"No." Her cheeks heat with embarrassment.

"Why not?"

Without taking the time to formulate her thoughts, she says the truth because if she can't say it here in her therapist's office, then where else can she? "Because I'm embarrassed."

"Can you elaborate?"

Sighing, she opens the cover of the box she's kept buried inside. The one she hoped she could ignore for a very long time. "Because I feel like I let it happen. I allowed Sam to treat me the way he did. I didn't push back or question his actions. I allowed him to separate me from my friends and family. To take over my life. And all that is embarrassing. I was raised by a strong woman. I believed I was one. And then I let some pissant of a man strip all of that away from me. A man who couldn't even be bothered to get on a plane after I needed a major surgery to make sure that I, the woman he apparently loved, was okay." She pulls the sleeve of her sweater over her hand and uses it to dab at the stray tears that have worked their way out. "And this," she says, motioning to her face, "annoys the fuck out of me. Because I feel like every tear I shed in relation to him lets him continue to win. That he continues to have hold of me. It's exhausting. I want to live a normal life."

"That's a lot. And everything you're feeling is valid. Normal even."

Eliana scoffs.

"It's true." Leaning back, he brings one leg up and rests the ankle on the opposite knee. His casual pose is in opposition to his words, but perhaps that's for the best, as it helps this moment stand out to Eliana as one that she'll remember for some time. "Hear me when I say this. You are strong. You are worthy. And you are valid." She sucks in a breath. "You have been through so much and are sitting here today on the other side. You got out. You recognized the situation you were in, and while, yes, it may have taken you a while to leave, you did. Relationships with friends and family can be repaired as needed. Though, from the sounds of it, your family loves you deeply, and your friends are the same. So it's you, Eliana, who needs to recognize your strength. Because everyone else around you already sees it. I guarantee your fella sees it too."

"I–I don't know what to say."

"You don't need to say anything. Because I mean every word of it."

Sniffling, she responds, "Thank you."

He smiles back at her and makes a few more notes on his pad. He calls the session to an end shortly after, and as her hand finds the doorknob, Dr. Colson has perhaps the most important parting words for her. "Tell your family, Eliana. They deserve to know, and you don't need to carry it all yourself."

"Hi, honey, it's so good to see you."

Tossing her coat on the railing, she says, "It's only been a few weeks, Mom."

"Yet, still feels like a lifetime."

Eliana rolls her eyes at Cora's dramatics as she leads them into the kitchen. "Do you need any help?"

Her mother turns, briefly surveying the assortment of pots and pans she has on the go with what's sure to be another delicious dinner. "No, I think everything is under control here. But if you could set the table, that would be great."

"That, I can do." She steps over to the cupboard, pulling out the required items.

Her mother shuffles behind her, reaching around her to pick up a wooden spoon. "Oh, and set an extra plate."

Confused, Eliana responds, "Why?"

"Everest said Declan is coming. Something about

Declan seeming sad and in need of some good home cooking."

Nerves flood her system, making her feel like she's suddenly been dipped into a boiling cauldron. She dabs the back of her hand on her cheeks—burning hot. And her back? Feels already drenched in sweat.

"Declan's coming?" she says, hoping her voice sounds steadier than she feels. Almost getting caught by Everest last night was enough to have her consider asking one of the local witches to make her disappear forever. But here? At her parents? With her whole family around? Fuck, that's enough for her to expire on the spot.

"Yes, darling," her mom says before turning to look at her. "Are you alright, dear? You look feverish." Cora's hand comes within an inch of her forehead before Eliana dodges out of the way.

"I'm fine, a little warm by the stove. I'm gonna take these to the dining table." Eliana doesn't wait for her mother's response or look back to see if she believes her. As she sets the table, she does her best to keep calm, but knowing that she is going to be in the same room with Declan while her eagle-eyed mom is around isn't helping. Thankfully, Everest is generally oblivious, and her dad will be too occupied talking cars or something else manly with the boys, to notice.

Maybe that's what she needs to do—make sure the boys stay occupied with their own conversation so there's no chance that the attention could shift to her. Yes. That's it!

With her plan for making it through dinner in place, she takes a moment to pause and breathe, ensuring she is fully calm and ready.

And then the door opens, and Declan walks in, looking like the sexiest demon alive in dark jeans that hug his thick thighs so perfectly. The light gray sweater he's wearing brings out the blue in his eyes while also accentuating the strength in his frame. The softness of his stomach is hidden by the way the fabric sits, but her body remembers what it felt like to be held against him. Her body attempts to betray her by letting out a tiny whimper, which she manages to disguise with a slight cough as though she meant to clear her throat. Declan catches her eye, and the smallest quirk of his lip lets her know he heard it.

Fuck me, this is going to be a long dinner.

CHAPTER 29

Declan

He didn't plan to go to the Oaks residence, but Everest was already at his place and asked if Declan wanted to join him for Friday night dinner. It's been a while since he's attended one, and Ev's parents always enjoy having extra people over. So it was a pleasant surprise when they pulled in, and Eliana's car was there. And the look she gave him when he walked through the door... well, it spoke volumes. And that needy sound that she tried to cover. Oh, it told him everything he needed to hear.

He doesn't like that she essentially ran off like a dirty secret when they were interrupted. The shop was wildly busy today, which meant he barely had a moment to think, let alone text with Eliana. Figuring he could come to dinner and call her when he got home, he put it off until later, knowing he'd prefer a chance to have more than a quick chat. But of course, there she was, looking gorgeously flustered when he walked in the door. It took all his strength to refrain from immediately stalking over to her and kissing her breathless.

Her eyes have followed him since he entered the house, and he'd be lying if he said he didn't enjoy the feeling of her watching him. Her gaze roaming over his body. Hungrily following his hands as he rolled up his sleeves. Hades, all it takes is a look from her to set him on fire. It really is a gift that Everest is as oblivious as he is, or Declan would be in a whole cauldron of trouble.

Which is exactly why he made sure to sit at the opposite end of the table from her. The more physical distance between them, the less tempted he is to find a way to touch her.

As Everest, sitting to his left, passes him a dish of mashed potatoes, Eliana clears her throat. His eyes glance her way, taking in the tautness in her shoulders and the way she swallows nervously before she speaks.

"So…uh… Did I hear you guys talking about some car engine or something before dinner?"

"Yeah," Everest says, stuffing a carrot in his mouth. "Why?"

She spoons some vegetables onto her plate. "Well. I. I was curious. What kind of car was it?"

Everest's eyebrow quirks up. "Since when are you interested in cars?"

Moving her fork around the plate, seemingly poking at everything and nothing at the same time, she answers, "I thought it was time I took an interest. It might help me someday, way down the line, when I need to get a new one."

Her brother and father eye her skeptically, but don't push. Declan, though, can see and feel the tension rolling off of her. Watching her be this uncomfortable creates an ache in his chest, knowing that there's not much he can do to help.

"So, was it a big car or a little car?" she asks, evidently trying to keep the conversation going.

Everest snorts amusement beside him, while Declan's left hand moves to rest on his knee under the table and lets a nearly invisible wisp of smoke flow from his fingertips. He pushes it forward, edging ever so carefully toward Eliana, careful not to let it touch anyone else along the way. It softly wraps around her ankle and slides up her leg to rest on her thigh. Her eyes flick to his while he takes a bite of potatoes, and he does his best to give her a reassuring smile.

As realization blankets her features, the thrum of her nerves settles under his faint touch. The conversation at the table quickly turns away from whatever it was she was trying to do, and he feels her relax further. The tendril of smoke stays resting on her thigh throughout the meal, which appears to help her feel more at ease, while also still allowing him to feel her. To touch her.

The smoke can be surprisingly sensitive, and it has helped him pick up on people's moods, which is great when working with the public. But with her, it seems to be extra sensitive. Sometimes, he feels his power drawn to her. Eager to seek her out. To connect. It's something he's never felt before and is both intriguing and unsettling. Lachlan spoke of feeling like there was a thread that bound him and Petra together, and as Declan soothes Eliana under the table, he wonders if this pull toward her is that thread his brother referred to.

His watchful gaze lands on her again and he can't help but think about all that she's been through. Not only did she move away to pursue her lifelong dream, but when that dream ended, she had to heal from a massive injury and deal with a shitty partner. And as far as he knows, she went through it all on her own. Remarkable.

She's remarkable, his demon counters.

"Earth to Declan!" Everest says, tossing a dinner roll at him, breaking him from his thoughts. A second tendril shoots out and catches it before it hits the floor.

He clears his throat as the roll is placed on the table beside him. "Sorry, I missed what was said."

"Clearly," Ev jests.

"It's alright, dear. I was asking about the shop. Business doing okay?" Cora asks.

"Oh, yes. We're doing great. Since word seems to be getting around that we're helping out with the showcase for Eliana's studio, we seem to have a bit of an influx. But we're happy to be kept busy." The tendril still resting on Eliana's thigh gives it a gentle squeeze before edging up a little higher on her leg and turning ever-so-slightly inward. He lets his eyes flick to her, catching a soft, rosy hue as it dusts her cheeks.

"That's wonderful." Cora turns her head to look at her daughter. "Why didn't you tell us that Declan was helping?" She turns back to Declan, "What are you all helping with?"

"Because I don't tell you everything," Eliana says under her breath at the same time that Declan says, "We are helping to build the sets. We are about done, though. Maybe another day or two, and it should be ready for the big night."

"That's so exciting, dear, and I'm so happy that you were clearly able to get such fine helpers," Cora says, glancing between him and Eliana.

There's no way she knows.

She can't know.

Can she?

Eliana leans back, and her head dips, her eyes lingering on the space between the table and her body as his tendril continues to move toward her center. "Yeah, my littles are particularly excited about dancing in front of everyone. The teen groups tell me they dread it, but I'm doing my best to hype it up for them."

His smoky limb stops before it makes contact with her core, but he still catches the soft breath of anticipation she lets out. Declan has no intention of playing with her at the table while her family sits around her, but if his touch helps to distract her from whatever she's worked up about, that's good enough for him.

"When is it again?" Cora asks.

Placing her utensils on her plate, Eliana replies, "Two weeks tomorrow. We will use next week as an opportunity to practice with the stage pieces, and the week after for full dress rehearsals. It's a tighter schedule than we would like, but assuming there's no big hiccups, we should be okay, timing-wise."

"Wonderful. I'll put it on the calendar."

Elliana's head lifts, and her expression changes to confusion. "Why?"

"Well, so we can come watch your show, lil' foot," her father says as if it were obvious.

He watches as a series of emotions floods her features. Moving quickly from confusion to shock, back to confusion, and then landing finally on embarrassment.

"You don't have to come. It's a silly children's showcase," she says unconvincingly.

"But it's *your* showcase. So we will be there to support you and your work, dear. We have always regretted not getting the chance to see you perform on the big stage in Hollybrook. So we will be there to support you for this showcase."

A flash of grief passes over her eyes. Realization dawns

on Declan. Her family never saw her achieve her dream, presumably because of her shithead ex. He not only kept her from friends, but also kept her family from her.

Rage builds rapidly in his chest. His muscles tighten as what feels like a block of anger settles inside. His demon roars angrily in his head, wanting to take over. To protect her. To avenge her. All of it.

Declan sucks in a breath, reluctantly drawing the tendril away from Eliana's lap as he focuses his energy on keeping the demon at bay. The last thing he needs right now is his angered demon making an appearance. Clearing his throat, he excuses himself and steps out of the room.

He finds his way to the backyard and steps around the corner to give himself some privacy. Shutting his eyes tight, he takes a few deep breaths to calm the rolling river of animosity. It doesn't take long before he hears soft steps approaching.

"Are you okay?" she asks.

Hearing the concern in her tone squashes any remaining bitterness inside him. His eyes open, and she stands before him, her eyebrows scrunched in, creating the most adorable little wrinkle between them. She crosses her arms over her chest and softly rubs her arms to keep warm. It is a bit chilly out, but the cool air has never really bothered him, despite running hotter thanks to his demon.

He steps toward her, glancing behind to be sure they are out of sight.

"Can I hug you?" he asks.

She smiles at him. "Yes, Declan, you can hug me. You don't need to ask every time," she says, letting a soft chuckle loose at his expense.

He takes two steps to close the distance and wraps her in his arms. "You should have a coat on," he mumbles into the top of her head before breathing her in. Peppermint and grapefruit are quickly becoming his favorite scents.

"Thanks, Dad."

A rumble sounds from within. "Careful, Oaks."

Her head turns, and she laughs softly, resting her cheek on his chest. "Or what?"

"You're so lucky we are at your family home. That's all I'm gonna say."

She laughs again, and it's officially a sound he never wants to stop hearing. Her laugh is melodic and bursting with sunshine. His chest warms each time he hears it, and he's realizing more and more that he wants to keep hearing it. That *he* wants to be the one who makes her laugh. "We should get back inside before Ev comes looking for us."

"Yeah. You never answered my question, though."

"What was that?"

"Are you okay?"

"I am now." He kisses the top of her head. "I had to calm the beast after realizing why your family never saw you dance after you moved away," Declan responds, managing to keep his demon calm.

"Oh," she says.

"Yeah. But I'm okay now," he says, kissing the top of her head again. "Thanks for coming to check on me."

"Anytime, Grace."

CHAPTER 30

Eliana

"Where did you go?" Everest asks as she enters the kitchen, startling her.

Hand to her chest, she replies quickly, "I wanted to go and see how Mom's roses were doing."

His eyes narrow.

Please believe me. Please believe me.

Everest shrugs his shoulders, apparently deciding it was an acceptable response. He picks up a chocolate from the bowl on the counter and pops it in his mouth before turning away. "If you see Dec, tell him we're playing cards and I'm gonna win my money back," he says over his shoulder as he steps into the dining room.

Fuck, we need to be more careful, she thinks, feeling her face flush.

"Will do," she replies as Everest disappears around the corner.

"What will you do?" her mother asks from behind her, startling her again. *Did they suddenly learn how to walk without making a sound?*

"Holy Hades, Mom. You scared me half to death."

"Sorry, dear," Cora chuckles. "Anyway, what is my lovely daughter going to do?" She asks, taking a bottle out from the wine fridge.

"Oh. Yes." Eliana swallows, trying to calm her still slightly racing heart. There's too much going on right now. Too many people. Too many feelings. Too many opportunities for her to slip up. "Ev wanted me to tell Declan we are playing cards, but I don't know where he went off to."

Cora uncorks the bottle, pours herself a glass, and looks at Eliana questioningly. *Shit. Did she see something?* If she did, she doesn't directly say anything. Instead, she says, "I think he went outside, dear. He might be around the corner by the hedges."

Fuck. She knows something.

Her mind spins, wrestling with itself. Everest can't find out. At least not yet. And not from her. Her mother wouldn't say anything would she? Eliana glances outside, paying attention to the sightlines and possible windows that face the hedges.

No, we were definitely out of sight.

"Should I go get him?" Eliana asks, pointing behind her with her thumb.

Cora sips her wine, taking a moment to respond. Her gaze still feels suspicious, before she replies, "No, no, love. You head into the family room, and I'll gather the demon." Cora shoos Eliana away with one hand, places her glass on the counter, and saunters toward the door. She turns her head, looking at Eliana right before she exits, and Eliana swears there's a knowing little smirk on her traitorous mother's face.

Fuck me.

Her group of teenagers strut onto the floor, possessing all the attitude she wished she had when she was their age. They take their starting positions and she counts them in before pressing play on her phone, allowing their chosen music to boom throughout the studio.

Despite the tough times they sometimes give her, she's so proud of how far they've come this season, and their idea to combine pointe and jazz is marvelous. They've selected a pop music compilation, and while she was skeptical at first, their ideas have really flourished. It's been so wonderful to help them bring it all together.

She walks around the room, watching closely and pointing out any necessary adjustments. With each group and each pass, the performance gets cleaner. More precise. And with each run through of the routine, she can physically see their confidence grow. They hold their heads higher, lengthening their arms and legs, achieving the perfect mix of attitude and grace.

"Sona, turnout from the hip more before you go into the first pirouette."

Sona does the move again, turning her leg out from the hip and pushing off exactly as she should. She's more stable this time, and when she comes down from her turn, she beams.

"Much better," Eliana praises.

They've run through the routine in smaller groups a few times, but they are doing it all together for the showcase. Large group dances are challenging, and even more so with the complexity of leaps and turns they wanted to incorporate. With that in mind, Eliana walks the room's perimeter, pushing all bags and gear as far away as possible.

When the music stops, she calls out to the group, "Alright, it's time for us to practice this as an entire group. You already know your formation, so Group A will be on the right, Group B in the middle, and Group C on the left. We will have more room on the stage, but practicing in a slightly tighter formation is helpful. It helps you to keep track of your positioning and ensures you don't travel more than you should, because if you do, you'll take down one of your peers, and trust me, you don't want to be responsible for someone else's injury."

The students find their starting positions, she counts them in the same way as before, and then starts the music. As they dance through the routine, her heart swells with joy, seeing their vision come to life. Eliana may take pride in being a talented dancer. But as she watches them carry out the story they chose to tell, she feels a unique sense of pride. Coming back home was never in her plan, and yet, she seems to be finding her footing again. By channeling her energy into teaching, she's rediscovering that sense of joy. That feeling she's been missing since her own injury took her off the stage. As much as she may hate to admit it, Dr. Colson was right; her joy can take on a different shape.

She watches them work through the sequence as a large group, noticing where different students need to refine their moves or where adjustments need to be made in the choreography to help it run a little more smoothly.

This group worked incredibly hard, collectively deciding on the story they wanted to tell, which they chose to adapt into their own version of how Petra became the new premier witch. Only instead of Grog being a combative council member, he is younger, and a former lover trying to win her back. The routine concludes with a dramatic dance-off between the Lachlan and Grog characters, ultimately ending with the three of them journeying into the underworld together to live happily ever after. The students sought out Petra's permission to ensure they would not get in trouble, and Petra, being the good sport that she is, laughed and shared that she couldn't wait to see it. Eliana, frankly, can't wait to see Lachlan's face on opening night.

Their rendition of the love story to guide all love stories is quite comical, and once the final orientation of the routine is set, they will surely entertain everyone in attendance.

The music rises, and it's time for the final battle between lovers. The lead dancers, Hova (playing Lachlan) and Benni (playing Grog) take the center as others back up to give them room.

"Remember," Eliana calls over the music, "passion. You are fighting for the woman you love; have it come through in your movement."

She steps to one side of the room, watching their entanglement. "Good. Good." She moves to the other side. "Benni, a little more force and extension. Perfect." Back to the center. "Alright, big finish."

The three leads complete their final sequence, bringing the piece to a close with perfect timing as the music comes to an end. "Well done!" She claps alongside the ensemble. "A couple of minor tweaks and you're all set."

Looking around the room, she's met with broad smiles and looks of accomplishment. They pat each other on the back, and she overhears celebratory comments, and she has to agree with every single one of them.

"Alright, all, that is the end for today. We will meet again on Wednesday for our first rehearsal in the theater."

The students clap for themselves, and maybe for her. "Oh, and one more thing," she yells over the chatter, "you all should be so proud of the work you've done. This story you've created is fabulous, and I can't wait for everyone to see it on the stage."

She claps, and others join. As she watches them pack up, there are definitely a few blushing cheeks. She knows how hard it is to accept the accolades. But with any luck, she's not the only one leaving tonight with a fuller heart and a deeper love of dance.

CHAPTER 31

Eliana

DECLAN

Hi beautiful.

I hope you have a great day.

ELIANA

Thanks 😔

Can I see you tonight?

I have another rehearsal

That's fine.

I'll pick you up. What time are you done?

8:30

I'll be there.

Her face warms as a blush creeps up her neck and rosies her cheeks. Her fingers find their way up to her lips and lightly brush them, remembering the feeling of his on hers.

As she slides her phone into her back pocket, arms wrap around her from behind, and her body freezes on instinct. Kaia's face appears in her peripheral vision, and she feels her shoulders relax and the knot in her stomach loosen. She's never liked being surprised, let alone from behind, but some days it's worse than others, and unfortunately, today is one of those days.

Kaia hops in front of Eliana, bubbling with the energy of an over-caffeinated squirrel. "You ready for lunch?"

Eliana blinks and shakes her head to clear the lingering tension from being grabbed. "Yeah. Yeah, I'm good."

"Good, 'cause I am so hungry I could eat a troll," Kaia says, looping her arm around Eliana's and guiding them into the restaurant.

The host greets them and takes them to their table, then leaves their menus and lets them know their server will be over shortly. The moment they are alone, Kaia's eyes drill into Eliana. "Alright, spill the cauldron water." Kaia opens the bottle of water already on the table and pours each of them a glass.

Eliana laughs. Always right to the point. "About what?"

"Oh, don't play clueless gnome, you know what."

Eliana smirks, opening her menu. She hasn't been at The Grazing Hag in some time, so she's curious to see what's new. Kaia, clearly not amused by the lack of response, kicks her under the table.

"Ow!"

"You deserved it," Kaia says, sticking her tongue out.

"There's no cauldron water to spill."

Kaia attempts to kick her under the table again, but Eliana anticipates it this time and manages to move her leg aside in time. "Ha!" Eliana teases.

"Don't *ha!* me. We haven't had a good dish session in a while, and from the gooey look in your eyes, you have something to tell. Do I, as your forever best friend, trusted confidant, and fellow woman-in-arms, not deserve to know what has you looking, well, like this?"

Eliana looks at her friend, trying to decide if she wants to say it out loud. They talked about him before, so it's not like its anything new. But she hasn't shared with anyone other than her therapist that whatever is going on between her and Declan has progressed. To what, she has no idea, but it's more than a passing curiosity. Or at least it feels that way to her.

"Well?"

Eliana sighs and readies herself to spill it all, but they are interrupted by the waitstaff. Kaia and Eliana quickly give their orders, and when the staff walks away, Kaia's eyes are back on Eliana, staring her down.

"Fine. So you know Declan and I kissed," she starts. Kaia nods, confirming what they had already discussed. "Well, things have progressed a little past that."

Kaia's eyebrows perk up with interest. "How little?"

She feels a blush rising again. "Only a little. I haven't been ready for *that* yet. But we've gone out a couple of times, and he's going to pick me up from work tonight."

"And?"

Eliana picks up her water glass, sipping slowly. Kaia's eyebrows continue to rise with interest, to where Eliana knows that if Kaia has to wait any longer, those eyebrows will belong to someone else. "We made out a bit on his couch, and then I messed up the moment by saying I didn't want to go further."

Kaia's expression instantly shifts to anger. "Did that demon dipshit try to pressure you to do anything? If so, I will go and kick his ass myself."

"No, not at all," Eliana replies, her hands out to stop Kaia from getting up right now to go and tell Declan off. "He was so kind about it, and assured me that he would never ask me to do anything I didn't want to. It was... unexpected."

Calmer now, Kaia leans back, resting her arm on the back of her chair. "Okay. So what's the problem?"

"Well, aside from my therapist, and maybe my mom, but I'll come back to that, and you, no one else knows. Sure, it's fun to kind of sneak around, but at what point do we no longer have to? At what point does it become a dirty secret rather than a fun one?"

"I don't know. But is the only reason you're hiding it because of Everest?"

"Yeah, I think so." She tries to think of any other reason, but her brother is the only one that makes sense. That's the only reason they've talked about, anyway. Could he be trying to hide a relationship with her because of something else?

"Do you really think Everest would be that angry about you and his best friend getting together?"

She considers it for a moment. "I don't know. He's never really cared about who I dated before. But he's always been so protective. You should hear him going on about my car," she laughs. "He never knew about Sam."

At the mention of his name, her phone buzzes in her pocket. She pulls it out and looks at the illuminated screen.

UNKNOWN

You've been avoiding my calls.

I want to talk, Ellie.

The edges of her vision start to blur, and goosebumps rush over her skin as if she's had a bucket of ice water dumped on her head.

Sam.

CHAPTER 32
Declan

"This looks wonderful," June praises as she walks through the final set pieces with Declan. He and his crew stayed late last night, and those who could came in early this morning to help finish up painting and assemble all the pieces. Looking around at what they've built, a sense of pride, not for himself but for his team, wells up inside him.

"Are you okay, boss?" Sebastian asks. "Did you get dust in your eyes?"

Clearing his throat, Declan nods. "Yes. Must have been a stray fleck that was floating around." June eyes him, not believing the lie for a second, but Sebastian buys it. "Can you grab a broom and do a final sweep to make sure we got it all? Can't have a child getting sawdust in their eyes..." he trails off.

"Yes, boss. Right on it, boss." Sebastian scampers off in search of a broom as Declan turns away and quickly dabs at his eyes with his sleeve.

He hears June approach before he feels her hand lightly touch his shoulder. "You and your team did great work."

Turning to face her, he replies, "Thank you. They—we —were so happy we could help."

She steps toward some fake trees off to the side that are to be used in one of the contemporary pieces, according to Eliana. Her hands run over painted wood. "This looks so real. I could have sworn it was actual bark here."

"I know. I never knew my staff were so talented. I fear that now that I've opened this door for them, I may lose their expertise at the shop to more creative endeavors. The sheer joy they exuded every time we were in here was palpable. Like its own living entity in the room."

"I can tell. It takes true passion to create pieces like these. Perhaps your true calling lies beyond the machinery, Mr. Grace."

He chuckles. Not uncomfortably, but the idea had never occurred to him. He's had a love of cars and machinery, of figuring out how things worked and how to put them back together, for as long as he could remember. It's part of why Lachlan helped him to set up the shop in the first place. He knew that if Declan was that passionate about something, that he'd never let it fade to the wayside. That Declan would put whatever he could into it to make sure it succeeded. And that he has.

Hellbent Motors, as much as it can be a time sink and source of frustration and exhaustion, is where his passion lies. It's where he finds peace. Solace. It helps him calm the beast inside that constantly wants to rage.

June watches him consider the idea of being an artist, and the corner of her lip knowingly quirks up, "Something to think about."

"Perhaps. Though I think my preference is still with machinery. I may have a skill with a saw and wood, but to me, the mechanics of machines, the whirring and buzzing, the clicking and spinning, is its own kind of art."

She nods. "Fair enough."

"Anyway, we are thrilled you like it all. Eliana shared your vision and was a great guide in the process. We would consider it an honor to partner with your studio again in the future. But until then, the stage is yours."

"Thank you. And I will be reaching out soon to see how we can team up in the future," she replies, heading down the stairs at the side of the stage.

"I look forward to it."

She waves over her shoulder and heads up the aisle toward the door. Stopping before she leaves, she turns back to him and, projecting her voice, she says, "Don't let her get away, Mr. Grace. She's a good one."

She doesn't wait for him to respond before she exits, leaving him alone on the stage.

Declan pulls into the grocery store parking lot, turns off his motorcycle, kicks the kickstand down, and slides his helmet off. Locking his helmet in place, he darts inside to the flower display. He's not sure what her favorite flowers are, but he knows she reminds him of the bright orange and yellow ones, so he chooses a bunch of each and makes his way to the checkout.

A buzz from his pocket catches his attention. He switches the flowers over to his other hand while he digs out his phone, not so subtly hoping it's a message from Eliana.

EVEREST

Hey Daddy. You free tonight?

Declan groans. With the frequency at which Everest interrupts Declan's plans, he wouldn't be surprised if Ev is secretly some kind of magical being with the ability to tell the future. Of course, he only uses those powers to ruin Declan's plans.

He steps to the side, placing the flowers on a stack of cereal boxes, and types out his response.

DECLAN

Hey

Yeah I'm not feeling the greatest. Gonna call it an early night.

You need anything?

Fuck. Even when he's unknowingly a pain, the guy still cares.

Nah. I'm good.

At Lach's right now, picking up some sleeping potion from Petra.

Alright, well, let me know if you need anything.

Will do.

Thanks.

No prob.

Oh! Are you coming to this showcase thing for Ellie? Mom wanted to know.

Apparently we need to get tickets or some shit and she wants to make sure we have enough seats together.

Sure. Count me in.

Really?

Yeah?

I mean, I did help build the set

I'd like to see how it all comes together.

Alright 😌

I'll let her know.

Anyway, feel better, big daddy.

Despite lying to his best friend—again—he laughs as he slides his phone back in his pocket and steps into the checkout line. He knows he needs to tell Everest what's going on between him and Eliana, but frankly, he doesn't know how. Everest has always been protective of her, though he doesn't always show it, masking it as the older brother teasing and general pain-in-the-ass shenanigans. But he cares, and he cares deeply. So, telling Everest that Declan's dating his sister won't go over well.

As his mind wanders to Eliana and the anticipation that builds in his stomach knowing he's about to go see her, he knows that she's worth it. She's worth whatever Everest wants to say to him. All he can hope is that Everest sees how much Declan cares for her.

Digging out his wallet from his back pocket, the last voice he wants to hear right now calls his name.

"Well, if it isn't Declan Grace," Charlie says, her tone laced with venom. Or at least it would be if she could actually spit it. Thankfully, that's not a power she possesses.

"Hi, Charlie," Declan responds, flatly.

"Are those flowers I see? Surely, you, the master of sneaking out of a woman's bed, can't be getting flowers for someone?"

His jaw clenches. This is not what he needs right now. "Yes, these are flowers. And no, they are not for you. Now, if you don't mind, I need to get going."

Her voice rises. "I do mind. I mind *a lot*. I mind that you slept with me and left me while I was still sleeping, like some dirty deed you wanted to forget about." People around them start to look on, watching as this unfolds. Anger starts to bubble under his skin, twisting and turning, needing to release. He tries to step away and get in line, but she follows. "I also mind that you then treated me like dirt when I attempted to see you again. Like I was worth less than the scuff on your boot. Yes. I fucking mind."

She continues to yell at him as he steps up to pay for the flowers. Flowers, which he was excited to give Eliana, that are now tainted with the memory of Charlie screaming at him. Not that he'll tell Eliana about any of this.

"What? Am I not even good enough for you to acknowledge me now? Does the person you're getting those for know how much of a dickbag you are? How you only want to fuck someone? That you don't have the ability to actually engage with them like a human being?"

Without warning, smoke fills the space, enveloping them in a thick fog. His demon growls in his head, as anger floods his system. The demon inside wants to shift. To show the perceived threat what she is really dealing with, but he manages to keep it at bay. He fights the urges pulsing through him and the pain searing at his temples. The last thing he needs right now is a video of him shifting to presumably attack some upset woman in the grocery store going viral.

Charlie quickly silences as he steps toward her, menace lacing every movement of his body. His vision flickers gold as he rolls his head, cracking his neck in the process, in an effort to keep the vitriol he wants to spill under control.

His voice is tight, restrained, as he says, "That's the funny thing. I left you so that you wouldn't get hurt. Instead, you stand here making a fool of yourself, for what? In hopes that I'll give you the attention you so desperately desire, but which I can't fulfill? You don't deserve that, and I don't deserve to be locked into something I don't want to be a part of. Let. This. Go. Charlie. It was one night."

She squeaks as he retreats. The view around them clears, and the other patrons around them remain silent, unsure of how to proceed.

"And stop spreading rumors about me. Everyone knows you're lying." Declan looks up at the till and tosses more than enough money on the counter to cover the flowers and hopefully, the cashier's discomfort. Without saying another word, he picks up the flowers and steps back into the night.

It doesn't take long for him to get to the studio. His attempts to calm himself along the way have not helped. He was lucky that the only thing that happened back there was a cloud of smoke. Yes, he told Eliana that he had to practice to control himself and his demon abilities when he was younger, and that's true. But there are times, particularly when he feels threatened, that the demon inside him takes over, and he has no choice but to let the bastard lead.

He parks his motorcycle out front of the studio and swings his leg over the seat, turning so he faces the building and leans on the side of the seat, flowers in hand as he waits. He can't help but replay everything that happened over and over in his mind, wondering how he could have made it go at least a little more smoothly. No ideas come to mind.

A few minutes later, Eliana emerges, and his heart clenches at the sight of her. She looks as radiant as ever in her standard leggings and oversized T-shirt.

"Fuck, you're gorgeous," he says at the same time she softly says, "Hi, Mr. Grace."

He opens his arms. "Come here, Oaks."

Hades, he needs her.

Moving toward him, she drops her bag on the sidewalk next to him and steps into his arms. She slides her arms over top, wrapping her hands around the back of his neck as his arms close around her. Her peppermint and grapefruit scent mixed with the saltiness of sweat envelopes him. As he takes a deep breath, continually trying to imprint her into his brain, he finally feels the angry toddler within him relax.

Home, his demon internally states.

Fucking right, he agrees.

She pulls back and gazes into his eyes. "You alright?"

"I'm perfect now."

"But before?"

He pauses, hesitating. He had no intention of telling her what happened. Or anything that ever transpired between him and any other woman. As far as she is concerned, Declan is a virgin. But the concern painting Eliana's face is enough to break his heart. He can't have her worrying about him. He also doesn't want to keep secrets from her.

He takes a deep breath, deciding to at least give her the soft version of the truth. "I had a bit of a run-in on the way here with someone I dated. It wasn't pleasant. She wasn't happy. But I'm here with you, now, so that doesn't matter. You are the only one who matters. The only one who will ever matter."

She eyes him for a moment but doesn't push it further, which he's thankful for. She may be the only person he wants to spend time with, and he can't stop thinking about her, even when he shouldn't be, but he's definitely not ready to tell her that he loves her.

Wait, does he love her?

Oh fuck.

CHAPTER 33

Eliana

He releases her and she steps back to pick up her bag. When she stands, the beautiful bouquet he was holding earlier greets her. "These are for you. They reminded me of you."

He got her flowers. Not any flowers. But her favorite ones. Without even knowing. "They are beautiful," she replies, her voice thick with an emotion she doesn't want to identify.

"Like you," he replies, kissing her cheek, causing heat to rise to the surface of her skin at the exact location he made contact. "They are bright and pretty, but not too in your face. They remind me of sunshine and warmth. How it feels when I'm around you."

Well, Hades, come and take me now.

She swallows and blinks, trying to keep the emotion at bay. "Thank you. Gerberas also happen to be my favorites." Her eyes catch the look of pride that flashes across his features, also not missing the extra little puff in his chest. "They are perfect."

He steps forward, placing his finger under her chin and

kissing her softly on the lips. It's a brush of the lips, really, but it sets her stomach aflutter, and she lets out a quiet moan of contentment upon contact. When he pulls away and she opens her eyes, his face still lingers right in front of hers. Desire burns in those eyes. A desire likely mirrored in her own as the flutter in her stomach turns to more of a burning flame licking heat to her core.

"Shall we go?" he asks, his voice almost growling at her.

"Ye... Yes. Where did you have in mind?" she asks. He puts the flowers in his little saddlebag thing on his bike and holds his hand out. When she doesn't give him anything, he gently takes the strap of her bag off her shoulder and secures the bag to the bike as well.

"I thought we could pick up some ice cream? Or an actual meal if you want something more substantial? And then head back to my place and watch a movie or something?"

She smiles at him, finding his uncertainty endearing. Well, not so much uncertainty, as more of a concern for what she wants. She sees how he wants her to be comfortable. That the ultimate decision lies up to her. But he's also thought ahead enough to have a base of a plan in place. It tells her that he's considered her and her feelings and also isn't afraid to relinquish that control. That's something Sam never would have done. Frankly, he never would have picked her up in the first place, let alone had a plan to spend a casual evening together.

Ugh. Sam.

She's still contemplating whether she wants a full meal or an ice cream dinner, but thoughts of Sam and his stupid text from earlier pop back in her mind. Work kept her busy enough that she hadn't been able to think too much about him and now here he is, ruining a gentle moment with

Declan. Realization also dawns on her that she will have to tell Declan about Sam trying to contact her. Just not right now.

"Well, what do you say, Miss Oaks?" he asks, bringing her back to the present moment.

"Ice cream sounds great."

"Perfect. I know the place." He turns and swings a leg over the bike, seating himself. He slides his helmet on as she settles behind him and puts her own on. She's only been on the back of his bike the one time, but it already feels familiar. Like being with him. It's comfort and safety. Something she hasn't felt in far too long.

Her hands slide around his side and up his chest. He shivers under her touch. As they take off, she wonders if he's thinking the same thing she is as the vibrations flow toward a spot on her body that begins to ache in the most delicious of ways.

They stop not too far from Declan's home to pick up their ice cream. Declan opts for a pistachio base with almonds and Eliana chooses a sweet buttery base with salted caramel and chocolate-covered pretzels. The sample she tries in the store is so good that she audibly moans her satisfaction. She doesn't miss the slight adjustment Declan had to make afterward.

With the sweet treats stowed alongside her flowers, they climb back on his bike and head to Declan's place.

"Hello, Mr. Bucklesworth," Declan coos as they enter the front door. He steps to the side, allowing Eliana to enter, and then bends over to ruffle the large dog's fur with one hand, eliciting excited huffs and toe taps in response.

"Mr. Bucklesworth?" she giggles.

He stands again, turning to face her. His tone is light

and playful. "Yes, he is a refined gentleman who needed a proper title."

"Yes. Obviously," she jokes. Buckley pads over to her, his fluffy tail wagging happily back and forth. "Hi, Buckley," she says, patting the top of his head. "You are such a cutie, I see where your daddy gets his good looks."

His eyes flick to hers as she smirks. The searing heat in his gaze warms her. "Careful, Oaks," he warns.

Stepping around Buckley, she places her bag off to the side and moves toward him. "Or what?"

She doesn't know why she's suddenly feeling so brazen. She's never been this way and honestly has no idea where it's coming from. The last time she was here, she told him she wasn't ready for the next step, but right now, her brain isn't the one in the lead. The longer she's around him, the more her body responds. Fireworks under her skin. The desire to touch and be touched. The heat between her legs. It's all so much, yet not enough.

She's still not sure she's ready, but she does know that Sam—fuck, she hates to think of him, and wonders if she'll ever stop—never created this kind of response in her. If she had challenged him as such, it would have led down a very different path. *But Declan is not Sam,* she reminds herself.

The demon before her allows his eyes to roam her body as she approaches him. She places a single finger on his broad chest, tilting her head up to see him. His gaze takes on a golden hue, ever so briefly. *His inner demon.*

"Or. What?" she challenges again.

Wisps of smoke soar around her, taking the ice cream and flowers out of his hands and whisking them away. At the same time, his hands land softly on either side of her face. Before she has a second to breathe, his lips are crashing onto hers, bringing her life.

She meets his passion with her own. Her hands wrap around his back. They find the hem of his shirt and slide underneath, where she's met with the most comforting warmth. His tongue dances along her lips, asking for permission to enter, and she grants it easily. When their tongues meet, it's as if fireworks have been set off inside her. There's no other way to describe it. Pops, sizzles, and fizzes dance beneath her skin like the most spectacular display meant just for her. It sets her soul on fire in ways she never imagined, and she never wants this feeling to stop.

As her hands glide up his back, reveling in the strength beneath her fingers, a low growl rumbles in his chest. It's a sound of restrained hunger. But she doesn't want to be restrained. In fact, that's the last thing she wants.

Breathlessly, she breaks the kiss, putting the smallest bit of distance between them. His head falls forward, allowing him to rest his forehead on hers.

"You make me come undone, Oaks," he says, his voice rough and his breath short. "Best of all, you don't even realize you're doing it."

"What do you mean?"

"It takes an obscene amount of control when I am near you. I have to actively stop myself from doing this," he says, capturing her in another scorching kiss, before finishing his thought, "whenever you're around."

"Maybe it's time you let go of that control," she replies, having apparently lost all sense of decorum. *Who needs decorum anyway?* her brain challenges, evidently siding with the horny vixen below, who seems to be guiding this interaction.

His heated gaze bores into her, stoking the flames within. His expression a silent question. Seeking permission and reassurance. She nods slightly, giving him the acknowledgment he needs. His hands slide under the hem of her shirt and land on her side, lifting her into the air. Her legs naturally wrap around his waist as if she's done this a thousand times.

As he did before, he walks down the hall with her wrapped around him like she's a koala on the hottest fucking demon tree in existence. His hands are fire on her skin, surely leaving imprints, as they roam on her back, finding the back of her bra and unclasping it while his mouth kisses and sucks on any piece of flesh he can find. Lips. Chin. Clavicle. It doesn't matter. It all feels like heaven.

Buckley gruffs from behind them, eliciting a grunting noise from Declan as he continues to try to consume her. It must be a command as she hears Buckley click off somewhere else in the house.

Eliana has no idea how they manage to find their way to the kitchen without hitting anything, but they do. Her thighs hit the top of the counter, and despite wearing leggings, she can feel the coldness of the surface. The sudden coolness along her heated skin sends a shiver up her spine, creating goosebumps on her arms and pebbling her nipples.

His hands slide down her back and grasp the hem of her top.

"Arms," he grunts at her, as if he's lost the ability to form full sentences. She obliges, raising her arms above her head, allowing him to remove her T-shirt. With her bra already undone, she slides the straps over her arms and slowly holds it out in front of her, keeping her eyes connected with his, then drops it onto the floor.

The brazen being within takes further control as she leans back, placing her palms on the countertop, creating the perfect position to arch her back, drop her head back, and push her breasts out.

A rumble emanates from him as he presses against her center, grinding that glorious fucking bulge into her. "Perfection." One of his heated hands lands on her tit, rolling her nipple between his forefinger and thumb while his other hand slides into her hair, grasping it to keep her in place as he licks up her neck.

Every fiber of her being is alight under his touch. Fuck, he's barely done anything to her, and tension is already building in her core. She is already so wet and needy, and with each kiss or graze of his flesh on hers, she knows it will not be enough. There can never be enough.

The revelation is as mind-blowing as an orgasm itself. To feel as turned on as she is right now. To feel as safe as she does is so sexy. She doesn't know how, but deep down she knows he will never hurt her the way that what's-his-face did.

His lips move down her neck again, nipping at the flesh as he makes his way to her breasts, where he shifts his hand to the underside, exposing her pert nipple to the cooler air. His warm tongue flicks the end of the sensitive flesh. Her head falls back further as her back arches, pushing her tit further into his hand. Who knew a single flick of a tongue could feel so good? The mix of cool air from the room and warmth from his breath and tongue as he flicks it again sends goosebumps down her spine and makes her pussy clench in need.

"Does that feel good, Oaks?" he asks before sucking her nipple into his mouth. And fuck her if that doesn't make her see stars. He's going to make her come from tit play alone.

"Yes," she whimpers in response, pushing against him as she tries to seek more pressure where she needs it.

His perfect tongue flicks her nipple as he sucks, the combination of sensations continuing to bring her closer and closer to the edge. "More," she begs, bringing her head up to watch as he rolls her nipple between his lips. *Fucking hell.* She's never begged during sex in her entire life, but a few flicks from his tongue have her ready to make a bargain with Hades. Or whatever god or goddess Declan answers to.

His mouth tightens as he grins around her nipple right before he glides his teeth along her peak. Lights flash behind her eyes as she moans out, and her toes begin to curl. Her pussy slick and pulsing for more, she shifts her weight and brings a hand between her legs, sliding under her tights and underwear, seeking her own heat.

His mouth pops off her breast, and he smirks at her.

He fucking smirks.

"Tsk. Tsk. Tsk. I didn't say you could touch yourself."

"But..." she stammers.

"You must wait, gorgeous. The only one making you come tonight will be me. Do you understand?"

She blinks. *Fuck.* He has her so close to the edge, and she needs this release, or she will certainly combust right here on the counter. "I need to come," she finally says.

"You'll come when I'm ready for you to." The firmness in his voice makes her pussy clench. His commanding presence, strangely, doesn't frighten her. Rather, it's the exact opposite. She wants to do what he says. She wants him to lead. To make the decisions for her.

She pushes her core into his hardness again, hoping for some friction to help. "Does that cunt of yours need some attention, Oaks?"

She nods.

"Tell me."

She swallows. "Yes. Please. Give my cunt attention."

"Good girl."

That tiny comment heats her entire body as she flushes

under his praise. Her nipples peak again, hardening like beacons calling out in the night. He doesn't miss the reaction it causes, and he smirks at her as his eyes darken. He finally releases her hair and steps back, removing the pressure to her pussy that she was enjoying. Bending down between her legs, he places his hands on the inside of her thighs, pushing them further apart.

Despite the desire driving her actions right now, her brain manages to chime in, telling her they need to pause for a moment. Before she can think too much about it, she blurts, "I want you to know that I'm all clear. You know, sexually."

With his face mere inches from her hot pussy, he pulls back slightly, looking up at her. His head cocks to the side as he surveys her.

"Sorry. I thought I should let you know. You know, before you, well, you know," she says, lifting a hand and waving it in the general area of where his head is. "I was tested shortly after I moved back home because I wanted to be sure. I haven't been with anyone since." The words come out so fast she's nearly breathless when she finishes.

Smiling up at her, his fingers hook into the sides of her leggings. "Thank you for telling me. I was clearly preoccupied," he replies, staring at her cunt. Even as he's positioned, she feels his breath coming through the fabric, making her skin tingle underneath. His eyes come back up to hers before he clenches them tight, apparently needing not to see her for a second while he concentrates on what he wants to say.

Please say you're clear too. I don't know if I can stop this right now without dying on the spot from orgasm withdrawal.

"I have a habit of getting tested regularly. My last one was a few days before you came to my shop that first time. I am clear as well, and," he says, opening his eyes and gazing into her soul, and with a strained voice, he finishes, "you are the only one I have wanted to be with since that day. There is, and has been, no one else but you, Eliana."

A slight whimper escapes her. From where she does not know.

"Again, thank you. We probably should have had that conversation at another time… but with that said, do you want me to continue?" he asks.

This demon. Constantly asking for permission. Checking in to make sure she's okay.

Heat floods her system once more, and the only thing she can think of is his mouth on her pussy. The anticipation of his tongue on her has her squirming on the countertop. "Yes."

"Thank Hades. Tell me to stop, and I will. But I have to be honest; I have been dreaming about tasting this cunt of yours for weeks." Heat flares in his eyes as he orders her to lift her hips. She does as instructed, and in one swift movement, her bottoms disappear, leaving her bare before him.

He drops to his knees. "Fucking perfect." He spreads her open again, allowing him to see every inch of her. "And so wet for me." The first stroke of his tongue is magic. Or what she imagines magic feels like. A groan escapes him as he laps up her arousal, and it is perhaps the sexiest fucking sound she has ever heard. "You are delicious," he says, licking her slick pussy.

She lowers her back onto the counter at the same time that he wraps his arms around the outside of her thighs and pulls her closer to the edge. Her breath hitches as her back touches the cold countertop, but after a moment, she adjusts, and her brain focuses again on the demon between her legs.

His tongue plunges into her, devouring her heat as he buries his face. One of her hands finds the back of his head as she laces her fingers into his braided hair. Her hips buck into his face, following the rhythm he has set as he thrusts his tongue into her pussy. Her other hand lands on her breast, where she begins to play with a nipple, rolling and pinching it between her fingers.

As sensations roll through her body and pleasure builds, a wisp of smoke appears, removing her hand from her breast. Stopping only long enough to admonish her, he says, "I said, no touching yourself." The wisp gently raises her arm above her head and holds it in place against the counter.

As his mouth moves up to her sensitive clit, she feels a firm finger press against her opening. He sucks on her clit as he slides it in gently, taking his time. After a few thrusts, he adds a second finger, stretching her in delicious ways. His fingers curl up inside her, finding the perfect spot, and she bucks against his face again.

"More. I need more," she demands.

CHAPTER 34
Declan

She moans again, making his cock throb. Hades, he wants to bury himself in her, to feel her perfect cunt clench around his dick as he drives himself deep into her. But watching her writhe on the counter, pleading for more as he pumps his fingers into her, well that's got to be as great as what he imagines fucking her will be.

His smoky tendril keeps her hand in place despite her repeated attempts to move it. He wasn't lying when he told her he was going to be the only one to make her come tonight, and he plans to keep that promise. Fuck, if she keeps moaning like that, she may make him come in his pants like a goddess-damned high schooler.

Her hips buck, and the grip she has in his hair tightens as he sucks her sensitive nub, flicking it with his tongue.

"Yes. Please, Declan," she begs. Her legs start to close around his head, and two more tendrils appear to hold her open. Goddess, she's so beautiful like this. Presented perfectly before him with her delicious cunt glistening.

His fingers curl inside her, rubbing the spot he's quickly learned gets her close. He's edged her a few times at this point, getting her right to the breaking point and then backing off. But he's ready to see her fall apart.

Pulling his fingers back, he adds a third in and instantly feels her tighten around his digits. He slides them back and forth slowly at first, letting her adjust to the added thickness. After a moment, he begins to pick up the pace, not too hard but enough to bring her back to the edge. As she begins to squirm again, he curls his fingers, holding the pressure she needs.

Her back arches and her legs tense. "Yes, I'm so close. Let me come."

And he does. He buries his face in her cunt at the same time she pulls his face into her core, using his hair as leverage. She grinds into him and he groans, loving that she's taking what she needs. His lips seal around her clit as he sucks and flicks.

"I'm. Gonna. Come. Declan. Fuck!" she yells out, as her walls clench around his fingers. Fuck, she feels amazing. His cock pulses in his pants, aching for its own release.

Soon, he tells himself. *This is about her.*

As her legs relax around him, his smoky tendrils release their hold on all of her extremities. Her hand flies up and immediately lands on her tit, where she pinches her nipple before rolling it between her fingers. Her walls clench around him again in an aftershock before he withdraws his fingers.

"Taste," he says, more as a question than a command, but he'd be lying if he said he didn't want to see her lick her own fluids from his fingers.

Without hesitation, she removes her hand from her breast, grasps his wrist, and pulls it up to her mouth. Her heated lips wrap around his cum-drenched digits, and she slides them all the way to the base, her tongue gliding along the underside. She swirls it around his fingers and sucks. Hecate help him, but all he can picture is her mouth wrapped around his cock.

"Fucking Hades, Eliana," he groans.

His dick is so hard it's almost painful.

She hums around his fingers, and he has to stop himself from releasing right here. Instead, to try and distract himself from the beautiful woman sucking herself off his fingers, he plunges his tongue into her pussy again and laps at her fluids as if he will never drink again.

She's quickly grinding into him again, and though muffled, he tells her, "Claim me. Make me yours, Oaks."

She doesn't hesitate this time. She grips the back of his hair with both hands, pulling him into her cunt, doing exactly what he said. Eliana taking charge of what she wants—what she needs and deserves—is the hottest thing in the fucking world, and he would happily die here. She moves a hand to her clit and comes undone again, clenching around his tongue with her fingers still rapidly rubbing her nub.

"You're fucking succulent," he says after she releases her hold on him.

Breathless, Eliana moves her other hand from the back of his head, placing it at the side of his face, and draws him up. He stands, leaning over her, bringing his face to hers. Their tongues meet in a clash of passion and mutual satisfaction. He hadn't planned for this tonight, but he's more than happy that it's happened.

She catches his tongue in her lips and sucks, tasting the remnants of herself on him. *Goddess, she's perfect.*

He sends out one of his tendrils as they continue to consume each other. A moment later, it returns with a warm, damp cloth. As much as it pains him, he pulls away from the kiss, and he's pretty sure she whimpers when he does.

"I thought I would clean you up," he says, holding the cloth out. He backs away, and holds her legs apart. Taking a moment, he admires the wonder before him. When his eyes cast up to hers, he sees a tiny bit of embarrassment, which he will not stand for. "You. Are. Beautiful," he says, punctuating each word with a kiss down her thigh.

His hand gently places the cloth over her pussy and swipes over her, cleaning up the mess both of them have made.

"I am honored that you have shared yourself with me."

"Stop that," she says, blushing as she waves her hand vaguely in his direction.

"It's the truth. You are immaculate, and watching you come is by far my new favorite thing."

Once she's cleaned up, he reluctantly helps her get dressed again. He tried to convince her to continue walking around naked, and that he would join her but much to his disappointment, she didn't agree.

As he grabs the ice cream out of the freezer, she takes out a couple of spoons and joins him on the other side of the counter.

"We should probably disinfect that," she says, motioning to the countertop she came all over mere minutes ago.

"But what if it erases the memory of how great you taste? I'll never be able to verify that it actually happened," he teases.

She pops a spoonful of the dessert into her mouth, and his eyes become fixated on her lips and tongue as she licks the remainder off. "I'm sure I could help you with a memory refresh if you asked nicely."

He swallows. "I would appreciate that." He scoops his

own bit of ice cream and sends out his smoke again. If floats to the other side of the kitchen, cleaners in hand, and does the naughty work for him. A minute later and any remnant of how he feasted on her cunt is gone. At least for now.

"So not to burst the feel-good bubble right now," she says, a faint blush appearing on her cheeks, "but are you sure Ev won't stop by and have me running out the back door again?"

"He shouldn't. I told him I wasn't feeling well and was at Lach's picking up some sleeping potion. So, unless he plans to come by to watch me sleep, which I don't think he's that desperate, we should be okay."

"Good."

He hesitates, the words sitting on the tip of his tongue. She's here now, and given Everest and his propensity for stopping by unannounced, he doesn't know when they will get a chance like this again. Before he can think too much about it, the question "Do you want to spend the night?" is out of his mouth, and he's left waiting for her response.

Eliana turns her body to face him properly. Her hand lands on his thigh, and it's as if he's back in seventh grade again, being picked first on the dodgeball team. His heart races, and a nervous sweat begins to build at his temples. He wants to put his hand on hers, but with his hands now clammy, it will be too gross. No one likes clammy hands.

Answer, his demon barks internally.

Give her time, he mentally backfires.

"I'd love to," she responds.

All of his nervousness dissipates as if it were never there in the first place. Her expression is reassuring, and her presence is calm. If he was Eliana, he'd be freaking out right now. Hell, he was a moment ago. He's spent the night with many women before. Well, not many. A few. He's never been a fan of the overnight stay, worried that it would send a mixed message about intentions. But her... oh, asking Eliana to stay is something different entirely. It's opening himself up to something he never thought he'd have. Or something he didn't even know he wanted.

He's been content for so long in the pattern he's in. The late nights with Everest. The whole game to pick up a new partner and take them home. Only to repeat it again the next weekend. It was fun. For a time, anyway.

But as he sits here, with Eliana gazing deep into his eyes, he realizes that maybe he wasn't as content as he thought. Going through the motions doesn't breed happiness. Being with her, though? It's the best thing in the world.

CHAPTER 35
Eliana

"Here," Declan says, handing Eliana a folded T-shirt. "For you to sleep in."

"Thanks." Her eyes threaten to well up as she holds the soft fabric between her fingers. She tilts her head back, looking up at the ceiling, willing those tears to stay put. Now is not the time for a big emotional response. Bringing her head back down, she's met with Declan's concerned gaze. His unbound hair flows softly over his shoulders in loose waves thanks to the braid he always wears, and he scrunches his eyebrows together. His eyes search her, looking for what's wrong, and not finding it.

"Are you—" he says, at the same time she says, "I'm okay. A moment of overwhelm."

He steps toward her, closing what little distance there was between them. "Did I push this too fast? I can totally take you home if you would rather be in your own space."

This demon of hers.

Wait.

Hers.

Nope, not going to interrogate that right now.

Her hand comes up to rest on his tattooed forearm. "Declan, I'm fine. Sometimes the thoughts get to be a lot, and they come all at once. I needed a moment to collect myself, that's all."

"Oh."

"I promise. I'm okay and I want to be here." Eliana pushes up on her tiptoes and kisses his cheek. "I'm gonna go get ready for bed."

He nods. Sensing his eyes following her as she walks away, she makes sure to give her hips a little extra sway with each step, evoking a growl from behind her. "You're gonna be the end of me, Oaks."

She laughs, light and airy, enjoying the impact she has on him. And that he has on her.

As she changes, she can't help but be thankful that she has an appointment with Colson in the morning, which will allow her to unpack all of this. That thought causes her to pause, realizing the progress she has made. Not only does she *want* to unpack it, but she's almost excited to tell him about everything she's feeling. Her mind flashes back to her lying spread out on the counter—well, maybe not *everything*.

She uses the mouthwash on the bathroom counter to rinse her mouth as thoroughly as possible. Bundling up her clothes in one arm, she opens the door and walks back into Declan's bedroom. When she looks up, he's already lying on the bed, wearing only a pair of dark gray sweatpants. She's seen him topless before while at the theater, but here, in his bed, well, the sight makes her mouth go dry.

Holy fucking hell, he's hot.

His arms are thick with muscle, and his chest and stomach are more rounded and not perfectly defined. He looks like comfort and safety, like a life-sized stuffed teddy bear that she wants nothing more than to snuggle up with.

As she takes him in, she finds the spot on his chest that would be the perfect place to rest her head. And his tattoos. Oh, his tattoos. The gray-scale decorative swirls and flowers dance up his arms and onto his chest, adding a delicacy to him that is unexpected. It's such a soft design for someone like him, someone who seems larger than life, with such great power, yet it suits him perfectly. It's balanced and gentle, like him.

His eyes catch hers as she continues to ogle him, and the corner of his mouth quirks up into the sexiest smirk she's ever seen. "Are you planning to come to bed?" he asks teasingly as Buckley snorts from the corner, curled up in his own bed.

Swallowing, she nods. She steps toward the bed, then awkwardly turns to either side, trying to decide where to put her clothes. "Here," he says as a smoky limb appears beside her. She opens her arm and it takes the clothes from her, bringing them to the bench at the end of the bed, where it proceeds to fold her clothes nicely, and places them gently on top.

She was telling the truth when she told him she wanted to be here, but it doesn't remove the fact that this is their first night together and the unspoken expectations that hang in the air between them. Is he expecting her to sleep with him, given what they did earlier? Does she want to sleep with him? Well, yes, but it seems like such a bigger step than some oral. And as giddy as she was feeling a moment ago in the bathroom, she can't help the hesitation she's experiencing now.

The last man she had full-on sex with was Sam, and that continues to loom over her head as much as she doesn't want it to. That she trusted him as much as she did, and that he ended up diminishing so much of her.

Her mind continues to waver back and forth on what she wants from tonight, leaving her frozen beside the bed.

Declan, noticing her growing distress, crawls over to her. "Oaks. Are you okay?"

His voice is calming, but his hands, rubbing up and down her arms, are what help to bring her back to the surface. It takes her a moment to respond, and when she does, her voice cracks a little as it's still filled with all the emotion and confusion she was fighting. "I'm sorry..." she starts, but he interrupts, "Eliana, you never have to apologize for having feelings."

"I—I'm sorr—" she starts again, before seeing the stern look in his eyes and correcting, "no, I'm not sorry, but it hit me that the last time I spent the night with someone, it was my ex and..."

"Hey," he says, putting a finger under her chin so she can look at him, "that's okay. I'd love to say I understand, but I know I never really will. Look, I know I invited you to stay, but you can back out at any point. I will take you home, as I already said. However, I want to be clear; I have absolutely no expectations about tonight. I just wasn't ready to say goodnight yet. If you want me to sleep on the couch or on the floor, I will. I want you to feel comfortable here. So what would make you feel comfortable?"

Goddess, she doesn't think she's ever been asked that before. What does she want? It's such a simple question, and yet, it still causes tension to build in her chest.

She smiles at him, hoping it comes across as endearing, as she says, "I don't want you to sleep on the floor."

"Okay."

"I think I'd like to cuddle," she adds.

"You think?"

Her hands fidget with the bottom of his shirt that she

wears, and as she breathes deeply, his scent envelopes her, giving her the confidence she needs. "I want to cuddle. You looked like a teddy bear when I first came in, and it was the first thing I thought of. That you'd be perfect for a cuddle."

"Alright, then, Miss Oaks. Let's snuggle." He leans back, smiling lovingly at her, and extends his hand out for her to take as she climbs into his bed.

She tosses the blankets back and takes his hand, pulling her into the comfiest of clouds. His bed is like heaven. Soft and pillowy. It immediately forms around her as she settles in. He lies back and says, "Where do you want me?"

"On your back. I thought I'd put my head on your chest."

"Perfect."

He opens his arm, giving her access. She scoots herself over, already feeling sleepy. She turns onto her side, and her head finds that perfect spot on his chest that she noticed before, while her free arm wraps over his stomach and her leg hitches over to settle between his. His open arm wraps around her back, hugging her in closer. The feeling is immaculate. It's exactly as she imagined, and as he reaches over with his other hand to turn the light out, she lets out a hum of contentment.

Being wrapped in his arms is exactly what she needs.

Eliana is surrounded by a woodsy scent and weighed down by a heavy arm as she wakes the next morning. Disoriented and in an unfamiliar place, panic causes her chest to tighten. Her brain flashes back to living with Sam and the way she hated mornings with him. He'd always have some snarky comment about how she looked, what she ate for breakfast, or even how she slept the night before.

Opening her eyes, she notes the room, which is different from the one they shared back in Hollybrook. As she takes another deep breath, she breathes in the scent that is familiar to her now, and as her hand runs up the arm draped across her stomach, she sees the tattoos that run from the shoulder to the back of his hand. *Declan.* The tightness in her chest lightens as the world and current surroundings come into focus.

I'm in Declan's bed.

I stayed in his bed.

Her hand continues to caress him, running the length of his forearm and down to the tip of his fingers. Back and forth. Soft. Gentle. Soothing.

A low groan sounds in her ear before he takes a breath, his head moving over to nestle in the crook of her neck as he pulls her into him. Into *all* of him. "Good morning, Oaks."

Talk about oaks. He's packing a fucking tree in there based on what she can feel poking her ass.

"Morning, Grace."

Hearing their movement and voices, Buckley wakes with a flap of his ears and appears at the side of the bed, huffing his own morning greetings and thumping the side with his large tail.

"Good morning to you, too, Bucks," Declan says, lifting his arm to pet him quickly before wrapping it back around her.

"How'd you sleep?" he asks, his breath tickling her ear.

"Good. I honestly don't remember anything after curling up against you."

"That's good." His smile is warm against her skin. "I love how you smell, by the way. I'd love to bottle it up and carry it with me all day." A laugh escapes her, the sound happy, light, and playful as he holds her tight and draws in a big breath through his nose. "So good," he growls, matching her energy.

He continues to draw in breaths, causing her to laugh harder and before she knows it, she's lost in a fit of giggles as he flips himself on top of her, pinning her down in place and running his nose down the side of her neck, to the space between her breasts, and back up the other side.

Torn between continuing this little bit of play and not making a mess of his sheets, she finally sputters between giggles, "I. Need. To. Pee." He laughs in response, kissing up her neck a final time, but rolls off of her to let her up. While he didn't put all of his weight on top of her, the absence of his body leaves her feeling momentarily untethered. Like she's missing a part of herself. A limb. An extension. A piece of her being.

Her heart feels fuller than it has in so long, and looking back at the gorgeous demon sprawled on the bed, his wonderfully blue eyes are so clear, and in their reflections, she can see herself, but in an entirely new light.

Reentering the room, he wraps her in his arms and kisses her fiercely. "I never did give you a good morning kiss," he says when they break apart.

"True. I feel like you should do it again to make sure you did it right."

She doesn't have to tell him twice. He takes her hands and gently lifts them above her head, stepping her back toward the wall. His lips crash onto hers as her back hits the wall, and he holds her hands in place overhead. Her mouth opens as she tilts her head back, allowing him to deepen the kiss.

His tongue collides with hers in heat and fury, seeking,

claiming, and owning every bit of her. He's already shown her what he can do with that demon tongue of his, and as he licks along her bottom lip before nipping at it, she's reminded of how fucking good he felt between her legs. He pulls away, leaving her breathless, while he kisses down her chin and finds his way to the hollow at the base of her neck.

Her hands may be held in place above her head, but the rest of her body takes on a mind of its own. One of her legs lifts and wraps around the back of his knee, pulling him closer. He takes it as a hint and uses two of his smoky tendrils to lift her up, allowing his body to slot perfectly between her legs. Her panties may be wet with her arousal, but his boxers are doing nothing to hide the hardness underneath.

Despite the thin layer of clothes between them, she grinds into his stiff cock and whimpers, eliciting a rumble of satisfaction from his chest. She can't remember the last time she was this horny, and she knows she asked him to wait, but if he keeps this up, she's not sure how long she'll be able to be patient herself.

Continuing to kiss her neck, another tendril of magic replaces his hands, keeping hers in place. With his hands free, he uses them to roam her body. Cupping her ass. Caressing her breasts. Eventually, he lifts his shirt off over her head and cups one tit, rolling the peaked nipple between his fingers, while his mouth lands on the other. Declan flicks her sensitive flesh with his tongue before running his teeth along the tip. The slight pinch from his teeth met with the warmth of his mouth, coupled with the relief from how he sucks it after, drives her wild. She bucks into him as he rolls his hips against her soaked core; the friction is too good.

"Declan," she whispers, her head falling back as the

tension builds in her center, bringing her closer to the edge with each nip and drive of his hips.

"Let me hear you, Oaks." He thrusts his hardness against her core again, and she starts to see stars. Fuck, he's too good if he can get her to the edge so quickly.

Her skin tingles with the anticipation of release. The need to come. The desire to come *for him.*

"Come for me," he practically growls. "Let me see you come undone." Her hips push into him, seeking more pressure, needing to feel him.

He meets her thrust for thrust, grinding his hips into hers, finding the perfect rhythm, and sets her off. Her toes curl, her eyes pull tightly shut, and her jaw opens as she yells out her release.

"Look at me," he orders. She does as requested, her eyes pinging open, immediately meeting his heat-flooded gaze. His golden demon eyes stare back at her, molten and all-consuming.

She yells out, "Fuck, Declan. Yes," as her pussy clenches wildly, her orgasm overcoming her. Fire shoots up her spine and down to her toes as she falls over the edge.

His hand slides between them, finding her slick cunt. "All this for me?"

"Yes," she whimpers, riding out the aftershocks.

"Good girl." His adept fingers slide between her soaking lips, finding her sensitive clit. "Give me one more," he says, as his fingers circle her bud, bringing her right back to the brink. The smoky tendril holding her hands releases, and she brings her hands to the back of his head, gripping his hair, bringing his head to hers. Her lips crash onto his as she moans another release into his mouth, her legs twitch, and arousal drips from between her legs. He swallows her cries of pleasure like a man dying of starvation.

His hand slides out from between their bodies. As he goes to lick her fluid from his fingers, she takes his hand and redirects it to her own mouth. Her lips wrap around them, slowly sucking them into her mouth, relishing the look in his eyes as she swirls her tongue around the end and takes them in. "Fuck, you're gorgeous."

The smallest movement could have him sliding inside her, and the fact that he hasn't taken advantage of that is perhaps hotter than him demanding she come again. He has never made her feel that she's anything other than treasure; even in the heat of all this, he has kept it only about her. Showering her with attention. That thought warms her heart more than the multiple orgasms. It may be the satiated bliss talking right now, but as she gazes into his golden eyes, Eliana realizes it's entirely possible she's falling for this demon.

CHAPTER 36
Declan

Fuck, saying goodbye to Eliana this morning was tough. He would have loved nothing more than to stay locked away with her in his house, continuing to learn every inch of her body and every sound she makes while he makes her come again and again and again. Sure, he had to rub one out, okay, maybe more than one, after she left. But it was one hundred percent worth it. Seeing her let go is the hottest thing in the world.

He's barely been away from her a few hours, and it feels like his world is off its axis. That he's missing the piece to balance him. He's never seen himself as the boyfriend type, but with her, it's different. He wants to be the one there for her. To support her. To cheer her on. To keep her safe.

And he will do all of that. But first, Declan needs to find a way to tell Everest that he's fucking his little sister. Because, yes, while they haven't gone all the way yet, eating her out on his kitchen counter and humping her against a wall until she comes is just as good. But also, not only are Declan and Eliana fucking, but they have a relationship.

With everything bouncing around his brain, he knows what he needs to do.

"Bucks, wanna go for a car ride?" he calls out. Seconds later, the excited tippy-tapping of paws sounds as the furry beast comes bounding down the hall. Declan braces himself for the incoming attack as he waits at the door for Buckley to join him. Buckley bounces his way to Declan, jumping up and putting his paws on Declan's thigh.

"Alright, boy. Let's go," he says, running his hands roughly at the side of the dog's head, flopping his large ears back and forth as he squishes Buckley's face.

Bark!

"You're not old enough to drive yet. You need to be at least four."

Bark! Bark!

Declan closes and locks the door behind them, then opens the back door of his truck, lowering the custom stairs he had installed, and lets Buckley climb in. "Okay. Okay. I see your point. I'll teach you at three." Declan climbs in the driver's side and pulls his phone out to send a quick text.

DECLAN

Got time for your little bro?

The response is nearly instant.

LACHLAN

New number. Who dis'?

⊙⊙

Alright if the Buck-a-tron and I stop by?

😂😂

Yeah, that's fine.

Cool. See you in a few.

The drive over is short. As he turns the last corner onto Lachlan's street, Buckley perks up in the back, panting with excitement.

"Where are we, buddy?" Declan says, riling Buckley up even more. He pulls into the driveway, quickly parks, and as he opens the truck's back door, Buckley pushes his way out, running to their front door. He barks a couple of times before looking back at Declan as if to say, *what's taking you so long?*

Declan opens Lachlan's front door, and Buckley flies inside, nails clicking on the floor as he searches for his second favorite demon.

"Lach," Declan calls into the house as he follows Buckley in.

"Out back!"

Buckley makes his way to the door before Declan. When he catches up, Declan opens the sliding glass door and lets the dog loose. He's greeted by Petra's giggles and Daisy and Sloan yelling in unison, "Grab your drinks!" Buckley is adorable and so lovable, but his tail will absolutely clear a table.

Laughing as he watches everyone but Petra scramble for their drinks and clear the table before Buckley can do it for them, he grabs his own can of soda from the minibar fridge and makes his way to the seating area to join everyone else.

"Hey, you. Haven't seen you around the Acorn lately," Daisy says, giving him a once-over.

"Yeah. Been busy and haven't felt up to it."

"I'm sure." Her tone is dry, like she doesn't quite believe him. "Everest has been there plenty, though. He seems to find himself getting into more trouble when you aren't around."

He winces. "Hopefully nothing too bad."

"No, he does need to keep better track of his partners, though," Lachlan chimes in, earning a laugh-snort from Daisy and Sloan. "He keeps us entertained, and seems to know when to rein it in, at least."

"That's good. I think he's been feeling a bit lonely lately. But I'm not feeling that scene so much anymore."

"Oh?" Petra replies, perking up and shifting her attention away from the fur monster rolling onto his back for her to pet his belly. She turns to face them, crossing her legs in front of her as a hand passively rubs Buckley's fluffy stomach. "Is there something we need to know about, Dec?"

He hangs his head, trying to decide if he wants to do this here and now. He came here because he planned to discuss everything with Lachlan and seek his advice. But with everyone here? Is it too much? Too many opinions? Too much judgment?

Fuck.

He lets out a frustrated groan, raising his head. His gaze catches Petra's interested but caring expression, and that seals it for him. He knows she would never steer him wrong, and if anyone can help him with a fucked up situation, it's this crew.

"Yes."

"I knew it!" Daisy calls out, fist pumping the air. "Who is she?"

Groaning again, he wrestles with the words that want to fly out of his body. What he wants to shout to the world, but can't.

"Eliana."

All eyes are on him. The pressure of their stares weighing on him, but there is no response. He waits another beat, hoping they'll make the connection without him having to explain it. When they don't, he finishes, "Oaks. As in Everest's sister."

"No fucking way!"

"Your best friend's sister?"

"Didn't she move to Hollybrook?"

"For how long?"

They all ask their questions simultaneously, each voice layering over the other. It takes him a second to sort it all out before he responds. "Yes, my best friend's sister. Yes, she did. She moved away to be a dancer but got injured and recently moved back home. And it's been going on for like a month or so. But things have really picked up over the last couple of weeks."

"A MONTH!" Lachlan says, incredulous. "Wait, is that why you were asking me about how to know when to settle down?"

Declan sips his drink, putting his hand out for Buckley to walk under as he comes over to comfort his distressed human. "Yeah."

"Dude." Lachlan reaches over, playfully punching Declan's shoulder. "So why are you here?"

"Everest doesn't know. No one does. I'm tired of it being a secret, and I don't know what to do so that I don't lose my friend and the woman I'm crazy about."

Petra's eyes look like they are about to pop out of her head. "Hold on, your best friend doesn't know that you're in a relationship with his sister?"

"Nope. She was worried about how he would react, and I didn't want to risk not having a chance to see how things would play out with her. But now I can't stop thinking about her and want to be with her anytime we want without having to worry about him busting in and discovering us at any moment."

"How have you kept it from him for so long?"

He sighs, resigning himself to the truth. "A lot of lies. So many lies. I fucking hate myself for it."

"Aww, Declan," Sloan says, leaning forward and giving him her full attention. "You are in a tough position, but it sounds like this is more than fooling around."

"It is."

"Then you need to be honest with him," Sloan continues. "Continuing to lie to him and to yourselves, forcing what you're feeling to be a secret, isn't going to help anyone."

"I know," Declan says, his head dropping back in frustration. Buckley lays his head on Declan's lap, trying to soothe him. His hand lands on Buckley's head, petting it to reassure him he's okay. "He's gonna fucking hate me."

"Maybe," Lachlan says. "Or maybe he'll be understanding. If anything, knowing what I know of him, he'll likely be more upset about you lying to him than you being in a *relationship* with his sister." He puts extra emphasis on the term relationship, and while Declan knows it's his brother trying to tease him, because in the past that would have sent him running, he's relieved to feel no tension in his body. The idea of a relationship with Eliana doesn't scare him. It does the opposite, actually. It excites him.

"Maybe. But how do I even broach the subject with him?" Declan asks. "It's not like I can hand him a beer and be like 'by the way I'm in love with your sister' and expect it to go well."

All of their eyes go wide at that revelation. His own body

freezes as he plays back what he said. As he looks around, he sees nothing but knowing smirks looking back at him. "Fuck off," he retorts to their unspoken reaction.

The group busts into laughter, and Lachlan claps him on the shoulder. "Welcome to the club, Dec. It's a whole new world on this side. You're gonna love it."

CHAPTER 37
Eliana

"How are we doing today?" Dr. Colson asks as she takes her customary seat on the small couch.

Unable to fight the smile on her face, she says, "I've been good."

Colson laughs. "From the look on your face, and the way you're blushing right now, I'd say you've been more than good since we last spoke."

"Shut up!"

"I will not," he playfully gasps, feigning hurt. "Why don't we start with what has you feeling this way?"

Happy bubbles bounce under her skin as she repositions herself on the sofa, sliding one leg underneath her and pulling the other one up to rest her foot on the edge. She wraps her arms around her now-bent knee, putting her forehead on top so she can attempt to hide the stupidly cheerful grin that seems to be plastered on her face while she talks. "I had a really good night. With the guy I'm seeing."

"I figured he had something to do with it," he teases. "Things are going well then?"

"Very well," she says, the smile even evident in her tone. "I'm happy to hear that."

"Thank you. I'm honestly surprised. He's surprised me in every way possible. I can't think of a time I've felt this way. Or at least it's been such a long time that I don't remember when I last felt this way."

"The beginning of a relationship is usually exciting. Did you ever feel this way about your ex?"

The happy bubbles within her begin to burst, popping and fizzing like a high school volcano at the mention of Sam. Eliana shifts her body again, moving to sit cross-legged and folding her hands in her lap, playing with the hem of her sweater as she stares down at them. She hasn't told anyone about his last text. Not even Kaia, even though she was with her. She played it off as a scam and put it aside as best as she could. He hasn't tried again since, but she knows it's coming.

"Not that I can think of," Eliana responds, her voice more somber.

"Interesting."

"What?" She asks, pretending she doesn't understand.

Colson doesn't miss any of it. "There was an instant shift in your demeanor when I mentioned your ex. From body language, to your voice, to the literal light you were exuding a moment ago. It's all gone. Why do you think that is?"

Rolling the hem of her sleeve through her fingers, she takes a moment to think it through. There's so much difference between Declan and Sam. For one, Declan actually cares. He wanted to tear the world apart when she told him about Sam. During dinner at her parents', he used his power to try to calm her, placing a comforting touch on her when he knew she needed it, without her actually having

245

to say so. Sam never would have done that. He never would have noticed. But as happy as Declan makes her, Sam makes her just as angry.

"Because I can't seem to let Sam go."

Colson's head tilts to the side, surveying her. "What do you mean?"

"There's still so much of me tied up with him. I resent him for how he treated me. I'm still angry that I had to leave my career behind. I know he didn't have a role in that, but knowing he never really supported me to begin with, and that he then refused to help me in my time of need... I have so much anger toward him. And then on top of that, he won't let me go either."

"It's good to hear you start to acknowledge his behavior and how it makes you feel. You've spent so long defending him or being indifferent. But what do you mean by he won't let you go either?"

She sighs. "He's been trying to reach me. He sent me a text a few days ago."

"He did? What did he want?"

Leaning back, she kicks her legs out in front of her and drops her head onto the back of the couch, looking to the ceiling. She's done this so many times before that she's pretty sure she knows the exact number of ceiling tiles up there. "He said he wants a chance to talk. I haven't responded to him, though."

"Why do you think you haven't responded?" he asks, even though she knows he already knows the answer.

"Because I'm scared."

"What is causing the fear?"

"I think that he'll somehow pull me back in. I know we talked about my feeling like I was missing something, but I think I was missing what I felt like was my place in the world. And I am starting to feel like I've found it. I've loved being able to put the showcase together for work. I'm happy teaching, even if it means I'll never be on the stage as I was before. And I'm making connections again."

"And you've found someone who seems to show you what's possible."

"And I've found someone who shows me what's possible." She smiles again, feeling the light Colson mentioned coming back to her at the thought of Declan.

"So my question then is, if you're happy now, or at least on the way to happy, why do you fear that he'll pull you back in? That you'll let him take control of you again?"

"Honestly? Because I don't believe I deserve to feel this way. I haven't done anything special to be worthy of it. I was with him for years, and there's still that part of me that believes I belong with him."

Silence settles between them as her words sink in. Eventually, Colson looks at her and waits for her to meet his gaze. "I am going to break my role a little bit here, but I want to be perfectly clear. You, Eliana, do not need to do anything special to deserve to be treated with respect, care, and affection. You do not need to do anything special to be worthy of happiness. Of love. You deserve it because you exist. That's it."

Wiping a tear from her cheek, she nods. Inside, she knows he's right. She knows Sam is bad for her and would never treat her as well as Declan has, but there's that part of her that will always love him. Despite everything. He was her first real love, and for better or worse, he's become a part of her being.

"You said before that my body had a memory," she says between sniffles.

"I did."

"I don't think it's only my body. I think it's my heart as well. And I know you've said we need to talk about how Sam treated me and the abuse he subjected me to—"

"Good job calling it abuse," he interjects.

The corner of her mouth quirks up, a tiny smirk, showing her acceptance of his praise. "But I think it's so hard for me to let go because he made a home in my heart. He was the first man to show me what love was—even in the form he did—and that is the constant model I compare this new relationship to. As lovely as Declan has been, there's a part of me that's waiting. Sam was lovely at the start, too. At least that's how I remember it. How do I know that Declan won't shift like he did?"

"You don't. That's unfortunately the reality. But is there anything in your current relationship that makes you think he's likely to behave as your ex?"

She opens her mouth to respond, but pauses before any words can come out. No, there's not a single thing that has made her question him. Rather than accusing her of being cold or telling her to get over it, when she explained why she shut down as she did, he began to ensure that he asked for her consent. Making sure she was comfortable every step of the way. He's respected her body and autonomy since that moment on. Declan's been gentle and has not pushed her to do more than she was willing, and he's felt like home every time she's been in his arms.

"No. I can't say there is," she eventually responds.

"So trust that. Trust that feeling. You've been through a great ordeal and have experienced a lot of upheaval in your life over the last little while. The fear and hesitancy are to be expected. But…" he pauses, as he makes a note on his pad, "you, Eliana, have also made great strides. Recognizing and naming your trauma is an important step."

Trauma. She hadn't thought of losing her career and her relationship with Sam as such, but it feels right. It has shaped who she is now. But it also doesn't need to be what defines her. Her head turns, and she looks out the window, watching the wind rustle through the rust colored leaves. And it's here that she decides that's all Sam is to her now, the wind rustling through.

"I'd like to talk more about Declan now," she says, her voice soft.

"Absolutely."

Dr. Colson was right when he told her she didn't need to carry everything she's been through alone, and it's far past time that her parents actually knew everything she's been through. Which is why she is currently parked outside her family home, trying to work up the courage to go in and tell them everything. Well, everything about Sam, at least.

Slapping her hands on the steering wheel, she groans in frustration. It shouldn't be this hard. "Alright. Do it. Get out of the car and go inside," Eliana commands herself. Taking a deep breath, she opens the car door and follows her command. It takes her an extra second at the door to muster the courage to walk in.

Cora walks around the corner, appearing at the end of the hall as Eliana closes the door behind her. "Ellie!" her mother exclaims, surprised. "What are you doing here?"

"I was in the neighborhood and thought I'd stop by," she replies, being pulled into her mother's arms. Her mother's hugs are always something special. She gives them out freely, but they are filled with warmth and affection. Some days, Eliana swears they contain magic, able to melt away the worst of feelings, stress, and any ailments the receiver is experiencing, which is exactly what Eliana needs right now. She knows this conversation will not be easy, so she'll take any sense of comfort she can.

With her face still smooshed against Cora's shoulder, Eliana mumbles, "Is Dad home? I'd like to talk to you both about something."

Cora instantly pulls away, holding Eliana at arm's length. "Is everything okay?" she asks, her brows furrowed with concern. "Amos," Cora calls over her shoulder.

"Yes, dear?" he answers from somewhere deeper in the house.

"Can you come to the living room, please? Ellie's here and needs to talk to us."

Rather than answer, her dad can be heard walking through the house. He meets them in the living room where Cora and Eliana are already sitting on the sofa. "What's wrong?"

Eliana laughs awkwardly, her mother's hands resting on top of hers. "Nothing's wrong. Well, not anymore."

"What do you mean?" Cora asks.

"I'll get to that, but before I start, I want to apologize in advance for not sharing this with you earlier. I thought I could handle everything on my own at the time, and honestly, I was embarrassed. But after talking with my therapist—yes, I've been in therapy—it's time you know the truth about why I moved back to Leeside."

"Okay. What do you have to tell us, dear?" Amos asks.

She takes a deep breath, steadying the nerves rushing through her body, reminding herself that Colson was right, she doesn't need to carry this alone anymore. "So I was in a relationship while I lived in Hollybrook. His name was Sam. We were together for a couple of years and he's the reason you were never able to come and see me dance while I lived there. While the relationship started nice as they all do, he became manipulative and controlling." Her eyes flick to her father, seeing his chest puff out with anger as he leans forward, ready to interject. She holds her hand up to stop him. "You can ask whatever you want after, but please, let me get this out."

He hesitates a moment before nodding his acceptance, but doesn't change his position, still prepared to fight for her.

"He never hit me, but sometimes he would get rough, grabbing my wrist or arms to keep me from going places he didn't want me to go. Through his manipulation, I lost contact with you all, friends, and was only allowed to be with him if I was going anywhere other than work. I believe he didn't want you to come and see me because he feared that you would pull me away from him, making him lose his control over me. It wasn't until I was injured on stage and needed surgery that I realized everything he had been doing to me. How he had separated me from my world. My people. He was away on a work trip at the time and refused to come home to help me. I moved back here as soon as I was able and haven't talked to him since. I couldn't afford to stay in Hollybrook on my own without working full-time, so yeah. That's why I moved home."

Tears fill her mother's eyes as she envelops Eliana in her arms. "Oh, honey, I wish you had told us sooner."

"I know. I'm sorry." Eliana sniffles, reaching a hand around her mother's back so she can wipe the tears from her eyes. "But I'm okay now."

"What do you need us to do?" Amos asks, his voice still showing his anger as he shifts into fix-it mode.

"Nothing really. I'm safe now and away from him.

Therapy has been helping me so much to be able to work through it all and to recognize that it was an abusive relationship." She laughs awkwardly. "My therapist would be proud of me for saying that."

"Does your brother know?" Cora asks.

A chill falls over her, making her shiver. "No. And I would prefer to tell him myself when the time is right. I know he'll instantly go into his protective mode, and I don't need him doing that before being reassured that I'm okay."

A look passes between her parents, one she knows means they've silently communicated something she will never be privy to. "Alright," her father says after a moment, "we won't tell him, but we also can't keep this a secret forever."

"I wouldn't ask that of you. But thank you for allowing me to share it on my own terms."

"We love you, honey. We only want what's best for you."

"Thank you."

Telling her parents about her history with Sam lifts an invisible weight from her chest. While she knows it didn't erase the experience from her past, sharing it with them helps her feel lighter. Less consumed by the secret and shame.

Of course, she now has to prepare herself to tell Everest about Sam. And Declan, too. But that will need to wait for another day, as she looks at the clock on the mantle over the fireplace and realizes she needs to get to the theater for the final rehearsal before the showcase tomorrow night.

With a quick hug goodbye, Eliana dashes out of her family home, feeling more hopeful than she has in a long time.

CHAPTER 38

Declan

Declan lies down on the mechanic's creeper, making sure he has the head clearance he needs, and pulls himself under the raised car. The client popped in for a quick oil change, and rather than make them wait until a lift was available, Declan popped a jack underneath and got to work, much like he did in his younger years while doing maintenance on friends' vehicles in their driveways. Thankfully, he doesn't need to crawl around on the ground too often these days.

As the oil drains, he slides back out, wiping his hands on the rag from his pocket. Sebastian pops out from the reception area a moment later. "Boss. Someone's here to see you."

"Thanks, Seb," Declan replies. "Can you check on this in a minute if I'm not back? Filter is ready to go."

"Got it, Boss."

Grabbing a new rag from the shelf, he wipes his hands again, trying to get as much of the grease and oil off as he can, as he walks through the door to reception.

"Hey, daddy," Everest calls from behind the counter.

"Daddy?" Cole, his staff at the desk, asks at the same time Declan gives a firm "nope" and turns to walk back through the door.

Everest runs around the desk, preventing Declan from leaving him behind. "I kid. I kid." He laughs with a smug look on his stupid face. Declan ignores his friend, turning his back on him and facing Cole. "Do. Not," he says, pointing a finger at him, "tell anyone what you heard this dipshit say. Last thing I need is a rumor going around the shop that I'm a daddy."

Cole smirks, but nods. *Good choice,* his demon confirms. Evidently, Everest rattled the monster inside a little too.

Everest cackles behind him, drawing Declan's attention back to the asshat who is supposed to be his best friend. "What do you want?" Declan asks, trying to make his voice as cold as possible, but failing.

"Oh, come on. You know I didn't mean anything by it."

"Yeah, yeah." Declan steps around him, heading back into the shop area. Everest's footsteps quickly follow behind. It's definitely not the first time he's been back here, though Declan tries not to make a habit of it. He doesn't want his staff to get the idea that they can bring their friends around to hang out. Usually, Everest respects that boundary. But not today.

Lowering himself back down on the creeper, Declan slides under the car to check on the drainage. Noting that it's done, and that Seb has already put the new filter on and resealed the plug, he slides back out and heads to the shelf to grab the oil he needs. "Aside from trying to ruin my reputation, why are you here?" Declan eventually asks, his tone friendlier, letting Everest know he's not really mad.

"I felt like coming to see you."

"We're seeing each other tomorrow night, for the showcase thing, remember?"

"Yeah, that. I can't say I'm particularly excited to see a bunch of kids I don't know dance around, but Mom seems to think it's important we all be there." He picks up a small, sealed bag of caramel popcorn that was on one of the side benches, which one of the others must have left lying around. "Can I have this?"

Declan laughs. Dude would be lost without snacks. "Yeah, sure."

"Cool." He rips open the bag, popping a couple pieces in his mouth, before continuing, "Anyway, I don't really consider that hanging out. Like, I've barely seen you these past couple of weeks, man. If I didn't know you any better, I'd say you're avoiding me."

Shit.

"What's been going on, Declan?"

Declan's eyes turn to his friend, and what he sees reflected back at him is hurt. As much as Everest likes to play the goofball and gives off the air of being an easy-going guy, Declan knows he's really sensitive underneath. He should have known that continually giving him excuses to not hang out would come back to bite him in the ass. Even knowing that his friend is here now, trying to figure out what he's done wrong to make Declan push him away, Declan can't say he wouldn't do it again for the chance to get to be with Eliana.

Turning his back to the car and leaning against it, Declan crosses his arms over his chest. Looking Everest square in the eye, he says the only thing he can do to make it better, "I'm sorry." The words are simple, but the weight they carry is heavy. He knows he's fucked up and, looking at Everest now, the clown mask dropped, he can see the real harm he's done. Even feeling as bad as he does, Declan can't tell him about Eliana yet, at least not without her approval. If anything, they should tell him together.

"I've missed you. Missed us hanging out."

"I know. I've missed it too. I haven't been in the right headspace lately for all the nightly games." *Fuck, another lie.* "Aren't you tired of it?"

He watches as Everest rolls the thought around his mind, his eyes closing briefly while he thinks. Opening them again, he says, "Maybe? I don't know. I still find it fun."

"What part do you find fun?"

"All of it?" Everest questions. "Why do I feel like you're judging me and what I, no, what *we*, do?" His voice takes on a more agitated edge.

"I'm not judging. You can do what you want, as long as you're still enjoying it and people aren't getting hurt. But I've been feeling at sea with the whole playboy life as of late, and I think it's time I grow up." Immediately, he knows the words are wrong.

"Grow up? Really Declan? I'm not the one with rumors swirling around town that he fucks 'em and leaves 'em before they even wake up. I at least have the decency to spend the night with the women, so they don't end up feeling completely used."

Fucking Hades.

"That's not what I meant, and you know it. I think it's something I'm not interested in anymore. I've been enjoying the quieter nights, the less stress, less booze, and overall, less."

"Well then, I guess tomorrow night will be right up your alley. A quiet night with the family." Everest tosses the now-empty popcorn bag into the trash as he walks to the open bay door. Fuck, he hopes no clients heard their conversation.

"See you at the theater," Everest says sarcastically as he walks out.

"Fucking hell," Declan groans to himself, running his hands over his face before locking them behind his head as he looks up at the ceiling.

Pulling out his phone, he opens his ongoing chat with Eliana.

DECLAN

Just a heads up

Ev was at the shop. He's upset that me and him haven't been hanging out as much.

It didn't go well.

We need to tell him about us.

A response comes quickly.

ELIANA

I know. I'm sorry it was a shitshow.

I told my parents about Sam today. I want to talk to Ev about it and about us after the showcase.

I'm proud of you

Do you want to talk to him together?

I don't know.

I feel like he'll take it better from me?

Maybe.

Whatever you want to do, I'll support.

Can I see you tonight?

Do you even need to ask?

😏 silly me.

My place - 8:30?

Can't wait

💋

💋

Sliding his phone back in his pocket, he's overcome with a sense of dread. There's no way Everest is going to take this well. Especially not when he realizes that Declan's been lying to him to spend time with his sister.

But then... then his mind wanders to Eliana. It eases the feeling of impending doom enough that he can allow himself to be excited to see his girl tonight.

His girl.

CHAPTER 39

Eliana

A rriving home with only a few minutes to spare before Declan is expected, Eliana dashes through her house, tossing whatever she can into hiding spots, hoping he doesn't move cushions or open cupboards. It's not that she keeps a filthy house, but between the showcase, her own training, and spending time with him, cleaning hasn't been a priority.

With the house looking somewhat presentable, she heads into the kitchen, taking out a container of leftover rice and stir fry to pop in the microwave to reheat. When it beeps a minute later, she takes it out, cursing to herself as the steam stings her fingers.

"I don't have time for this," she says, taking a forkful of the mix and putting it in her mouth. "Ah. Hot," she pants around the food, sucking air into her mouth to try and cool it more quickly. Normally, she'd bring it to the living room, toss on her favorite show, and allow it to cool, but with Declan coming over—for the first time—her stomach flutters and her energy is chaotic.

Why did she ask him here? Into her space. She could

have suggested that she go back to his place again. His place is nice. Well, furnished. Clean—especially for a guy who works with grease and dirt all day. But no, her stupid brain invited him over, and now it has her convinced that he's going to hate it. And with the showcase tomorrow? Fuck, this was a bad idea.

Shoving another forkful of food into her mouth, a knock sounds at the door, pulling Eliana from her meltdown. Shit! He must have followed someone into the building. Swallowing, she opens the door to spot the hottest fucking demon she's ever seen. Not that she's seen many. And she may be a little biased because this one is hers.

"Hi," he says, stepping through the doorway before tilting his head down to kiss her lips. As if he's returning from work, and it's an everyday occurrence. Even so, it still makes her tingle all the way down to her toes. "You look great." He slides his foot around the door and swings it shut behind them, dropping his bag by the door.

Blushing, she waves her hand at him, brushing off his compliment as she walks them back into the kitchen. "I haven't even had a chance to change yet. I only got home like ten minutes ago."

"Oaks," he rumbles. "You look great all the time. Sweats. Dressed up. Naked on my counter. All of it. Fucking. Great."

Holy shit.

Well, if she was blushing before, she must be scarlet now. Heat floods her entire body like a furnace come to life after a long, cold winter.

"Do—do you want something to drink?" she asks, in an effort to change the subject and allow the desire that's building inside her to subside.

"Sure."

"Okay," she pauses, going to the fridge. "I have water, soda, a couple of beers Ev left here, and some juice."

"Water's fine," he replies. Getting out two glasses, she senses his body behind her before she feels his touch. It's a gentle caress of his hand down the back of her arm, but when his chest presses against her back, she melts inside. His lips graze her neck, and it's as if the key she's been missing has been found. Something unlocks inside her, and she tilts her head to the side, granting him better access while she moans a sigh of contentment.

She's longed for this. Wished to be cared for in ways that make her feel whole, appreciated, and loved. It's such a simple gesture, but the ease with which he did it, and that he does it because he wants to, that he wants to be close to her, and that he couldn't wait for her even to get him a glass of water before he needed to touch her. It makes her well up with tears.

When she sniffles, trying to hold back the rush of emotions, he stops. His arms wrap around her, crossing over her stomach as he leans down to rest his chin on her shoulder. "You okay, love?"

Love.

She doesn't miss the term of endearment. But doesn't question it either.

"Yes. I... You make me feel so much."

"Do tell," he says. She can hear the playful smile in his tone and feel the way his cheek pulls up as he nestles his head into the crook of her neck.

Eliana places the glasses on the counter, grasps his hands, and pulls them away from her stomach. He lets out a tiny whine of disappointment, but when she turns to face him, he almost purrs back at her.

Do demons purr? Not important.

His arms come around to either side as he places his hands on the counter behind her, caging her in. If he were Sam, this position would have her fearing the worst. Usually, it was so he could keep her in place while he told her how shitty of a person she was. But with Declan, it's different. It doesn't *feel* like a cage. Instead, it's a home. A space meant for her.

He leans down, kissing her forehead. "Wanna tell me what's going on in that beautiful head of yours?"

Bringing her hands up to rest on the back of his neck, she wraps the end of his braid around her index finger and begins to twirl it around absent-mindedly. "You make me nervous. Like minutes before you arrived, I was panicking about you being here, in my home. Worried about what you'd think about my space. I literally ran around hiding things so it looked a little cleaner." She notes how he turns his head, eyes scanning the room. "No, you can't go looking." He laughs so fully that the rumbles roll through her own chest. "You make me feel things I wasn't sure I'd ever feel." His eyebrow quirks up. "Not the nerves. That comes naturally." She laughs. "But you make me feel whole. Like, I didn't know who I was before you."

His lips easily find hers, and she gets lost in the heat of his hands as they slide up her back, pulling her body against his. She loves the way his softness feels against her, how he molds to her curves. She's never been one for the super ripped guys. No, she loves the soft belly. The cushion. How he feels under her hands. It's perfect. *He's perfect.*

Her head tilts back, allowing him better access as his mouth opens and his tongue slides out to meet hers. Breathing in, his oak scent fills her, making her sigh into him. *Home.* His hips push against her, and feeling his hard cock against her makes her knees want to buckle. Knowing she causes that reaction in him is intoxicating.

As their tongues and lips continue to collide, the kiss growing more and more hungry, her clit pulsing with need, and feeling the safest and most secure she has in who knows how long, Eliana knows to the depths of her being that Declan Grace is her beginning, middle, and end. It's here, with him, that she is the best version of herself, and that by his side is the only place she wants to be.

When she pulls back, breaking their connection, her chest heaves, seeking air. She swallows, giving herself a second to back out. But she doesn't need it. She doesn't *want* it.

"Do you want to go to my room?" she asks.

His eyes widen quickly before narrowing and surveying her. "We don't have to do anything you aren't comfortable with." He looks down at his crotch. "Please don't take his reaction to mean anything other than me finding you absolutely divine."

"Declan," she says, pausing so he knows she means it, "I want to sleep with you. Please come to my room so I can feel that cock inside me."

He swallows, appearing almost as nervous as she had been before he got here. But he nods and takes her hand, following as she leads him down the hall.

CHAPTER 40
Eliana

His hands are on her as soon as they make it to her room. Strong, hardworking hands grip her hips, pulling her body against his, before sliding down and firmly gripping her ass. "Perfection," he growls, digging his fingers in. "Do you know how hard it is to keep my hands off you? To fight the urge to follow you around staring at this perfect ass all day?"

"About as hard as it is for me to keep from climbing you the moment I see you."

"Harder," he says, pushing his hard cock against her stomach.

Two smoky tendrils emerge, lifting her so she is better positioned as she wraps her legs around his middle. *Ah... that's the spot.* She hums with satisfaction at the pressure of his cock against her hot pussy. His fingers splay across her ass, holding her firm against him, and her hands go up the back of her shirt, unhooking her bra. She slides an arm out of it and pulls it out through her shirt sleeve, tossing it over his shoulder.

Eliana's head tilts back as his lips kiss across her shoulder and up her neck. As he reaches her chin, she brings her head back up and meets his lips. Their lips crash together, eager and hungry. Tongues collide and teeth nip while her hands clasp behind his head.

Shuffling forward, his knees hit the edge of her bed, and the world tilts as they collapse onto it. Tendrils of power land beside her head as another floats underneath her, softening the impact. She laughs into his mouth, amused that he felt the need to protect her from falling onto the soft bed.

"What's so funny?" he asks, as he nips her lip again.

"You," she replies, half-heartedly trying to squirm away as his hands move to her side and begin to tickle her.

"Is that so?"

"Yes." She giggles.

"Well, is it funny when I do this?" he asks, placing his mouth over her breast and sucking her nipple through her shirt.

The dampening fabric mixed with his hot breath and the friction as he rolls his tongue over her peak has her wrapping her legs around his middle again as she arches into him. "Yes," she gasps.

"Really? How about when I do this?" His hand slides down her stomach and over her pants, landing on her cunt, where he runs a finger over the seam. "Look at you. Already soaking through for me."

Her hips buck, needing more. Pressure. Friction. Him. "Please."

"So eager." His finger slides down her pussy again, pushing harder than before, giving her more of the delicious pressure she needs. She doesn't know how he does it, or what sexual magic he may possess as a demon, but she can already feel the tension building in her core. The need to release quickly taking over. "But you seem to be mistaken, Oaks. I'm not going to rush this. Don't get me wrong, I am putty in your hands. I will do whatever you want of me, *except* rush through making you come as many times as I can." His teeth pinch her nipple through her shirt while his hand finds the hem of her pants and slides underneath. Declan's finger slips between her slick lips and begins rubbing her clit in perfect circles, and it's like someone set off a sparkler inside her. Electric heat shoots from her clit to her toes, causing them to curl while she fists the bedding above her head.

"Oh, god," she moans lowly.

"No, love, I'm a demon." His tone is dry, as if simply stating a mathematical fact. A giggle escapes her at the same time that he slides a finger into her wet cunt, quickly changing the giggle to a whimper. His thick digit slides languidly in and out of her pussy, curling in ever so slightly, hitting that sensitive spot on her inner wall as he uses his thumb to give her clit the attention it craves.

"More," she pleads.

"Patience, Oaks." His free hand lifts her shirt, exposing her breasts. "Beautiful. So beautiful." Turning her head to look at him, she sees nothing but pure admiration staring back at her. It's as if he is staring at a revered piece of art, long locked away and only now getting to see it for the first time.

His lips work their way across her chest, taking time to stop at one nipple and suck it into his mouth, nipping at it he does. A lap of his tongue quickly eases the slight shock of pain as his teeth pinch and grate on her sensitive peak. Soothing the sting with warmth. The mix of quick pinches and soft licks makes her mind swim with pleasure. She never thought she would be into anything resembling pain or discomfort during sex, but this, this is so good. So unexpected. It takes her out of her head, allowing her to be here in the moment with him. Because yes, she wants this. She wants him. But that doesn't mean she's still not internally freaking out, wondering if this is the right choice.

"I can hear your brain going," he says, before licking the underside of her breast. "Perhaps I am not doing a good enough job."

"No," she breathes. "It feels great." He increases the pressure on her clit as he flattens his thumb on it at the same time as he slides a second finger into her cunt. "So good."

"Is that so?" Letting go of her shirt, he pushes himself up and moves down her body, kissing a trail down her stomach as he goes. "Lift your hips." His command is strong, pulling her attention completely to him. She does as instructed. His free hand and a tendril of magic work together to free her from her pants and underwear. "Look at this pussy. Glistening for me." Without waiting, he bends down, planting his face into her cunt as he removes his fingers and replaces them with his tongue, plunging deep into her core. He laps up her arousal like a man starved, moaning into her pussy. The tension that has been rumbling under the surface spikes, bringing her to the edge faster than she thought possible.

His arms hook around the back of her legs, and before she asks what he's doing, he flips them over, balancing his shoulders on the edge of the bed, with her soaked cunt hovering above him. "Sit."

"I—but—"

He growls at her. But it's not frustrated. It's hungry. "Oaks. Fucking sit on my face and come on it." He pulls her down, and her cunt lands on his face. His tongue is already waiting, burying it into her center. Her hands splay out in front of her, helping to keep her steady as he holds her in place.

Low moans and pleas leak from her as he feasts between her legs. Hot coils of tension ride up from her clit and cunt, making her nipples harden. He shifts below her, sealing his lips around her clit, and she bucks her pussy into his face. He hums his praise, the vibration delectable. She grinds into his face again and he growls, sending more shockwaves throughout her body, leaving goosebumps in its wake. Tendrils of magic slide over her legs, taking the place of his arms as two fingers pump into her. It only takes a few slow pumps as she rides him, filled with his thick digits, for her to fall over the edge.

"Yes. Fuck. Yes," she yells as she comes on his face.

His lips release her clit, and his fingers withdraw, leaving her feeling empty, but his tongue languidly collects every last drop. "Fucking delicious," he says, groaning into her.

"You're so fucking good at that," she says, her legs feeling like jelly and her breath ragged as she comes down from the clouds in which he launched her.

"Hard not to be when you sound like that. I live to hear you screaming in pleasure."

Pushing herself up and away, she looks down at him, still glistening with her fluids. She leans down, kissing him deeply, tasting herself on him. *Hottest. Thing. Ever.* When she pulls away, there's that look of admiration staring back at her. "Well, Grace. I think it's time I get to hear what you sound like."

"Is that so?" he asks, cheekily.

"Ab-so-fucking-lutely." She steps back, putting distance between them, with no idea where this sudden brazenness is coming from. It always has an interesting time of showing up, that's for sure. "Pants off."

He stands, undoing his belt and pants. They drop to his ankles, leaving him in his boxers. Fuck whatever he's packing there must be huge. A flush of heat rushes up her neck. Thank fuck she's already rosy from an orgasm or else he'd think she's embarrassed.

"Now what?" he asks, a mixture of curiosity and teasing as he palms his cock through his boxers.

"Crawl to me."

CHAPTER 41

Declan

" **C** rawl to me." *Hades, if she only knew what I would do for her.*

Declan falls to his knees, long ago ready to submit to her. To give her anything and everything she wants. She steps back again, moving to the cushioned chair that sits in the corner. She sits, crossing those gorgeous legs, looking like the powerful woman he knows she is, even if she doesn't yet know it herself.

Bending at the waist, he puts his hands down on the floor, keeping his eyes trained on Eliana as he crawls on his hands and knees to the siren who has completely wrecked him in the best way possible. The look on her face as he makes his way across the floor is hot as fuck, and knowing that she feels comfortable enough to play this out with him makes his rock-hard cock throb with need.

Knowing everything she's been through, he has been careful to ensure that she has felt nothing less than cherished, and watching her now, he can see that it has worked. She's confident. Strong. And sexy as fuck.

Stopping before Eliana, his gaze stays locked with hers, waiting for the next direction. Lifting her feet, she turns sideways in the chair, swinging her legs over the side as she arches her back over the other arm, letting her head hang down. Her eyes are so heated with desire he can feel the flames from where he kneels. "Fuck my face, Grace."

He nearly chokes at her words. Whatever he expected, it wasn't that. But there's no fucking way he's going to deny her what she wants.

Declan pushes himself up onto his knees, shuffling over so he's within reach. His hand slides around the back of her head, winding into her loose hair. His lips crash onto hers, his tongue pillaging and claiming her as his, letting all that he has left unspoken flow into her. When he pulls away, he's breathless and sweating harder than he was before. Her tongue slides along her bottom lip, licking remnants of her come from her lips. "I said, fuck my face."

"Are you sure?"

"Declan, if I don't get your dick inside me, I'm going to take matters into my own hands," she replies, her hands drifting between her clenched thighs.

Declan stands, slipping a hand into his boxers and freeing his cock. "Well, then, I can't leave my lady wanting, now, can I?" He moves to the side of the chair, positioning himself above her. "Open wide, Oaks."

He swears he sees fire flash in those pretty hazel eyes of hers. She swallows, licks her lips, drops her jaw, and takes him into her hot mouth. One of his hands flies out to brace himself on the window frame beside him because, holy fucking shit, she feels amazing.

Fucking hell, his demon groans internally.

With her head hanging upside down, her tongue glides

along the top of the head of his cock. She swirls it around the tip, spreading her saliva down the shaft as she adjusts to his size and sucks him in.

One of her hands comes up and cups his balls that dangle over her face, while her other hand reaches behind him, grabbing his ass. Her nails dig in hard enough that he's sure she's going to leave marks. The thought of her marking him, and claiming him, makes his cock twitch inside her beautiful mouth. He pulls back, giving her a bit of a breather, but she hungrily pulls him back toward her, taking his dick deeper down her throat. As she nears the base, she begins to hum in satisfaction while she pulls gently on his balls.

Breathing out through her nose, Declan feels her throat relax further. With her perfect mouth full of his cock, she nods her head, telling him to go for it. So he does.

He pulls back almost to the tip and thrusts back into her mouth, overcome with how good she feels wrapped around him. And fuck, her mouth is making his spine tingle in ways he never imagined.

She gargles around him, moving her tongue along the base of his cock, sucking, licking, tasting every bit of him. Letting go of his balls, she brings her hand around to his other ass cheek and grips hard, digging her nails in further, spurring him on.

He leans forward, towering over her, and brings both hands to rest on the arm of the chair next to where her legs rest. Using the new position as added leverage, he raises his hips, pulling his cock back, and slides it back down her throat to the hilt. She moans around him, sending fireworks to his spine. He does it again and again, and each time she moans louder, wanting more and more of him.

Looking down, he sees her rubbing her thighs together,

and as much as he's fucking loving the feel of her around him, he swore to himself that he wouldn't leave her wanting. Lifting a hand from the chair arm, he slides it between her legs, finding her cunt slick with arousal. He runs his fingers through her pussy, gathering her fluid, and brings it to his lips. "Fuck me, Oaks. You are delectable." She moans again as his fingers slide between her legs and into her pussy. *Mine,* his demon growls.

Pumping his fingers into her, he matches the rhythm with his hips as he continues to fuck her face. Her walls begin to tighten around his fingers, and the tension builds at his spine. He's so close.

"Come. With. Me. Eliana." He pants, punctuating each word with a thrust of his fingers and hips in unison. Her walls clench around his fingers as she moans around him, and he releases down her throat, feeling her clamp around his thick cock with each swallow.

"Fucking, Hades, you're gorgeous."

When she's swallowed everything she can get from him, he pulls out, already missing her warmth. Eliana takes his hand and wraps her mouth around the two fingers he had plunged inside her.

"I need to fuck you. Now," he says. A stream of smoke extends out from him, returning a moment later, holding a condom aloft. Taking the packet in his hand, he opens it and rolls the condom down his shaft. Then, bending down to lift her off the chair, she swings her legs around his middle as he turns and makes to take the seat she occupied. As he sits, he lines his cock up with her soaked pussy and pushes inside her.

Even with how wet and relaxed she is from having come a couple of times already, he still has to take it slow, letting her adjust to his size. "Breathe," he says as she moves her hips, taking him in deeper. Not even fully seated, she feels like heaven wrapped around his dick. "You're taking me so well, love."

"So big. So good," she pants, like filling her prevents her from being able to form proper sentences. "So. Fucking. Good." She punctuates each word with another wiggle of her hips, bringing him further into her heat.

She leans back and his hands lift her legs, spreading them open to give more room, and helping her rest them on the chair arms. Once she's comfortable, he moves his hands to the back of her ass. Using the hold he has on her to help lift her, he draws his cock back and then brings her back down, plunging into her perfect pussy. Each time he repeats the action, it's torturously slow, but it allows his cock to go deeper and deeper with each thrust. With one final pull, he's fully seated, and her head falls back, with her hands on his shoulders, allowing him to easily bend his head down and suck on her perfect peak.

"Again," she says.

With his mouth still sucking her nipple, he lifts her ass back, withdrawing his throbbing dick to the tip, and then pulls her back down, painfully slow.

"Yes," she whimpers. "Again."

And he does. Each time, eliciting a more guttural sound from her as she takes every last inch of his cock. He has waited what feels like forever for this moment, and as amazing as she feels around him, it's how she looks right now that takes his breath away. Head tossed back, skin dewy, lips parted as she lets the pleasure wash over her. "You're perfect. So fucking perfect." He thrusts again, feeling his own release building again at the base of his spine. "You want me to fill that pussy?"

"Please," she begs.

"Come for me first. Let me feel that sweet cunt of yours clench on my cock." One of her hands moves between their bodies as she begins to stroke her clit, the movements quick and purposeful.

"So close."

He holds her in place as he thrusts into her from below, keeping the pace slow and steady. Her pussy starts to clench around him as she finds the ledge. "Look at you. So beautiful. Taking my cock so well, like the goddess that you are." With a final flick of her clit, she tumbles over the edge, screaming out her release as her cunt grips onto him, pulsing firmly.

"Yes, Declan. Yes."

Her name on his lips as she comes undone sends him over the edge. An additional thrust has his balls clench, and he grunts out his own release as she continues to milk every last drop of cum from his cock.

Breathless, she removes her hand from between her legs and wraps her arms around his neck, pulling her body against his. His lips paint kisses across her collarbone before their lips meet. Her hips swivel on top of him, his cock still firmly lodged inside her delicious pussy.

"This should be illegal," she says.

"What?"

"How good you feel." She kisses him, continuing to grind on him. "I fear I may never get enough."

He pulls her bottom lip between his teeth, nipping it lightly. "Oh really?"

"Yes."

Declan grips her hips and lifts her far enough to free his dick from her cunt. She whines, confused. "Patience." He doesn't explain, as two little tendrils of smoke roll a new condom on. Still gripping her hips, he lines himself back and slams his cock into her pretty cunt again.

Right where I belong.

Eliana moans out his name, and it's the sweetest sound. One he never wants to stop hearing. "Well, I'm up for the challenge if you are," he says, as he finally allows his demon to come through.

CHAPTER 42

Eliana

Declan's eyes shift to molten gold, his skin toughens up under her fingers, and two dark horns about six inches in length appear on either side of his forehead. And if she's not mistaken, given the increased stretch in her pussy, his cock has grown too. And holy shit, it's fucking delicious. The stretch from him in human form was already amazing, but this, this is unreal. Eliana didn't think she could take any more, but apparently she was wrong, as her pussy clenches around him, hungry to be fucked by his demon cock.

She's never seen him in his demon form, but if it's possible, he may be even hotter than he is in his human shape. Those eyes could melt her on the spot with how heated his gaze is, and the added roughness of his skin brings a new sensation she wasn't expecting. Like a scruffy beard, but all over. The feeling makes her already sensitive nerves light up all over her body. At this rate, it won't take long for her to come again, and frankly, she can't wait.

"Hold on," he says, his voice deeper. Raspier. When she

looks at him, confusion must be evident on her face. His eyes flick up. Her gaze follows. Ah. His horns.

Eliana's hands reach up, wrapping around the thick protrusions coming from his head. He shudders under her touch, and she recalls an earlier conversation. They are extra sensitive. "Do you prefer a light or firm touch?" Eliana asks, wanting to make sure she doesn't hurt him.

His voice in this form is like lava flowing over her entire body, heating her up, and setting her alight. "Firm is better," he says.

She nods, then grips harder. Or as hard as she can without her fingertips being able to touch. He groans beneath her before he rises, lifting her, still speared by his cock, and putting her back against the wall. Eliana flinches as the cool surface touches her back, sending a shiver down her spine straight to her cunt, causing her pussy to clench around him. Her hands stroke his horns, feeling the power within him hum as she does. Declan's lips crash into hers, and then he's grinding his hips into her, slowly. Oh, so slowly.

She never pictured him as a slow lover, one who wanted to take his time. Fuck, history would tell her that guys want to get off as fast as possible. But not Declan. Each stroke is deliberate. Drawing as much pleasure from her as he absolutely can.

If she didn't think he was perfect before, she certainly does now. "You will ruin me," she says, her back bowing off the wall as he withdraws achingly slow before taking his time to seat himself again.

"Good." He growls, thrusting into her again. "You. Are. Mine. Oaks."

Goddess, her name, in whatever form he uses, is enough to bring her to ecstasy.

"Tell me," Declan demands.

She whines, his cock filling her in the most delicious of ways. The stretch almost too much, and yet, as she told him before, she knows she will never get enough. "I'm yours."

He thrusts again. "Damn." Thrust. "Fucking." Thrust. "Right."

"Make me come, Grace."

"With pleasure."

And he does. He grips her ass, holding her in place as he thrusts into her again and again. Each thrust, each pivot of his hips, is deliberate, making his cock brush against that spot inside that makes her see stars.

When a smoky tendril lands on her clit, cool against the heat of their bodies, it only has to brush it a few times before she explodes. He doesn't let up as she moans her release, drawing out her orgasm as she comes all over his thick demon cock. No, his demon is hungry as Declan plunges into her cunt over and over. She strokes his horns, gripping hard, and matching his rhythm, thrust for thrust. When he finds his release, it's like her world comes apart and then stitched back together. Suddenly, everything she was worried about no longer matters, and it's only him. Filling her. Connecting with her. She's never experienced anything like it, but the world seems to go quiet and all that's left is their ragged breathing as he whispers, "*Mine,*" into her ear.

"Yours," she responds.

A marathon sex session when she hasn't had sex, let alone a session like last night, in a very long time, means she is more than a little sore the next morning. But as she watches

Declan sleeping peacefully in her bed, she knows it was all worth it.

Of course, doing that the night before the big showcase probably wasn't the best idea, but it wouldn't be the first time she's had a poor night's sleep before a show, and looking at him, she knows it won't be the last.

Carefully lifting the duvet, she slides out of bed, and makes her way to the bathroom where she uses the facilities and brushes her teeth before she sneaks to the kitchen and starts a pot of coffee. Halfway through making breakfast, heavy footsteps make their way toward her. She senses his presence as he fills the small kitchen before he slides behind her, wrapping his arms around her midsection and nuzzling his nose into the crook of her neck, sending goosebumps down to her toes.

"Good morning, Oaks," he mumbles into her flesh before sucking in a deep breath. "You smell like me."

"Really? How odd," she teases, mixing the scrambled eggs in the pan.

"I like it."

Eliana turns hers and kisses him quickly before turning her attention back to the eggs. "I do too," she says. "Coffee is ready, I wasn't sure how you took it, or really if you drink it, which sounds silly as we've slept together now and I feel like I should know your coffee order before that happens—"

His hands turn her to face him and lightly touches the side of her cheeks. "Breathe." His steady gaze helps to recenter her. He breathes in slowly, holds it, and releases it in a controlled manner. She mimics his technique and within seconds, she's calmer.

"Thank you."

He leans in and kisses her forehead before releasing her face from his soft hold. "Anytime."

She watches Declan out of the corner of her eye as he takes the mug she left on the counter and opens her fridge. Returning with the milk, he pours a little bit in and then fills the cup with coffee. He puts the milk back and, leaning against the counter, watching her, he sips.

Just milk. Got it.

The oven timer beeps, so she puts on an oven mitt and pulls the tray of bacon out, putting it on top of the stove. She stirs the pan of hashbrowns and the one with eggs one more time before turning the elements off and plating their breakfast. A wave of realization rushes toward her. "I'm sorry, I should have asked first if you wanted breakfast. Again, I don't know these things…"

Before she can get herself too worked up, Declan brings her back down. "It's perfect. Breakfast is my favorite meal, and frankly, bacon should be its own food group."

She smiles. Thankfully, he doesn't seem to mind, and also doesn't find her sudden nerves to be a turn-off. "Let's eat, then," she says, picking up their plates and taking them to the dining table.

A comfortable silence falls over them as they eat.

She wasn't wrong in saying that there's so much she doesn't know about him. Eliana understands that they don't know all the ins and outs about each other. And as scary as that feels, she still knows this demon is hers as much as she is his.

It's absolutely terrifying, the idea of opening herself up to someone else like she did with her ex, but perhaps Dr. Colson was right in that she can never truly know if things with Declan will end up the same way as they did with Sam. It doesn't mean it isn't worth trying.

What she does know is that Sam would never have helped her regulate the way Declan did. Declan didn't ask any questions or try to insinuate there was anything wrong with her. Instead, he used their connection as a tool for comfort. To Declan, her nervousness is not a sign of weakness. It's something that is a part of her. That, in itself, confirms what she can see now she's known for a while. Something wonderful. And scary. And exciting.

She loves this demon.

Everything else she needs to know, she can learn as they go.

CHAPTER 43

Declan

With their fabulous breakfast complete, Declan brings up what they should have talked about last night—mind you, he's not complaining one bit about anything that took place.

"So, Everest," he starts.

"Everest," Eliana replies, her voice turning distant. "I know, we need to tell him."

"We do. He was so angry at me for lying to him about not wanting to go out all the time anymore. I don't think I've ever seen like that."

Pushing away from the table, she comes over and sits on his lap, draping her head on his shoulders. Instinctively, his one arm slides around her back and lands on her hip, while the other rests on top of her thighs. He flexes his hand on her hip, loving the feel of her. "I'm sorry," she says.

"It's not your fault. I should have been honest with him earlier."

"It is my fault, though. You wouldn't have been lying to him if you weren't trying to hide the fact that you were spending time with me."

"Look at me," he says. She lifts her head, and he instantly wants to melt when her soft, hazel eyes meet his. "I don't regret any second of the time we have spent together." He kisses her lips softly. "Yes, I should have been honest with Everest, but we," he gestures between them with the hand that is on her thigh, "needed time to figure things out."

"I know. I'll talk to him after the showcase tonight."

"We can talk to him together."

She lays her head back on his shoulder. "Thank you. But I feel like he may take it better coming from me. I think he's less likely to feel betrayed or lied to if I'm the one telling him."

Declan doesn't quite believe that to be true. He thinks Everest is likely to still blame him and that he'll see it as Declan not only lying to him, but targeting his sister as a long game conquest. As he pulls her further into him, trying to soak up as much of this contact as possible before heading to work, he promises himself that he will do anything he has to to prove to his best friend that this thing going on with Eliana is the furthest thing from a fling.

Rather than tell this to Eliana, though, he rests his cheek on the top of her head and says, "If that's what you think is best."

"Thanks."

Shortly after their conversation, Declan heads home to check in on Buckley and shower before getting to the shop. Thankfully, as the owner, the only one who can give him shit for being late is himself. And as he parks in the lot behind the building, Declan decides that he'll be generous this time and give himself a pass.

Shuffling into his office, he drops his wallet and keys on his desk and checks for any messages. After he's caught up, he heads out to the floor and gets to work. Knowing that Eliana is going to tell Everest has his nerves on edge. He wants to be there to support her. To show Everest that he's serious—more than serious—about Eliana, but he also respects her decision. So, he's going to do what he does best—get lost in his work—as a way to distract himself and get through the day as quickly as possible so that he can get back to the woman he loves.

Thankfully, the day is packed with service, keeping Declan busy and his mind occupied. Despite coming in later than usual, it's soon time for him to head home again, and he does so with glee, perhaps for the first time ever. He loves his work. He looks forward to coming in every day and would stay longer most days if he could really get away with it. But not today. No, today he's the first one out the door at the shop's closing, ever grateful that he has staff he can count on to finish what needs to be done.

Practically flinging himself out of his truck, he runs inside, greeted by an excited Buckley. "Hey, Buckatron. Sorry, I didn't come home last night, but I know you love spending time with Uncle Lachlan and Aunt Petra," he says, ruffling the pup's fur. After letting him out, Declan gets Buckley's dinner together and feeds him, then dashes off to clean himself for the second time today. The last thing he wants is to go to Eliana's showcase smelling like oil and grime.

Dressing himself in a pair of black dress pants and a soft blue button-up, he pats Buckley again and heads out the door. Checking his watch, he knows he's going to be cutting it close, but he can't not get her flowers. He stops at a shop along the way and picks out a bouquet with her favorite gerberas and sunflowers. Bright and hopeful, like her.

He parks across the street, taking the last spot in the lot and jogs across the road, meeting Everest outside.

"Aww, for me? You didn't have to," Everest teases, fanning himself like an old-timey lady being courted.

Declan looks down at the flowers in his hand, then back at Everest. "Well, if I'd known you'd appreciate them so much, I would have grabbed you some too."

"Pssh! I always appreciate gifts." Declan is happy that Everest seems to be in a better mood compared to yesterday. Or at least he's doing a great job pretending not to be angry. Whatever the reason for the shift in demeanor, Declan will accept it if it helps tonight go well.

"Valid. Hey, are we... good?" Declan replies as they walk into the building and are directed to their seats.

"Depends, are those for me?" Everest says, his voice dry enough that Declan isn't sure whether or not to take him seriously.

"Nah, these are for Eliana. Figured she could use them for all the work that she's put into helping this happen."

"Shit, you're probably right." Everest leads them to their seats, where Cora, Amos, and Kaia are already sitting. "I'm still hurt. I don't like being lied to, Dec. But Mom wants us here, so... we're okay." He says before they do the awkward sideways shuffle to get through the few people at the end, and then finally sit as the lights go down.

Declan can hear the hurt in his friend's voice. Even so, he appreciates the honesty.

"You wouldn't mind if we said they are from both of us, would you?" Everest asks, sliding the invisible mask back on and shifting into his regular playful demeanor.

Declan laughs, happy to see his friend being himself,

even if it's a facade. "Fuck that," he whispers, "You aren't getting credit for my idea."

Everest chuckles next to him, but Declan's eyes are only for the woman walking across the stage. Eliana wears a black leotard, pink tights, and a flowy sheer pink skirt. She is radiant.

The crowd cheers loudly as she raises the microphone, and he joins along with them, happy to share his affection and excitement for her. She waits a moment for the cheers and clapping to settle down before she begins. "Good evening, Leeside. Thank you so much for joining Strike a Pose for our end of season showcase. Our students are so excited to show you what they've been working toward all season, so I won't keep this going too long. We hope you'll enjoy all the stories to be shared tonight, from the little fireflies to the dramatic reenactments. I am sure you'll be well entertained. So without further ado, I bring you our opening number, *Dance of the Wood Nymphs*, performed by our intermediate contemporary class." The room erupts into applause again as she tips her head in a bow, confidently walks off stage, and is replaced by a group of preteen students dressed as wood faeries.

CHAPTER 44

Eliana

The first number finishes, and Eliana helps usher the next group on while Lola introduces them. The other performers continue to get ready, some putting finishing touches on makeup or hair—they really should take out stock in glitter—or doing a final run-through of their set, ensuring they have it all down pat. These kinds of nights are always a kind of organized chaos, but the looks on the children's faces as they come off the stage are worth it all. All the late night planning, choreographing, scheduling, and so on. She'd do it all again to see the look of pride on their precious little faces.

After the next group goes on, Eliana takes her place to go on next, doing some last-minute stretches in the wings. No one but June knows what she has been planning, but she has been working after hours for the last week, preparing for this. She may not get to dance on the big Hollybrook stages anymore, but after her parents said they were sad that they never got to see her dance, she knew what she needed to do.

A few, too short, minutes later, Zoe's group of preschoolers come off chattering away excitedly. She gives them all congratulatory high fives as they pass, and then it is time.

"Alright, friends and family. We hope you have enjoyed the show so far." The audience claps enthusiastically. "But we now have a bit of an interlude. One of our instructors wanted to do something special for her family, who are here today, and so it is my pleasure to introduce our own little star, Eliana Oaks." June nods to her and then walks to the other side of the stage.

Eliana sucks in a breath and walks onto the stage, the toes of her pointed shoes softly tapping on the wood. The spotlight follows her across, and as she finds her starting position, she looks out to the audience, spotting her family, best friend, and the demon that has helped make all of this possible. Her chest fills with air as the music starts, giving her life and connecting her to a world she has loved for so long. A world she was so scared to leave. But as she looks out, seeing the sheer joy on her mother's face, she knows that while that injury a year ago may have ended her career in Hollybrook, it's brought her back home. Which was exactly where she needed to be.

Up on her toes, Eliana feels free. Emoting everything she hasn't been able to express for months. The pain. The joy. The fear. All of it.

Her arms extend out and contract back in as she spins, and each time her eyes land on Declan. Her center. The force that keeps her steady. That holds her up. The demon she never saw coming and the one she now can't live without.

She leaps across the stage, and the audience lets out a collective gasp as she soars, giving her the breath she needs. With a final flourish, she finishes. Gasping, Eliana leaves behind a past version of herself on stage in preparation for who she is becoming.

The crowd erupts into roaring applause. Declan's face glows with admiration, her parents look at her like she is their shining star, and Everest and Kaia hoot wildly, yelling, "That's my sister," and "That's my best friend."

Eliana bows and then kisses her hands, extending them out in thanks. She mouths *I love you*, hoping that both her family and Declan know it's for them. That all of this is for them.

Jogging off stage, June wraps Eliana in her arms before Eliana comes to a complete stop. "You were wonderful." June releases her and holds her at arm's length. When Eliana looks at her, June's eyes are watery, and the tip of her nose is red. "What you did up there… it was magical, Eliana. There's not a dry eye in the house."

Heat rises up Eliana's neck as she pulls away, waving her hand dismissively, not wanting to take the compliment. As she makes to step away, June's hands land on her shoulders and turn her, forcing her to look back at the crowd from the side of the stage. "Look," June says.

Eliana's eyes scan the audience and June's right. Many of the attendees are wiping under their eyes or dabbing at the corners with tissues or their shirtsleeves. She finds Declan in the audience and catches him sniffle as her mom hands him a tissue. Everest must say something to tease him as Declan's shoulders shake in a brief chuckle.

"I-I don't know what to say," Eliana says, her voice thick with emotion.

"You don't need to say anything. We were all honored to have witnessed what you shared with us. You'll be an inspiration to so many of our students."

"Thank you," Eliana says, dabbing away at her own tears threatening to spill over.

June wraps her in another hug. "I don't know everything that brought you back to Leeside, but I am grateful you found your way home. And if my intuition is right, there is a certain someone out there who feels the same way."

Eliana sucks in a breath, surprised that June knows about them.

"You haven't hidden it quite as well as you thought, dear. And that's okay. It's okay for you to be happy. If anyone disagrees, that's on them, not you."

Eliana squeezes her back, relishing the love this woman has given her and how she welcomed Eliana back into the studio with open arms. "Thank you, June. For everything."

"Anytime, dear."

Zoe comes hustling over with the next group of students, ending Eliana and June's conversation. Eliana looks back at the crowd one last time and lets the emotion flow over her, knowing she's right where she needs to be.

The rest of the showcase flows relatively smoothly. The audience absolutely loves Eliana's group's retelling of Petra and Lachlan's story. In fact, Lachlan could be heard laughing the loudest out of everyone.

As everyone enters the stage again for a final bow, the audience roars with applause and joy. Exactly what she wanted to have come out of tonight. This was intended to showcase the student's growth, while also serving as an opportunity for the community to gather and share in the love of dance.

Her eyes scan the crowd a final time as the curtain comes down. She finds Declan beaming with as much pride as her parents—June was so right—as well as a blond-haired woman who looks familiar, and next to her... Eliana's breath catches in her throat, as if it's been frozen in place.

Sam.

CHAPTER 45

Declan

"I'm gonna go to the washroom while we wait," Declan says, pointing awkwardly down the hall as he backs away. Cora looks at him, her expression saying she knows he's lying through his teeth, but he smiles back.

As he moves down the hall, he peeks inside every open door, trying to find Eliana. Eventually, he bumps into June. "Oh, hi. That was a fantastic show. You all should be so proud."

"Thank you, Mr. Grace. If you're looking for Eliana, she's in the office on the left." He nods at her, and she smiles back before turning and continuing on her way.

He closes the few strides needed and turns into the office door. "Oaks, you were great—" His joy drops the instant he sees her, changing to a mix of fear and anger as his demon rises inside him. Declan is at her side, wrapping her in his arms faster than he thought imaginable. "What's wrong?"

Her breaths are short and rapid as she tries to find her words. "S-s-Sam. H-here."

The world beneath his feet falls away as rage suddenly boils under his skin. As gently as he can, despite the fire roiling under his skin and his demon fighting to shift, he places his hands on her cheeks, gazing into her eyes. "Love. I need you to tell me. Where is he? Did he say anything to you?"

Her breathing slows as she stays focused on him. After a few deep breaths, she's composed enough to speak. "He— he was in the audience. He's been trying to reach me, and I've been ignoring him, hoping he'd go away. I was wrong. Oh, so wrong." Sobs burst from her as she fists his shirt and buries her face in his chest.

Mine, his demon demands.

Yeah, I know, dipshit, Declan responds.

Protect, his demon commands.

Declan pulls her away, taking her face in his hands again and kisses her, tears and makeup running down her face. "I'll get rid of him."

"He left already. I saw him walk out with a woman. Charlie, I think her name was. I had brunch with her weeks ago when Kaia and I bumped into her and a friend of hers."

Charlie. Of course. Anger flares inside him, and closing his eyes, he turns his head, forcing his demon to stay inside. This is not the time or place.

Declan goes to kiss her again when the only thing that could make this worse walks into the room.

"Hey, Dec, did you get lost? Zoe said you were—" Everest says, turning into the room, his words trailing off. "What. The. Fuck." If they could, Everest's eyes would certainly be blazing red right about now.

"Ev, I'm so sorry," Eliana says, panic taking over her voice.

"Everest, this isn't how we wanted you to find out."

"Find out about what?" Everest says, raising his voice. "Are you fucking my sister? Is she another trophy to you?"

"It's not like that," Declan and Eliana say together.

Declan steps forward, but Eliana interlaces her fingers with his, grounding him. Even though this isn't ideal, and not at all what they had planned, her touch reassures Declan that they are in this together.

"So what is it like then? Is she why you've been lying to me?"

Declan lets loose a resigned sigh. "Yes. Eliana and I needed time to figure us out."

Everest doesn't pay attention to Declan's response before facing Eliana, his face contorted in anger. "And you? Do you know what everyone says about him? Do you honestly think he's good enough for you?"

Everest's words are a punch to the gut. They land. And hurt. Poking at his insecurities. Not that Everest has been any better than Declan. He's been by Declan's side the entire time, through all the shenanigans, encouraging the one-night stands, not that Declan needed it. No, he and Everest are one and the same.

"Ev! That's not fair," Eliana says.

"Do you know he's fucked like half the women in town?"

"So?" she says, wiping a tear from under her eye. "Haven't you fucked the other half?"

Everest scoffs, flailing his arms in the air and turning away dramatically. "Please. I at least stay the night. I treat my partners as actual human beings. Besides, it's different."

"How?" Eliana asks.

"Because *he's fucking my sister*." The vitriol rolls off of Everest in waves. There will be no reasoning with him right now. Not in this state.

Eliana takes a step toward her brother, reaching out a hand as an offer of affection. "Please, listen," she pleads. He steps back, looking at her like she's disgusting. She flinches away as if she's been slapped. Declan understands Everest is angry and shocked, but that's no reason to treat his sister like garbage. Everest can throw whatever he wants at Declan, but he won't hurt her.

"No," Everest barks. "He's a monster, and you're only going to get discarded like any of the other women he's been with."

"Everest. That's enough," Declan says, his voice booming. His vision is turning gold, and with already being agitated, he's not sure how much longer he can hold his demon back, given everything his supposed friend is throwing at him. Through a clenched jaw, Declan says, "I know I am not perfect. Fucking far from it. But Eliana," he turns to look at her, as she wipes a tear from her cheek, "makes me a better person. She's brought me a sense of calm when I felt like I was wading through a storm. She is the light to my darkness, and I love her."

The room falls silent.

"You love me?" Eliana asks, her breath hitching as if she doesn't believe it to be true.

"Yes, Oaks. I love you," Declan says. He didn't want to tell her like this. But it's out now, and he's not taking it back.

"I love you, too, Grace."

"Fuck you both. I'm done," Everest says before leaving the room.

Declan pulls Eliana toward him and kisses her fiercely. He doesn't give a flying fuck that his best friend is still raging. No. The only thing that matters is her.

When he breaks the kiss, her hand comes up and wipes away a tear from his cheek that he didn't know he shed.

Huh. Maybe the beast has a heart after all.

The ride to Eliana's apartment is quiet.

What should have been a celebration after the showcase turned into a shit show with Everest storming off, and her parents and Kaia left confused. Eliana didn't want to talk about any of it, and so Declan offered to take her home.

As he parks in front of her building, he hears her sniffle beside him. "Do you want me to come up?" he asks, knowing it was a big night and she may want to be alone to process it all.

She smiles weakly at him, tears rolling down her cheek, which he reaches over and wipes away with his thumb. She leans her head into his touch, her eyes closing slowly as she does. "That would be nice," she says softly.

He leans over, kissing her forehead, before opening his door and climbing out. He runs around to her side, opening her door for her, and holds out a hand to help her down. Her fingers interlacing with his, she steps next to him and rests her head on his arm as he tosses her bag on his other shoulder as they make their way to her apartment.

Declan grabs a drink from the fridge and sits on the couch as she goes and changes. He takes a sip, and then his head tips back on the back of the sofa, and he huffs audibly. He knows he's gonna have to have a talk to Everest, not only to try and repair their friendship, but to try and convince him that what Declan said at the theater was true. It's not a game to him. He loves Eliana—more than he can even say.

Her footsteps pull him back into the room. Even in a pair of oversized sweatpants and a T-shirt with her hair in a messy bun, she's the most beautiful woman he's ever seen.

She comes over to him and kisses him quickly before lying down, placing her head in his lap. His hand comes to rest on her hip, where he finds a slice of exposed skin that he begins to caress with his thumb.

"I don't care about what Everest said about you," Eliana says, breaking the silence.

"I…"

She rolls onto her back, looking up at him as his hand slides across her soft stomach. "I don't. We all have a history. A past. The important thing to me is that it is in the past. It's you and me."

"I know I'm not perfect, and I know people say shit about me. They always will. But I swear, there has been no one else since you walked into my shop. It's only you. It will only ever be you, Oaks." He leans down, awkwardly kissing her. Breaking away, he says, "What Ev said was true. I've been a dick and I've been a player, but it's not who I am. At least not anymore. I think I was afraid to get attached to someone, for fear that they wouldn't stick around or see me as worthy. So I made it a thing to leave before I ever had the chance to. I mean, one night can't hurt anyone, right?"

"You don't give yourself enough credit, Declan."

His thumb rubs a circle on her stomach. "How do you figure?"

"You didn't see yourself tonight, when I said Sam was here. You didn't see the fire in your eyes. How you wanted to tear the world down. It was the same when I first told you about him, and when you realized something was wrong after the drive-in. When you care, Declan, you care so deeply. It's what I love about you. Well, one of the things I love about you."

He's not sure how to respond. Declan can't think of a time he has ever had someone say something like that about him. For years, he's tried to stay detached, doing his best to be the fun friend who goes along for the ride. But if he's honest with himself, that hasn't been who he really is for some time. Sure, it sucks that Everest is angry at him, but the anger is worth it if Declan can finally allow himself to feel. To have what he's been missing.

"I'm gonna have to square things away with your brother."

"I know," she says, tilting her head down to look at her hands as she places them on top of his. "Maybe we could go together? Maybe if he knows everything, he'll understand."

"I think that's good. United front and all. Let him see us together in a different situation. Hopefully, it will help him see how serious we are."

"Sounds like a plan," she says. Her fingers intertwine with his, and she rolls over onto her side, bringing their hands up to nestle between her breasts. A smoky tendril brings him the remote from the table. He turns on the TV, and she picks out some comedy movie to watch.

Declan shifts, scooting down a little to get comfier and allowing her to snuggle in further, all the while trying to figure out how he got so fucking lucky.

CHAPTER 46

Eliana

"You ready?" she asks, fidgeting with the cuffs of her sleeves.

"Like ripping a band-aid off, right?"

The corner of her mouth quirks up in a forced semi-smile. She is hoping they come out of this conversation all right, but Everest was so fucking pissed. Which she understands. They lied to him. But she's also realized that as a grown woman, she doesn't need his permission to date anyone. Even his best friend.

"Something like that, yeah."

Declan steps forward, opening the door to her family home, then lets her walk through first. Thankfully, her parents were on board with their plan and agreed to convince Everest he needed to come over. It feels like a bit of an ambush, but it's the only way she could think of to get him in the same room with them.

Declan closes the door behind them and then clasps her hand in his as she follows the sound of voices to the kitchen. Rounding the corner, she spots her mom first, standing at the counter with a glass in her hand. Dad comes in from the dining room next, followed by Everest.

It's like time stops for everyone. Not a breath is released or a sound made for what feels like minutes, despite being only seconds.

"Oh. Hell. No." Everest turns on his heel and makes to leave the room the way he came in.

"Everest, honey. Come on," Cora says, following him, while Amos exits the kitchen and goes down the hall that she and Declan came through, to try and head Everest off. "Hear them out."

"No. I don't listen to liars."

"If my memory recalls, you've been known to tell a lie or two yourself, son," she hears her father say.

"Dad, move out of the way, please."

"No. You will stop acting like a child who had his ball taken away and listen to your sister and best friend. They deserve at least that."

"But dad—"

Amo's voice is firm. "I said no. Now sit." They both know that tone with him. It's his no-nonsense voice, and he only pulls it out when he means it. Clearly, even at thirty-two, Everest still understands it, because as Eliana and Declan enter the living room, she sees him sulking his way over to the couch. He sits roughly, crossing his arms over his chest like a child being admonished.

Cora sits in one of the armchairs at the side, with Amos taking the one across from her and near the exit closest to the door, leaving the loveseat facing Everest open. Sitting opposite him feels more formal than she would have liked, but she'll take what she can get.

"Well. Say what you need to say so I can get out of here," Everest says, his words clipped.

Her tone is soft, not timid, but soft nonetheless, as she starts, "We know how you found out about Declan and me wasn't the best." He grunts. "But, you need to know we didn't want to hurt you. Which was part of why we kept it to ourselves for as long as we did. I was coming off an abusive relationship and a career injury." Everest perks up. His eyes widen, and his mouth parts ever so slightly, like he wants to say something, but she presses on, knowing she needs to get this out. "I was a mess. In many ways, I still am. It was a chance encounter that led to us coming together when my car was towed to Hellbent Motors. The attraction was pretty instant, and when we realized there might be something there, we wanted a chance to figure it out ourselves before it came under scrutiny from anyone else. So yes, we lied, and for that, we are truly sorry. But, and I mean this from the bottom of my heart, I love you; however, you don't get to have a say in who I or Declan choose to spend time with."

Glancing at her mom, she catches Cora's nod. Everest is silent for way too long, with the room starting to feel uncomfortable as the quiet grows. Declan fidgets beside her, and she squeezes his hand, trying to comfort him the way he's done to her many times before.

Eventually, Everest clears his throat. "What do you mean by an abusive relationship?"

Her gaze flicks to her parents and then to Declan, each of them giving her a nod. Their support means everything. This story is never easy, but each time she shares it, a little bit is lifted off her shoulders. She swallows and goes into her history with Sam and all that happened after her injury. Everest interjects a couple of times to ask a question, but when she's done, he's fuming almost as much as Declan was when she told him.

"I'm sorry you had to experience all of that. And alone. I should have been there," he says, his contained anger evident in his tone.

"There's nothing you could have done. But I appreciate the sentiment. I'm telling you all of this because I want you to see how much Declan has helped me. He's been there for me since we started seeing each other. When I have moments of panic or when I shut down, he's been wonderful. Patient and understanding." She turns and looks at Declan, squeezing his hand. "He's shown me what it's like when someone truly loves you."

Declan brings her hand to his mouth and kisses it, sending goosebumps all over her body. "It's true, Everest. I have never felt this way about anyone, and honestly, I didn't think I ever would. When she told me about Sam, I wanted to tear the world apart looking for him. And when she said last night that he was at the theater, all I saw was rage—"

Everest jumps up, steam practically billowing from his ears. "What do you mean?" he says through a clenched jaw. "He was at the theater?"

"I, um, saw him at the end of the show. He's been trying to reach out to me, but I haven't responded."

"So the fucker shows up, to what, intimidate you?" Everest paces the living room. "Not on my fucking watch." Turning to Declan, he points aggressively at him, "Use whatever powers you have and track the shithead down. We have a special message to deliver."

Declan laughs, but stops when Everest glares at him. "That's not quite how it works."

"Surely your sister-in-law could find him."

"She likely could, yes. But I'm not going to ask that of her." Declan stands, letting go of Eliana's hand, leaving her feeling temporarily unmoored in this emotional storm. His hands land on Everest's shoulders, holding him in place. "As much as I would love to have a word with this so-called man," he looks to Eliana, "I am not going to do something that she doesn't want me to. Now, if he approaches her, well, that's a completely different story." He winks at her, and she winks back. Knowing he would protect her somehow makes the implicit violence on her behalf endearing.

"Now, Everest, honey. Do you think you can overcome your feelings about these two being together? Knowing everything that you do now."

Declan joins her back on the loveseat, taking her hand. She smiles at him, knowing that whatever Everest may say, she has no intention of leaving this demon.

"Yeah. It's fine." Everest waves in their general direction as if trying to brush them away. "Don't be all lovey-dovey around me. I don't need to see or think about what you two do on your own time."

"Everest!" Eliana says, tossing a pillow at him as a blush creeps up her neck. She doesn't need anyone in her family to know she has any kind of adult relations, let alone with the person sitting next to her. Despite the embarrassment, she gets up and hugs him. "Thank you," she whispers into his ear.

"I want you to be happy, even if it is with him."

After the conversation with Everest, Declan and Eliana stick around to have lunch with her family before heading back to his place. Buckley greets them at the door as usual, tapping his claws on the floor as he spins in circles, unable to stand still. Once he's deemed the pets sufficient, he scampers off and finds a sunny spot to lie down for an afternoon of sunbaking.

Pushing herself up to sit on the counter while Declan gets them drinks, Eliana says, "I'll admit, I was a bit scared about how that conversation was going to go."

"Only a bit?" he laughs.

"Okay, more than a bit."

Declan chuckles before admitting, "I was, too. But you handled all of that perfectly."

"I did?"

"You did," he says, handing her a drink and placing his beside her before sliding his arms around her. "You're so strong. I admire many things about you, like your brains, your compassion, your beauty," he says, kissing his way up her neck with each compliment, "but most of all, your strength."

"Is that right?"

"Mmm…"

"Well, thank you, Mr. Grace."

"If you're up to it, I'd love to show you how much I admire you."

She puts her glass down on the counter and reaches her hand between them, palming his cock through his pants. "If I'm not mistaken, I'd say you already are."

He growls into the hollow of her neck, his hot breath sending a heatwave straight to her core. "Love, I have so much more in store for you." His hands move to her ass and lift her off the counter, her legs wrapping naturally around his hips as he carries her upstairs.

Despite having his face buried in her chest, nipping at the flesh through her shirt, he finds the way to his bedroom without issue. As he sits on the edge of his bed, she unwraps her legs from around him and bends her knees, straddling his broad form. Goddess, she'll never tire of the feeling of being wrapped up in him.

His hands grip her ass, surely leaving more fingerprints, as she grinds into that delicious bulge she grabbed onto. Not wanting to prolong the feel of him against her skin, her hands roam to the hem of his shirt, forcing him to lift his arms as she pulls it off. She then repeats the action with her top and tosses both behind her. His hands roam up her back, feeling like a brand on her skin. Hot and permanently marking her as his, but in the best way possible.

With a quick flick of his fingers, Declan undoes her bra. His fingers dance up her back, grazing her exposed flesh as they hook under the straps. Guiding the material down her arm leaves a trail of goosebumps on her exposed flesh. She removes one arm from the strap and then repeats it on the other side. He lifts her bra above his head, twirls it on a finger, and launches it somewhere into the room. "Hades, you're fucking hot," he says, palming her breast and rolling her peaked nipple between his thumb and index finger.

Eliana widens her legs, allowing her to sink further on top of him. Despite being half-naked, there are still too many clothes, but she can sense the demon is starved, and she has nowhere to be. Her hips grind onto his cock, adding the touch of pressure she desires.

When he pinches her nipple, giving her that little hint of pain that drives her wild, it sends a jolt of heat to her pussy, making her clit pulse with need. "More," she says. He does it again, and her cunt clenches, eager for him as she grinds into him harder, riding the bulge his cock has formed.

Still too many clothes.

"So needy."

"I need *you*," she whines. Fuck, she's never been

someone who whines, but this demon brings it out of her. Desperate. Hungry to be filled by him.

"I'm right here," he says. "I'll always be right here." His free hand lightly grasps the back of her neck and pulls her face down to his. Their lips meet, and it's slow and torturous. Exploratory, not as if they haven't done this before, but as though they understand they have all the time in the world to learn about each other. His lips are soft and supple, caressing her soul from the outside.

"I love you," she whispers into his mouth.

He nips her lip. "I love you, too. Now, and always."

Pulling himself away, he stands, putting her feet on the floor.

"What are you do—" she starts to ask before his hands find his belt. He holds the buckle in one hand and slides the other behind, and in one swift motion, he whips the belt out of his pants in perhaps the hottest display she has ever seen. She continues to watch as he undoes his pants and lets them drop to his ankles. His thumbs then hook into the top of his boxers, and he bends over, sliding them down as well. Seeing him naked still takes her breath away, and perhaps makes her drool a little. She wipes her thumb across her lip to be sure as he palms his cock and strokes it slowly.

Eliana takes her cue and undoes her jeans and slides them down. She steps out of them, kicking the fabric to the side, leaving her in her soft yellow thong. He continues stroking himself, and watching him play with himself is hot and oh so enticing. The little bead of precum on his head keeps catching the light, and it's taking a lot of willpower not to drop to her knees and lick it off.

Maybe...

She does exactly that. She may have asked him to crawl to her, but dammit, she's more than willing to do the same.

Eliana falls to all fours, pushing her ass into the air like a yoga cow pose, and crawls to him. She stops in front of him and gazes up through her eyelashes, catching the fire staring back at her. Pushing herself to be on her knees, she places her hands on each of his legs, using them as support as they glide toward that delicious cock of his. A low rumble starts to sound from him. One of her hands clasps his balls and begins to massage, eliciting a short, pleasured hiss from him while her other hand replaces his on his cock. When she licks the precum from the head, she swears his knees almost give out. And when she takes him into her mouth, tasting his salt, he groans out.

"Fuck. Me."

Popping off his cock, she licks her lips before spitting on his head and using her hand to spread it down his length. "That's what I'm trying to do, Grace." She opens wide and takes him again, relaxing her throat and taking him to the base.

"Holy. Hades."

She moans around him, and he growls deeply. So deep she's pretty sure it vibrated his balls.

Declan's hands go to the back of her head, scooping up her hair into a makeshift ponytail before wrapping one hand around it.

"Touch yourself."

She doesn't need to be told twice. Her clit is throbbing with need, and her pussy is so wet she's certain there will be a damp patch on the floor when she inevitably gets up. She slides her hand from his balls down between her legs, where she's met with slick heat. Her fingers deftly find her clit and begin swirling around it, flicking it in rhythm with her head bobbing on his cock. As she finds herself getting closer to the edge, Declan takes over up top, using her hair as a handle to guide her head. With each bob, she takes him to the base, relishing the feel of him inside her.

When she looks up at him again, seeing his love reflected back at her, she comes undone. She moans around him as he slides to the back of her throat, spilling his hot cum down as she flicks her clit, riding out her own release.

"You're so fucking beautiful," he says. "Show me." He shudders before he spurts into her mouth again, then withdraws.

She pulls off of him, still breathless from her own orgasm, and opens wide, showing him the pool of cum gathered on her tongue.

"Good girl." The praise makes her shudder with need. She wraps her lips around the head of his cock again and sucks, swallowing down his deliciousness already in her mouth and gathering whatever else she can from him.

"Stand up," he says, putting out a hand to help her up. Eliana slides her mouth from his cock and then takes his hand. He swings it behind her back, pulling her against him. His cock presses into her stomach. He kisses her fiercely before breaking contact and telling her to get on the bed. She does as instructed while he turns around and grabs a condom, rolling it on with a swiftness.

"Ah. Ah. On your knees."

Her eyes flare. *Fuck yes.* She follows the command, putting her face into the pillows and pushing her ass into the air.

"Scoot forward."

She does.

"Hold onto the headboard, love."

She pushes herself up, putting her hands on the headboard ordered. She feels him crawl toward her, positioning himself behind her as he pulls the strap of her thong to the side. The head of his cock lines up with her cunt, and he pushes into her.

Slowly.

Purposefully.

He's so thick. The way he stretches her is unreal. She's not sure she'll ever get used to it, but oh, how she plans to try as often as possible. Thinking about last time and how he shifted inside her, she didn't think she could take any more, and yet, that's all she ever wants from him. More. There's never enough.

It doesn't take long for the tension to build again at the base of her spine as he withdraws unhurriedly before slamming back into her. Each hard thrust into her pussy sends shockwaves throughout her body, continually bringing to her next release.

"More. Harder," she grunts as he thrusts into her.

He growls behind her, and she feels it. His shift. His cock grows, stretching her further, setting all her nerves on fire. Wisps of smoke come around her, two landing on her breasts as they begin to play with her nipples, and a third one sliding between her legs to circle her clit.

"Holy. Fucking. Hades," Eliana yells, the sensations almost too much at once.

"Mine," he says, his voice deeper.

"Yours."

Demon-shifted Declan grunts behind her as his hands land on her hips and he picks up the pace. It's not punishing, but rougher and precisely what she needs. The tendril on her clit gives it a gentle pinch, and that's all it takes. She falls over the edge, her cunt clenching wildly around his cock. He thrusts into her again and again, taking every bit of her release from her before he growls loudly and finds his release as well. His cock pulses inside her as she continues to ride out her orgasm, each clench of her pussy milking his hot demon cum from his perfect cock.

Breathless and still seated in her, he leans over, wrapping an arm around her stomach and kisses up her back. "Mine."

"Yours," she says back, basking in the glow of love and multiple orgasms.

CHAPTER 47
Declan

I *'m gonna marry this woman someday.*

He nestles his head into her neck, breathing in her peppermint and grapefruit scent, pulling her back against his chest. They must have dozed off after the fourth or fifth orgasm, he's not entirely sure, and he lost count of how many times she screamed out his name along the way.

She groans against him, the sound causing his cock to pulse and poke into her ass. "Mmm. Time?"

A smoky wisp appears before them, holding his phone aloft. "7:42 p.m.," he says.

"Food?" she asks, clearly still groggy and unable to fully form coherent sentences.

"Sure. Wanna go to the Acorn?"

"Wonderful."

He can't see it, but he can feel her smile against him as she rolls over, throwing her leg between his and wrapping her arm over his soft belly as she squishes her face into his chest.

After a moment, her hand strays down to his cock,

standing at attention. She begins to stroke him, and his eyes close, wanting to commit the sensation of her touch to memory. Not that he needs to, but he never wants to take for granted how lucky he is that she chose him.

"Oaks. As much as I love you and how good you feel against me, if you want food, you're gonna have to let go of my dick."

She pauses for a moment and then seems to relent. "Fine," she huffs reluctantly. "But I want more of that when we get back, Grace."

"I think I can oblige that request."

She places her hands on his chest and pushes away from him, climbing across the bed. "You know, the view from this position is pretty fantastic," he says, fully ogling her ass.

"If you want food, you're gonna have to stop staring at my butt," she replies, throwing Declan's words back at him.

He chuckles, then flies out of the bed, chasing her to the bathroom as she squeals with glee.

After a quick make out session in the shower, they manage to extricate themselves long enough to get dressed. Declan lets Buckley out and gives him dinner before they head out for their own.

Walking into the Bittersweet Acorn with Eliana under his arm is exciting, but a touch unnerving. It seems like everyone in the room is watching them as they make their way to a table. As he looks around, he realizes it must be all in his head as the patrons engage in conversations at their tables. Having come here for so long and using this place as a bit of a hunting ground for nightly partners, he recognizes that coming in with a date would feel different. But then again, everything with her is different.

Daisy comes and takes their order shortly after they sit,

and as they wait for their food and drinks to arrive, to the surprise of no one, Everest walks in the door with Tai. Declan raises his hand, signaling to his friend. Everest's eyes light up, and they saunter over, pull out a chair, and join their table.

"Ellie. Declan," Everest says. His greeting may be short, but the smile on his face gives him away. This could have been such a problem, and could've caused a huge rift between Declan and his friend. Instead, Everest is here as his usual self, so Declan gets to hang out with his best friend, no longer lying to him, and spend time with the love of his life, Eliana, at the same time.

Daisy reappears with their drinks and takes Everest and Tai's orders, but not before winking at him as she disappears again. He turns his head and sees Sloan sitting at the end of the bar with a martini and a book as her wife floats around serving customers and barking orders at Lachlan.

It's a live band tonight, which is always a great time. The band takes the stage as their food arrives, and the crowd settles into the vibes as the acoustic guitar strikes up. The conversation at their table is light and flows well, feeling relaxed and natural, as if they've been doing this regularly for years.

As one song leads into another, one of those natural lulls in noise across the room occurs at the same time the bell above the door chimes, signaling a new arrival. Declan leans back, taking a sip of his beer, when he catches Eliana's body language shift from relaxed to rigid. His demon instantly awakens, becoming alert to the sense of a nearby threat.

"Love. What is it?" Declan asks, leaning in, his hand softly rubbing on her back.

"Sam." She swallows. "That's Sam."

Declan is up with haste, pushing his way to the door and the so-called man standing there with a shit-eating grin on his face. And next to him, of course, is Charlie. He doesn't need to look behind him to see that Everest and Lachlan are mere steps behind.

Smoke and shadow billow around them. This may be Lachlan's bar, and causing a scene isn't usually a great idea, but Lach knows that if Declan is reacting this way, it has to be for a valid reason, so he supports it without question.

"Get out," Declan bellows.

"Told you, you'd find them here," Charlie says. Goddess, what does he need to do to be rid of her?

"I think we're good, thanks," Sam responds.

"This is my bar, and if my brother here thinks you need to leave, I suggest you listen," Lachlan responds before saying out the side of his mouth to Everest behind him, "who are these fools anyway?"

"That would be Ellie's abusive shithead ex, and that would be the woman who has been spreading rumors about Declan for months," Everest replies. "Clearly, they've paired up to form the ultimate shithead transformer. Pity that never made it to market."

Lachlan rolls his eyes at Everest. "Ah. Yeah, then you definitely need to leave."

"Again, I think we're good. I'd like to speak with Eliana for a moment. Won't take long, I promise."

Declan allows his demon to rise to the surface, his eyes flashing gold, and his horns to come through. Lachlan must do the same, as Sam takes a step back. Apparently, the dingbat does know how to make a good choice. The bar behind them is silent as the patrons and staff watch everything unfold.

Eliana pushes her way through, her hand resting on Declan's bicep. "Sam, there is nothing I have to say to you. I thought my lack of response would have said enough."

"Please. There's no way you're happy here. With," he casts a look at Declan and Lachlan, then looks back to her, "them. You know they don't really care about you. Come back to me. We can start fresh and be better than we ever were."

"Come back to you?" Charlie asks incredulously. "I thought you said you wanted to show her what she's missing?"

"Shut up. This isn't about you," Sam responds.

Charlie's face goes beet red, and tears form in her eyes before she turns and runs out the door. Declan and Everest pass a glance between them, wanting to laugh, but knowing this isn't the time.

Sam smirks. "Thank fuck. She was a good lay, but that's about it."

Lachlan and Declan step toward him, deep demon growls rolling out of them as wisps of shadow and smoke work their way toward him.

Eliana steps forward. "No, Sam. I wasn't happy with you. You ruined my life. You destroyed who I was as a person and then refused to even give me the bare minimum in my time of need. Find someone else to abuse." She steps away, and Declan's chest swells with pride. She's come so far in such a short amount of time, and he can only imagine how tough it would have been for her to say all of that a couple of months ago. Let alone say it to his face.

Sam steps forward, trying to follow her as he yells, "Fuck yo—" but is cut off by the tendrils of shadow and smoke that wrap around him and carry him out the door, Lachlan and Declan following him out.

They carry him around the corner, out of sight of the bar. When they release him, Sam tries to charge them, but a smoke wisp quickly trips him, making him face-plant into the sidewalk.

"Oh, I'm gonna end you," Sam says, attempting to scramble back to his feet. If only Declan's boot hadn't landed on his back first to keep him in place. Lachlan steps back, crossing his arms, and watches as Declan leans down, putting his face level with Sam's.

"Listen here, shit-for-brains. Eliana has told you nicely to leave her the fuck alone, and you refuse to listen. So I am not going to be as nice. See, I am a demon. I have lots of power inside me at this very moment, eager for an outlet. The demon in my head is roaring with anger because you, you tiny little ant, decided to come and threaten Eliana. I could cause you so much pain with the snap of my fingers if I wanted to." He lets a tendril of smoke wrap around Sam's arm and bend it back far enough so he can feel the threat. "Oh, and on top of that, my brother here is the demon council representative, which means he has a whole fuck ton of power. Like miles beyond what I can do. And he could easily help me cover up anything I did to you. I want you to let that sink in for a minute."

Declan gives the asshole a moment before continuing.

"I want you to think long and hard about what comes out of your mouth next. See that fabulous woman in there, that's the woman I love. I will go to the ends of the earth and back for her. That means I have no problem making sure that *you* never become a problem for her, or anyone else for that matter, again. So you have a choice: cut your losses and leave of your own volition, or try and cause a bigger problem than you already have here tonight, and see what two sons of a former crime boss demon lord can do to you. What will it be?"

Declan lifts his boot from Sam's back and releases his arm before walking over to stand beside Lachlan, who looks at Declan as if he's witnessed a miracle.

"She's a fucking whore," Sam spits out. A smoky fist meets Sam's face with enough force to send him to his knees. His hand flies up and covers his quickly swelling eye. "Fine. I'll go. She's not worth it anyway."

"Smart choice. And you're wrong," Declan says as Sam stands up and brushes himself off. "She's worth everything."

Sam huffs and begins to walk away, but before he is out of earshot, Declan calls out to him, "Oh, and Sam. If we get word of you treating anyone else the way you treated Eliana, you'll be hearing from us again."

Sam flips them off as he walks into the night.

Declan turns to Lachlan. "Thanks. For all that," he says, vaguely gesturing around them.

"Anytime. I don't know the history, and I don't need to. But I have no problem sending him through a portal to some random location where hellhounds can feast on his balls if needed."

Declan chuckles, clapping his brother's shoulder. "Noted. Let's head back inside."

Eliana charges at him, leaping into his arms. Her hands clasp the side of his face, and she kisses him with fervor. It's hard and fierce as her tongue meets his, spilling all of her emotions into him.

"I love you, Grace."

"I love you too, Oaks."

He can see the streaks of tears she must have shed while he was outside. His thumb runs across them. "He's gone. He won't be a problem any longer. And if he is, Lach threatened to maroon him on an island."

"Works for me." She kisses him again. "Thank you."

"Anytime, love." Declan lifts her up, her legs wrapping around his waist.

"Drinks on the house!" Daisy calls out from the bar, causing the crowd to erupt in cheers.

CHAPTER 48
Declan

"**Y**ou ready?" Declan asks, kicking the kickstand on his motorcycle into place as Eliana releases her hold on his chest—a sensation he will never tire of.

She takes a deep breath before answering, "As much as I'm gonna be."

"You've met them all before. Well, everyone except Mom. But she's practically harmless."

"Practically doesn't mean she's not." She laughs, dismounting from behind him. "And I know. But it's still intimidating. You've been around my family for years. I'm new to them. And it's different, coming to an official meet-the-family meal. I'm not just out at a bar and seeing them, or in my comfort zone at the theater. This is scary. What if they don't like me?"

Declan swings a leg over and turns to face her. He can see she's getting herself worked up. Her breathing is picking up, and she's starting to fidget with her clothes. She's been working hard with Dr. Reid, and as much as she's made progress in talking about her feelings and everything, moments like these clearly still cause her to be overwhelmed.

Reaching forward, he pulls her into his space. She fit so perfectly between his legs. Like the space is meant for her. His hands grip onto her hips, and he feels the tension in her body ease under his touch. Looking up at her, he smiles, offering silent comfort.

"They will love you. Because I love you. But if you really don't want to go in there, we don't need to."

Eliana gazes down at him. Hades, he could get lost in those eyes. Warm. Comforting. Loving. Everything she is and so much more.

Declan's thumb draws circles on her hip, patiently giving her time to decide what she wants to do. After a moment, with her hand running down the back of his head and her fingers twirling the end of his braid, with confidence, she says, "I want to go in." A gentle smile breaks across her gorgeous lips, and his heart fills with even more love than he thought possible.

"Only if you're sure. I never want you to feel you have to do something."

She nods. "I'm sure." She kisses him softly, letting her lips linger on his. "And thank you for being so patient."

"Always."

She smiles at him. A smile that he knows is only for him. He's so grateful that she lets him see her. All of her. And that she lets him into the moments she thinks are weakness, but to him, are pure strength. It takes so much to come out the other side of what she's experienced, let alone to manage her anxiety on a day-to-day basis.

He stands, wraps his arm around her, and spins them, leaning her back over the bike as he kisses her again. Yes, they are expected inside, but they can all wait. His tongue slides along her lips, tasting her sweetness. Eliana's lips part, allowing him in further; he takes the invitation. Her hands slide up his back and clasp onto the side of his face as he deepens the kiss.

"Ahem," a voice sounds behind them.

Declan groans into her, both in frustration that their moment has been broken and in desire for this beautiful woman. Breaking apart, Declan stands them both upright again before looking up to see Lachlan standing on the steps of his home with a shit-eating grin on his face.

"Anytime you two lovebirds are ready to come in, we would love to see you," Lachlan says, amused.

Looking at Eliana, Declan notices the blush creeping up her neck. As they make their way to the door, he leans down and whispers in her ear, "Not gonna lie, the idea of bending you over that bike is all I can think about."

She gasps before lightly smacking his stomach and replying, "If we make it out of this alive, I'll let you tie me up and use a butt plug while you fuck me senseless on it." She winks at him, then steps through the door with Declan nearly choking at her response. *Goddess, she's perfect.*

"Declan, my boy, come here," Fenella, his mother, says, wrapping her arms around him as Lachlan closes the door behind them.

"Hi, Mom." Declan hugs her back and kisses her cheek before she pulls away completely.

She steps over to Eliana next and places her hands on Eliana's arms. "It's so wonderful to meet you, dear. I'm Fenella."

"Hi, Fenella." She leans in and hugs his mom. This isn't something he ever thought he would see. Hell, he never thought he'd settle down with anyone. Declan figured he'd spend the rest of his days hopping from one bed to another.

But the more time he spends with her, the more he gets to know her, the more he loves her.

He didn't lie when he told her shithead ex that Eliana was worth everything. She's the light in the darkness. The home he's longed for. The one person in the world who brings him peace and doesn't question or judge any part of him. But most of all, he loves being a sturdy place for her to land.

They follow his mom and Lachlan into the house, Declan placing his hand on the small of Eliana's back along the way, while his other hand pats his pocket, making sure the little box is still there. She relaxes into his slight touch and looks at him, making his heart leap and his demon chant *mine* inside.

Walking into the kitchen, hellos and hugs from Petra, Daisy, and Sloan greet them. Morris, Petra's troublemaker cat, scampers in front of their feet, nearly tripping Declan. Declan growls at the little beast, but the fluff ball meows back before taking off around the corner.

"So nice to see you both again," Petra says.

"Yes, you too," Eliana replies. Her tone shows she's still nervous. Hopefully, she'll relax a little further as the evening goes on.

"Drinks?" Lachlan asks.

"Please." Declan looks to Eliana, who nods in return. "Beer for me, and an espresso martini for Eliana."

Lachlan waves a hand over his head. "Coming right up."

A moment later, Lachlan hands them their drinks, and they move over to the kitchen table, taking a seat with his mom, Daisy, and Sloan.

"So tell me everything. How did this come to be?" Fenella asks.

It's so typical of his family to jump right into it. Declan leans back, smiling as he places an arm along the back of Eliana's chair. He delves into their story, explaining everything that has led them to where they are now, with his mom and the others chiming in with questions along the way. It seems to take a while to get through it all, but soon enough, dinner is ready, and the chatter shifts to more regular conversation, not solely focused on them.

Eliana, despite her nerves, carries herself with ease. Jumping from one topic to the next, as if she's been in the group for years. Which is a good thing, as he plans to be with her for the rest of their lives.

Dinner wraps up, and they move out to the patio, enjoying the fire pit in the cooler temperatures that have taken over Leeside.

With fire dancing in her eyes, and unable to break the feeling that she needs to be his forevermore, Declan stands. Reaching into his pocket, he pulls out the ring that's been burning a hole in it all night.

Declan turns around, kneeling in front of Eliana, and takes her hand. The conversational buzz around them stops, and all he can see and hear is the two of them. Her eyes reflect back the flames of love he feels for her.

"Eliana," he starts. "I love you more than I thought was ever possible. You are completely unexpected and bring light into my life that I didn't know I was looking for. You are the only one I want to be with and the only one I will ever love. I would be honored if you would agree to spend the rest of your life with me." He wipes a tear from her cheek before continuing, "Eliana, will you marry me?"

She sits before him, shock written all over her face, from the gaping mouth to the enlarged pupils. "Are you serious?"

"Marry me. I can't spend another day without knowing you'll be mine forever."

She stutters, having difficulty finding her words. She's so beautiful. Flustered, flushed, or flirting, it doesn't matter. She couldn't be any more perfect. "I-I—Yes."

"Yes?" he asks, shocked himself.

"Yes, I'll marry you."

"Hell yeah!" He slides the ring onto her finger before they stand up together. He lifts her up, spinning around with her legs wrapped around him as they kiss excitedly.

A couple of bottles pop in the distance, and various hands clap him on the shoulder, but all he cares about is that he has found the woman of his dreams.

Epilogue

BUCKLEY - 1 YEAR LATER

The humans are extra emotional today, but he's not sure why. The big one, his longest friend, Declan, or Daddy as he calls himself, put something big and pointy around Buckley's neck this morning. He called it a bowtie and made those high-pitched noises Buckley loves as he complimented his new attire. Despite the desire to scratch it and try to remove it, Buckley perseveres, knowing that it would upset Declan to see him do so.

His newest friend, Eliana, also known as Oaks, is glowing these days. Her belly has grown over the past few months to where it makes a wonderful pillow when Buckley lies on her at night. They sat him down a few months ago and told him he was going to be a big brother, but he knew long before that.

Sensing the new heartbeat in the room, Buckley made it a point to ensure it was kept warm and safe by being nearby at all times. He already knows that what grows in Eliana's tummy will be his new best friend.

Padding around the house, his nose takes him to the kitchen, where it is filled with delicious-smelling foods, including his favorite—roast chicken. Looking around, making sure no one can see him, he hops onto his hind legs, checking to see if anything is in reach. Spotting the prize, his head slinks forward, reaching for a tasty morsel. It's within reach, his teeth only an inch away, when he hears a voice off to the side.

"Hey! Get down!" the red-headed witch, Petra, yells at him.

Caught!

Buckley pops his feet back on the floor and scampers away as she continues to call after him, saying something about being a bad dog. But that's not true, because Declan tells him he's a good boy all the time, and he would never lie to Buckley.

The house starts to fill with more people, and as Buckley makes his way to the backyard, he's greeted by old friends and new. Many reach out to pet him and ruffle his fur. Hopefully, Declan and Oaks won't be too upset about his fluffy fur.

His nose takes him to Declan's brother, who holds a funny colored drink in his hand as he talks to some other beings. He doesn't know who they are, but if Uncle Lach thinks they are good enough to be here, then so does Buckley.

Sitting beside his uncle, he turns his head to look up at him, and Buckley's big pink tongue lolls out of his mouth as he parts his lips to pant excitedly. He swishes his tail back and forth, asking for some attention, which Uncle Lach thankfully provides him. He leans down, keeping his eyes on the beings he's chatting to, but manages to scratch behind Buckley's ear and under his chin. Buckley's large brown eyes gaze up at his uncle as he licks his hand, thanking him in the only way he can.

When Lachlan stands back up, Buckley takes it as his cue to leave. He wanders around the yard for a minute more, spotting the purple-haired lady, Daisy, and her dark-haired mate Sloan. Buckley barks, the sound deep and resonant from within, in their direction, causing them to look over and raise their glasses in salute. He barks again in recognition and pads off again in search of his preferred human.

It takes sniffing throughout the entire house before he finds him upstairs in their bedroom. He's dressed all fancy, with a dark suit and dress shirt. His hair is braided back like he likes to do, and his shoes are all shiny.

Buckley gruffs at Declan as he makes his way into the room and settles on his bed at the base of the bed.

"Hi, Buckster. You look so handsome!" Declan says, kneeling down to ruffle the fur behind Buckley's ears. "Are you ready for the big day?"

Bark! he says, letting his Daddy know he's ready to go.

"Good. I'm gonna need you on your best behavior, okay?"

Bark! Buckley replies in agreement.

"That's my good boy." He stands back up and checks the shiny device in his pocket. "Looks like it's about time. Are you ready to be the ring bearer?"

Bark! he responds, meaning he can't wait.

"Alright. Let's go get me married!" Declan claps his hands together, and Buckley jumps to his feet, following his Daddy out the door.

Daisy holds his leash, keeping him at the back of the aisle. She's positioned a little pillow in front of him and has told him that when it's time, he needs to pick it up and carry it to the vampire at the end of the aisle. Buckley ruffs in agreement, but as he looks at her, it doesn't seem like she believes he can carry out such an easy task. Does she know who he is?

Daddy stands at the front already, and when Buckley turns his head to look back, he can see Oaks ready and waiting. She looks like an angel in her off-white gown. It flows majestically around her, bringing special attention to his new friend in her belly as she moves in a little closer, but still out of sight of Declan.

"Alright, Buckley. Now it's your turn," Daisy says, unhooking the leash from his collar. Buckley bends his head down, picks up the corner of the pillow with the rings securely attached, and trots down the aisle to the cold man at the end. The crowd oohs and ahhs as he goes, commenting about how cute he is, and he knows he's done his Daddy proud.

The cold man takes the pillow, and Buckley moves to the side, lying next to Lachlan's feet. From here, he watches as Oaks walks down the aisle toward them. Declan sniffles overhead, and Buckley shifts, getting ready to go make sure he's okay, but Lachlan tells him to stay. He doesn't want to, but he listens, trusting that Uncle Lach would let him go if he was needed.

When Eliana gets to the front, she hands off her flowers to the brunette behind her, who wipes away tears with her free hand. So many here seem to be crying, but they don't feel like sad tears. Instead, the room seems to be filled with joy and excitement. Buckley thumps his tail twice, showing he's excited too.

The cold man says some words, which Declan and Eliana repeat after him. After what seems like a really long time, Declan and Oaks have a moment to speak for themselves.

"Declan. I will admit, I never saw you coming. You were

unexpected in the best of ways, and I knew from that day in your shop that there was something different about you. As hesitant as I was, I found myself hooked on a demon in an auto shop and knew I needed to be around you. Despite the trials to get to this point, I would not want to do this life with anyone else. You may not be one for the big gestures, but you are kind and show you care in so many little ways. I love how you pay attention to those around you. How you endeavor to be the best that you can be while also making those around you the best they can be." She looks down and places a hand on her swollen belly, "I can't wait for our next adventure together and to see you be the best father. I love you, and I am so excited to become your wife."

The crowd claps at her speech, clearly having enjoyed it. Then it is Declan's turn.

"Oaks. You are perfection personified. I would not be the man I am today without you in my life." He looks around the yard, "which many here can attest to." The crowd laughs. Buckley pants excitedly along with them, trying to show he's in on the joke as well. "I love your passion and perseverance. I love your willingness to try. Your drive for growth has shown me that it's okay to change and that it can be for the best. You said that I strive to be the best that I can be, but that, Eliana, is because of you. You make me want to be a better man, and you've helped me to see the man I can be. So I stand here today, in front of our friends and family, because I need to show everyone how wonderful you are. You are the love of my life, and I cannot wait to spend the rest of our lives together. I love you, Eliana. From this moment until the day we leave this plane, you will have my heart, my soul, and my entire being."

The cold man speaks for another moment and then tells them to kiss. When they do, the crowd cheers, and Buckley barks along with them, celebrating the love that fills the room.

As Declan and Oaks leave the altar, Buckley sniffles, not because he's sad, but because he's happy. His humans have found each other, and together they are the best parents he could ask for. His new little sister has no idea what she's coming into, but she's going to be loved beyond measure. How could she not be with this group of beings around her?

And of course, to my husband, who helps me to continue believing in love so that I can continue writing love interests who are inspired by him in some way. You are my reason. You are my only. I love you more, sweet cheeks buttercup biscuit boy bear.

Acknowledgments

Thank you so much for venturing back into Leeside with me. I have loved these characters immensely, and I am thrilled to share their stories with you.

To my readers, new and returning, thank you for joining me on this journey. I truly wouldn't be able to continue writing if I didn't have your support and encouragement. It means so much more than I can ever put into words.

Beavers, having a group of friends to be sounding boards during difficult times or just someone to share garden pictures with, means a lot. Being an author can be a very lonely experience, so I am grateful to be part of our group.

Maddi and Nicole, thank you for the early input and pointing out those pesky continuity errors (like how Kaia's name changed three different times, ha!). Your comments were always helpful!

Lisa, yes, our internet is working, and I love how you are always one of the first to jump in with excitement.

Amanda, asking for updates, eager for me to share, and excited alongside me with every little piece of it.

To other friends and family who have continued to support this journey with such great enthusiasm, thank you.

Shelly, thank you for your wonderful editing and for helping this shine. I love all the little notes and general encouragement you give along the way.

About the Author

Isla lives with her husband and their furry family in Southwestern Ontario. When she's not writing, she enjoys floating in the pool, reading, or tending to her zucchini and tomatoes (not a euphemism!).

If you'd like to follow along and receive updates for new stories or behind the scenes details, you can sign up for Isla's newsletter here: **Join Isla's Newsletter** or follow her on Instagram or Tiktok.